his SECRET

BESTSELLING AUTHOR
ISABEL LUCERO

WARNINGS

This story contains elements that some might find harmful to their mental health. You can email me if you have any questions.

Cheating

Homophobia from a parent.

Verbal abuse from a parent.

Mention of a side character's past miscarriage. This happens off page.

Mention of a side character's substance abuse history. This also happens off page.

The Past

Matías

CHAPTER ONE

MATÍAS

I watch the door, waiting for him to come in. I find myself in this position quite often now. Adrian and I became friends at the start of the semester six weeks ago, and I'm already at the point of looking forward to his arrival and being disappointed on the days he doesn't show.

Adrian always comes at the last minute, rushing in here like he had to run the whole way. The guy wouldn't know punctuality if it punched him in the face. In his stupid, perfect, sculpted by the gods face.

Okay, so maybe I have a crush on my new friend, but the attraction is anything but new. Only the friendship is. Last year we had a class together, but he only stayed in it for two weeks before dropping. I'm pretty sure he never saw me, but I was immediately attracted to him. Well, me and probably half the class.

Adrian Kennedy is the kind of attractive that doesn't make sense. Sea-green eyes that shine from between dark lashes. A jawline you could cut glass with. Full and symmetrical lips. You see him and wonder why he's not in movies or

1

on runways. On top of that, he's funny and charming and nicer than I imagined he would be.

When this class started up, he scanned the room and then took the seat next to me. I looked around to see if all the other seats were taken, but no, there were plenty of others. He *chose* to sit next to me. He also decided to call me by my last name—an athlete thing. It felt like he was already including me in his circle of friends, even though I'm far from athletic.

Since then, he always comes in with a new topic of conversation. He asks about my plans and then tells me whatever he got into over the weekend. We see each other every Monday, Wednesday, and Friday, and sometimes it feels like we're not so different after all. Then he tells me about a party he was at, catalogs everything he drank, tells me about the girls that were there, makes jokes about his friends, and reality comes crashing back. We're *very* different.

The professor begins talking, and I resign myself to the fact that this will be another day I don't see Adrian, but then he runs in, his phone falling from his hoodie pocket and crashing to the floor.

He reaches down to pick it up and one of his earbuds falls out. A few people snicker as the professor sighs.

"Sorry," Adrian says, rushing to his seat. He drops into it and gives me a bug-eyed look. "So, I was thinking—"

"Mr. Kennedy, can I start the lesson now?"

"Oh. Yeah. Sorry."

He's quiet for a little bit, but then my phone buzzes in my pocket, and when I don't reach for it, he starts making noise.

"Psst. Cruz. Psssst."

I angle my head over my shoulder and he points to his phone. I shake my head. He knows I don't get on my phone in class. Professor Edwards has a strict policy, and one that Adrian ignores.

He sighs and opens his notebook. I go back to listening to the professor, but several seconds later, a paper lands on my desk.

I unfold it and read his chicken scratch while the professor writes something on the smart board.

> You should come to a party with me this weekend. Before you say no, I know you don't have any other plans, so if you say no, you're just being rude.

I turn and look at him, but he's acting like the model student now, focused completely on the professor.

I write my response under his.

> I'm not a party kind of guy. I'll just end up being a wallflower. If you make me go somewhere where I'll be uncomfortable, you're just being mean.

I wait until I can hand it over without the professor seeing, and as he reads it, I hear him sigh. Then he starts scribbling again. The paper nearly slides off my desk a few seconds later, and I slam my hand down on it, effectively gaining the attention of the professor. After a while, I read it.

> I won't let you feel uncomfortable. You know me. We'll hang out.

I don't write back to him once I read it, not wanting to risk getting caught. As soon as we're dismissed, he starts talking.

"Come on. Why not? I think you'll have a good time."

"We're very different, Adrian. Your friends don't interact with people like me."

"What do you mean?"

I give him a look like he should already know. "I'm not under the notion that I'm anything but the quiet, nerdy guy that the athletes only go to for help with assignments. I'm not supposed to be at their parties."

He looks a little taken aback and then follows me as we head for the door. "Well, first of all, it's *my* party. You're welcome at my parties."

"I don't really drink."

"So?"

"Isn't that the whole point of a party?"

"And to have fun, play games, hook up, and hang out with your friends. You're not interested in any of that?"

I mull over how to tell him that, no, I'm never really thinking of any of that, and he takes my silence as the beginning of my acquiescence.

"Come on. I know you wanna," he says, nudging my arm and giving me a smile.

My stupid, childish heart flutters in my chest, and I know right this moment that I'll do anything for him. Anything to see that smile. Anything. Even if it's a bad idea.

"Fine."

"Fuck yeah!" he shouts, grabbing me by my shoulders and shaking me. "I'm gonna make sure you have the time of your life, Cruz."

I went the rest of the week thinking about that damn

party. I stressed over what to wear. I wondered how many people would be there. I plotted an escape plan. I even got excited over hanging out with Adrian outside of a classroom...

What I didn't do was expect everything to change that night.

CHAPTER TWO
MATÍAS

"IF YOU DON'T COME OUTSIDE RIGHT now, I'm turning around and going back home."

Adrian's boisterous laugh pours into my ear through the phone. "Okay, okay. I'm coming."

As soon as I see him make his way down the steps of the house, I finally exit my car and meet him in the grass.

"You were really gonna wait at the curb all night?" he asks with a laugh.

"You don't understand the anxiety I have just being here. Why are there fifty cars?"

"Because I'm popular," he says with a shrug and boyish grin.

"Aren't they drinking? I hope there's still fifty cars here when the night is over."

He snorts and chuckles, wrapping his arm around my shoulders and tugging me toward the door. "You always so straight and narrow?"

Not straight, I think to myself. I'm not necessarily in the closet, but I don't think many people know about my sexuality, because most people don't know anything about me. I keep to myself and talk to a few people in each class. I don't hang out and have a lot of extracurriculars. I've had a couple boyfriends here and there, but nothing too serious. I don't know if Adrian even knows I'm gay. I wonder if he were to find out if it would change anything between us.

"I obey the law, if that's what you mean."

He laughs again. "You don't want a drink?" he asks as we step inside.

"Just water is fine."

As we maneuver our way through people, we find ourselves in the kitchen where he dumps half a water bottle into a red Solo cup and hands it to me.

"Let me introduce you to some people."

"Do we have to do that?"

He chuckles. "Yes. We have to."

A minute later, we're in the living room where a group of guys are surrounding an out of place table. They're drinking out of plastic cups and then flipping them over.

"What's going on?" I ask, leaning closer to Adrian.

"It's a race. The guys on this side versus the guys on that side. You drink the beer inside, then put it on the edge of the table and flip it until it lands right side up. Then the next person goes. Whichever side gets to the last person first, wins."

"Wins what?"

He laughs again. "Just wins."

After the game is over, a couple of the guys turn around and start talking to Adrian. I try not to be as awkward as I feel and take a sip of my water.

"Hey, guys. This is Matías. He's in my project management class. This is Frankie and Tyrell. But I call them Barlow and Johnson. They're on the football team with me."

"Hey, nice to meet you," I say, inclining my head slightly.

"You wanna play?" Frankie asks, gesturing to the table.

I let out a nervous chuckle. "Oh. No thanks. I'll watch."

Instead of forcing me or making me feel lame for not wanting to play, they accept my answer and gather some other people around for a new game.

"You survived," Adrian whispers, amusement in his eyes.

"Just barely."

He shakes his head and heads toward another group of people that are mingling near the TV.

"Kennedy!" the guy shouts, lifting his cup in the air. "Great party, man."

"Thanks, D," he says. "This is my friend, Matías. This is D, Penelope, and Lara."

I smile and say, "Hey," and they do the same.

"I haven't seen you at one of Adrian's parties before," one of the girls says.

"We haven't known each other for long," I reply. "Are you Penelope or Lara?"

The girls laugh, then the redhead speaks again. "I'm Penelope."

I nod and take another sip of my water.

"Kennedy, we need your help real quick," someone yells.

He leans into me. "I'll be right back."

I want to say, *no, please don't leave me here*, but I simply nod and stand there with the group of strangers I was just introduced to.

"So, Matías, right?" Penelope asks, and I nod. "Are you a senior?"

"Yeah. You?"

"Yep. Thank god. I'm so ready to be done with college."

I nod in agreement before looking around to see if Adrian is on his way back. D walks away, and Lara is engrossed in her phone.

"This isn't really your scene, is it?" Penelope asks.

I give her a small smile. "Not really, no. In fact, definitely not," I say with a laugh.

"I don't mean for this to sound rude, but why did you come?"

"Adrian asked me to. Said I was being mean if I said no."

She laughs. "I see. Peer pressure."

"I won't stay too long," I reply. "And now I have something I can hold over his head."

"Exactly. He'll owe you one, so now you can get him to do something that's out of his comfort zone."

"Do you have any ideas?" I ask.

She taps her pink painted finger on her lips. "Hmm. Oh, you know what? Bowling. He sucks at it and refuses to go."

"Really?" I ask with a smile.

She nods. "Oh yeah. I saw him once and it was bad. Four gutter balls in a row."

I laugh. "Wow. Okay."

"He still needs to use the bumpers that are made for kids."

We fall into laughter just as Adrian approaches. "Oh, look at you. You feeling more comfortable?"

"Well, when it's just me and one person, it's a little easier."

Penelope smiles at me, her green eyes sparkling. "Well, I'm gonna go use the restroom."

I nod, grinning at her, and she winks before walking away.

Adrian lifts his brows at me before perching his butt on the arm of a nearby chair. "Oooh. Penelope, huh?"

My cheeks redden. "Uhh...no."

"I see you blushing."

"Really, really...no. Not that she's not nice. She is."

Adrian looks amused as he takes a gulp from his cup. "I've known her for a couple years. Do you want me to—"

"No. I..." I look around and wonder if I should even say anything. Now isn't the best time to reveal my sexuality, but I don't want him to think I'm interested in her, and yet, I can't let him know I'm interested in him. "Meeting people is one thing. Let's just be happy I'm here."

He chuckles. "Okay. You're right. I don't want to push you too far."

His eyes trace my face before he stands up straight. "We got a game of beer pong happening in the kitchen. Wanna team up?"

I scrunch my nose. "Beer?"

"I'll drink for you. Don't worry."

"Okay. I do have a good aim."

He looks at me. "Yeah?"

I nod. "Don't look so surprised."

Adrian flashes me his perfect white teeth. "I'm not."

"Okay," I say, rolling my eyes.

I sink my first shot and so does Adrian, so we get to go again. I make my second one, but he misses. Only one person on the other team makes his shot, so Adrian drinks up, and then we continue. Once again, I sink the ball into the cup, but Adrian misses.

"Come on, man," I tease, elbowing him.

"Hey, I'm the drunk one. The cups are blurring together."

The other team makes both of theirs, and then miss the next two. When Adrian finishes his second drink, I wonder if maybe I should drink some of these.

"Are you actually drunk?" I ask quietly. "Do you need me to drink some?"

He grins at me, his eyes a little red, but still clear and alert. "I'm not that drunk. I'm good."

"Okay."

We get down to three cups on their side, and they have five on ours. Adrian misses first, and as I'm taking aim, he creeps up to my side and whispers, "You got this, man."

His breath ghosts across my neck, and I have to fight back the full-body chill that runs through me. I toss the ball and it hits the side of the cup and falls to the side.

"Dammit."

The crowd watching lets out a collective "Aww," at my streak going down the drain.

"It's okay. I'll make this for both of us," Adrian states.

He doesn't. The other team ties it up, leaving us with three cups a piece. I start getting really into it, and my pulse spikes as the nerves take over. I want to win!

I make mine. Adrian misses.

They make one.

Adrian makes his, then comes over and grabs me, playfully shaking me while our bodies are pressed against each other. "Come on, come on," he says joyfully, basically humping my hip.

I miss, because of course I did. How can I focus after this man just grinded all over me?

The other team makes one.

"Okay, wait, wait, wait. I need to discuss strategy with my partner," Adrian says, pulling me away and wrapping an arm around my neck as he moves in close. "Who should throw first? If we make this, we win. Well, they can counter attack, but hopefully they miss. If we miss both shots, then our fate rests in their hands. One of us has to..."

I stop hearing him. His words fade into the background and the sound of my rapidly beating heart takes over. Adrian's hair brushes against my forehead, and his lips look so soft and inviting as he talks about this ridiculous game. He retracts his arm slightly, his hand squeezing the back of my neck. My eyes close.

"Cruz. Cruz." He shakes me and I snap out of my haze.

"Huh? Oh. Sorry."

"So, I think you should—"

"No, you," I say quickly, standing up straight and backing away from his hold. "You go. I trust you."

His lips form a crooked grin. "Okay," he replies, dragging out the word in a sing-songy voice. "But if I miss, you can't hold it over my head."

I think I smile at him, but my heart is thumping and my body feels hot, and I'm aware of everyone around me. I wouldn't be able to make this shot. Not with my body vibrating the way it is. I need to leave this party and stop dreaming about Adrian Kennedy.

Suddenly, the room erupts, and I'm once again yanked from my daydream. Adrian comes at me, his huge football player frame looking like he's about to tackle me to the floor. Which might be fun, if we were alone—and naked. But he doesn't do that. He lifts me from my feet, jostling me up and down his body as he bounces with excitement.

"We won!" he yells, halfway to being drunk.

"We did?"

I missed the rest of the game while stuck in my head.

"Thanks to you!" He puts me down. "I've never won one of these games."

I smile. "Well, yay!"

Adrian barks out a laugh. "Yes. Yay. Let's go get a drink."

I don't bother to tell him I'm *still* not drinking, instead just choosing to follow him wherever he's going.

Adrian opens the fridge and quickly closes it, spinning around. "Come with me," he says in a whisper.

"What are we doing?" I reply back in the same tone, following him toward the stairs.

"Stealing beer from Barlow's room."

"Oh, well, that's not nice."

He chuckles. "It's fine."

"Be the lookout," he tells me as I stand in the doorway. "Let me know if he's coming."

"I'm not gonna lie to you. I've already forgotten what he looks like."

"Big guy with long blond hair."

"Got it."

Adrian opens up a mini fridge next to a full-sized bed and takes two cans before coming back toward me.

"You want one?"

I shake my head. "I'm probably gonna leave soon, so I shouldn't."

Instead of going downstairs, he walks to another door down the hall. When I step inside the room behind him, he's already sitting on the corner of the bed.

"I take it this is your room."

"Yep."

"Much quieter up here," I say with relief.

"Yeah. It won't die down for a while. You can close the door."

With the click of the latch, my heart rate begins to spike again. He's putting one beer on the floor and then opening the other, completely unaware of how nervous I just became.

I know it makes no logical sense. He lives in a house with other guys, so I'm sure they visit each other's rooms often. I'm overthinking things because I'm attracted to him and because I like him, but he doesn't even know I'm gay. Being alone with him, in his room, means nothing.

"So, first party. How do you feel?" he asks with a wide smile.

I awkwardly lean against his dresser, not wanting to sit on the bed with him. "It's...good. I won a game of beer pong, so—"

"Damn right you did," he says, holding up his beer.

I laugh. "Yeah. I'm still alive, so that's a plus."

"Is death a usual thought when you're invited to parties?" he teases.

"Well, I'm not usually invited to them, so no. But social situations in general aren't my thing. Also, I'm dramatic, so when I say 'still alive' I just mean, not panicking and running for the nearest exit."

"Ah. I see." He takes another sip of his beer and the silence is thick between us for a bit. "So, Penelope?"

I let out a nervous laugh. "No."

"Come on. I saw the way you two were laughing together."

"I'm really not interested. Are *you* into her or something?"

"Me? No. No, no. She's the ex-girlfriend of one of my friends. That feels wrong."

Wanting to change the subject from Penelope, girls, and dating in general, I scan the room hoping to find something to talk about. He's got a calendar on the wall that holds a photo of a bikini-clad woman, so I keep scanning. There's a South River University flag on the wall surrounded by some football memorabilia. His desk is littered with papers, but his mirror has photos tucked in the sides, so I walk over there.

There's one of him holding a football with a girl standing next to him. There's a group photo of him and his friends, another one of the same girl from the other picture, except this time she's alone. There's a picture of a dog next to one of

Adrian and the same dog when they were both younger and smaller.

"Is this your dog?"

"Yeah. Well, my parents' dog, I guess. They got it when I was a kid, so I've grown up with him."

"What's his name?"

"Tyson."

"He's cute."

"The girl is my sister," he offers.

"Oh. What's her name?"

"Amelia."

"So, are you trying to go pro?" I ask, finally turning around to face him.

He snorts. "That would be a dream, but it's just that."

"You're not good?"

Adrian laughs, putting his open beer on the nightstand before standing up. "I'm good."

"What uhh...part do you play?"

His smile stretches across his face. "I play the defensive end *part*. A linebacker," he adds with a shrug, like that's supposed to help.

"Ah," I say with a nod.

He removes his T-shirt, his undershirt lifting in the process and showing off his torso. After tossing it into a hamper in the corner, he kicks off his shoes.

"So," I say, swallowing and looking away. "If not football, what are your plans?"

Adrian sighs. "Business with my dad. He has a company, and I already have a job lined up as long as I pass my classes and graduate."

"Oh, well, that's good."

"I guess," he says, propping himself up against the pillows on his bed. "What about you?"

I shift and knock something off his dresser. "Oops. Sorry."

I bend down and pick it up and then just stand in the middle of the room. "Well, I—"

Adrian laughs. "Why do you look so uncomfortable?"

With a little shake of my head, I say, "Uhh. I am."

"Why? It's just me."

Just him. Yeah, just him and his ridiculous body. Him and those full and tempting lips. Him and that smile that makes you want to join in even if you have no idea why. Him and those eyes that draw you in and keep your attention.

"I feel comfortable around you," he says. "I want you to feel comfortable around me."

Yeah, well, he's not harboring a stupid crush, so that's easy to say. Have you ever been around someone you're absolutely smitten with? You are never comfortable. You're concerned about your posture, your body, and what's potentially in your teeth. Is your hair doing that weird thing? Do you have something in your nose? What does your ass look like in your jeans? Are they looking at you the way you want them to?

"I mean, I'm fine," I say, making my way to the chair at his desk.

"Can I tell you a secret?" he asks.

My lungs seize. "Yes."

<h1 style="text-align:center">CHAPTER THREE
MATÍAS</h1>

HE SCOOTS UP, one leg dangling off the side of the bed. I find myself leaning toward him, wondering what the hell kind of secret he's about to reveal—to me of all people.

"I don't want to work for my dad."

I lean back. Was it ignorant to believe, even for the tiniest of seconds, that he was going to reveal he was secretly gay and also maybe had a crush on me? Perhaps. It could happen though. It does in books and movies.

"Oh?" I question, trying not to sound disappointed.

He nods. "I'm not saying that pro football is what I want to do either."

"What do you want to do?"

He picks at a string on his hunter green comforter. "I don't know. I've thought about a few things, but I guess they're mostly hobbies."

"Tell me."

"I like writing." He peers up at me like he's waiting for me to make fun of him.

"Really? Like stories? Poetry?"

"Stories, though I did start with poetry. I'm not too good at it. You'd think rhyming would be easy."

I chuckle. "What else?"

He beams. I can almost see light radiating off of him. "Come here."

Reaching into the drawer next to him, he pulls out a photo album. I'm standing in front of the bed, but he taps the spot next to him so I reluctantly climb on top of the covers.

"I do a little photography."

Inside the album are dozens of photos ranging from black-and-white candids to vivid landscape scenery.

I grab hold of the photo album and keep turning the pages. "Oh, my god. These are incredible."

"They're just pictures."

"No. These are really good, Adrian."

We look at each other, and he grins, a tinge of pink staining his cheeks. "Thanks." With a sigh, he continues, "But they're both hobbies. Dad says I can't make a living with writing or photography."

"No offense, but your dad is wrong."

"Wanna tell him?" he says with a laugh.

I grip the album, but angle my head to look at him. "You got strict parents?"

"Oh, yeah. Strict is actually very understated. I have dictator parents."

"That sucks."

"Yeah. What about you?"

"My parents are fine. I'm closer to my mom, but my dad is cool. They divorced when I was fifteen, and I stayed with my mom."

For the next two hours, we lose track of time as we talk about our families and what it was like for us in high school. I tell him about growing up in Detroit and why I plan on staying in South River after college. He tells me he's from Chicago and mentions some football rivalry between Detroit and Chicago's teams. Then he goes on to talk about his sister, and I tell him about the first time I drank and why I don't want it to happen again. It involved an embarrassing story about throwing up in a sink at a bar.

We talk about nearly everything and get to know each other so much more in just a matter of hours. I've never talked to someone like this before. I've never known so much about another person. I had some friends in high school, but I wasn't a popular kid. I didn't have sleepovers and birthday parties at skating rinks. I talked to other students at school and that was about it.

Adrian ignores his buzzing cell phone to continue listening to me talk about my failed attempt at fishing for the first time and why I'll never try that again either. He laughs when I tell him I threw the fish back in the water after catching it, because I felt bad, only to find out he died anyway.

After a quick bathroom break, he comes back in the room with a story about running away when he was twelve. He didn't last long; he went back home only hours later with his tail between his legs because he was hungry.

At some point we end up flat on our backs, Adrian throwing a small basketball in the air and catching it over and over while I stare at the blades of the fan spinning around.

"So, you want to get into software development?" he asks.

"I love anything to do with computers. I'm certified with CompTIA A+ and have been since high school. It's a basic understanding of IT. But I've always loved creating games and doing coding and stuff like that."

"That's cool."

I stifle a yawn and finally look at the time. "Holy shit. It's almost three in the morning."

"Is it?" Adrian asks, looking at his clock. "Damn."

"I should get going."

He puts the ball down. "Yeah."

I sit up and swing my legs over the side. "Thanks for inviting me."

"Of course. You ready to do it again next weekend?"

I grin as I walk to the door. "Maybe, but don't hold your breath."

The truth is, I can't do it again. I feel myself liking him way too much already. It's dangerous, this sort of thing. I'm infatuated. He's oblivious.

He gets up and follows me. "Want me to walk you to the car?"

I bite my lip before saying, "Would you?"

"Let me get my shoes on."

I yawn and wipe the wetness from my eyes.

"Maybe you should stay here. You know what they say, 'driving sleepy is driving impaired.'"

"Is that what they say?"

He nods. "Yep."

"Hmm." I tap my lips with my finger, realizing just how tired I am. My eyes do feel a little blurry. A slow, long blink might put me to sleep, but staying with Adrian is not the smartest move.

"Do you have class tomorrow?" he asks.

"If I did, I wouldn't be here. I'm not that irresponsible."

He laughs. "Okay, so stay. My bed is big enough. I can give you something to change into so you don't sleep in jeans."

"No, it's okay. I'll make it home fine. It's not too far away. Maybe right under thirty minutes."

"Just stay and stop being weird. It's not a big deal."

To you.

"Well—" I yawn. "I guess. Thanks. Um."

"Bathroom is down the hall to the left. I'll find you some pants. They'll probably be too big, but..." He shrugs, but doesn't finish his thought. "Okay, let me show you what to use in the bathroom."

I don't question what he means, choosing to quietly follow him instead. There are still people downstairs, but nobody sees us as we cross the hall.

Adrian opens the cabinet under the sink and pulls out a caddy. "This is my stuff. Soaps, mouthwash, toothpaste, deodorant, etcetera. Use what you need. I don't have extra toothbrushes, but you can use the floss and mouthwash." He hands over a pair of pants. "And here's these."

I take them and give him a small smile. "Thanks."

He turns around and goes back to his room, so I close the door and start my routine. I don't shower because I don't want some of the other guys to try to come in, but I do quickly undress and basically give myself a sponge bath with what looked like a clean cloth in a basket full of them, and some of Adrian's body wash. I focus on the important parts and toss the cloth in the hamper before using some lotion and mouthwash. With my own T-shirt and underwear back on, I take the lounge pants Adrian gave me and pull them up my legs. They are big on me, in both length and in the waist, but luckily there's a drawstring.

I quietly open the door and peek out, hoping nobody else is up here. I don't know why I'm sneaking like I'm going to get in trouble, but as soon as I realize I'm alone, I rush to Adrian's room before I see anyone.

When I get inside, I quickly shut the door behind me. Adrian's at the bed, pulling the covers down, but he spins around at the noise. "Someone chasing you?"

"No."

He laughs. "You're being weird."

"No I'm not."

"Pants okay?" he asks with a quick glance.

"Yeah, fine."

"Cool. I'm gonna use the bathroom now, but you can get comfortable."

Once he's gone, I remove my shirt and climb under the covers, turning to the side so he can't see my face when he gets back in.

The door clicks with his return, but he doesn't say anything. I hear some shuffling and a drawer close, and then the bed dips with his weight.

After a few seconds, he says, "You asleep?"

I hesitate briefly. "No."

I feel him roll around. "Did you used to date James Parrish?"

I stop breathing.

CHAPTER FOUR
MATÍAS

THE SILENCE STRETCHES for what feels like forever, and I contemplate two things simultaneously. The first is launching myself out of his second story window, and the second is pretending to have fallen asleep in the five seconds since he asked me if I was asleep.

Neither one seems great.

How in the hell does he know I'm gay? Or know anything about James? Why would he ask about him at all?

"No," I answer simply, hoping he'll leave it alone.

"Oh," he replies quickly. "He had mentioned—"

I sigh. "James had a crush on me. It wasn't reciprocated."

"Oh," he says again. "Is it because…" He doesn't know how to finish the question, but he wants answers.

"What do you want to know, Adrian?"

He's quiet for a little while. "I don't want you to think I care either way. I don't."

"But you need to know if you have a gay guy sleeping in your bed?"

"No!" he says loudly. "No. Not that at all."

"I think I'm gonna go," I say, sitting up.

"Please don't," he says, the bed shifting with his movement. "I'm really not trying to judge you."

"Not *trying* to," I say.

He reaches for me, his hand clasping around my arm as I go to stand up. "I just—I need to..." He sighs. "God, please just tell me I'm not alone."

My back stiffens and my eyes widen at the window. Did he just...

"What?" I question softly.

He falls back onto the bed with a heavy sigh and when I look over my shoulder, I see he has his hands over his face.

I take a breath. "Yes. I'm gay."

His hands fall away from his face, revealing an expression that melts from worry to wonder. "You are?"

I nod. "Yes."

He exhales, closing his eyes as his lips form the tiniest smile. "I'm not alone."

"So, you're..."

"Bi?"

"Is that a question?"

"Well, I've never actually done anything with a guy, so—"

"That doesn't matter."

"Nobody knows," he says, sitting up quickly, his eyes wild with panic as he looks at me. "Nobody. I've never even..." He shakes his head. "Nobody can know. Please don't say anything."

"I won't."

"Okay."

"Did you befriend me so you could know another queer person?" I ask, suddenly feeling sick. "So you could tell someone you'd think would understand and keep your secret?"

He sits up. "No. I didn't know until a week ago. I have James in another class, and I guess he saw you and me leaving project management together, so he started talking about you."

I relax a little. "Hmm."

"Will you lie back down? You can go to sleep. I promise I won't bother you anymore." He gives me a crooked smile.

"Fine. But going to sleep with this information is going to be hard."

"Why?"

I shake my head. "Never mind. Good night. Or morning."

He chuckles. "Night."

My mind will not shut down. It doesn't matter that I've been awake for like eighteen hours. I'm wired, trying to understand how the guy I've been crushing on is now telling me he's also into guys, and I'm in his fucking bed. Okay, it's not like we're sleeping together. We're still just friends. But come on.

"You're moving an awful lot for someone who's supposed to be asleep," Adrian says, his voice scratchy.

"Well, you're clearly awake."

"You keep stealing the covers every time you move. It wakes me up."

"Sorry."

"Turn around."

I roll over onto my other side and find him in the mirrored position.

"What do you want to know?"

"When did you know?" I ask, already having thought about twenty questions.

"Pretty early on. Middle school maybe."

"You've never thought to tell anyone?"

"No," he says, drawing out the word. "Remember me

mentioning my dictator parents? Yeah, well, they would never be okay with that. I couldn't risk them finding out. I overheard plenty of conversations that made it clear what they thought about gay people."

"That's sad."

"We can't choose our parents."

"No, but you can choose your family. You can find people who will accept and love you regardless, and you make a point to keep them close."

"Do you have a chosen family like that?"

"Not really," I say after a few seconds. "But I have my parents. They're good people. I'm just not good at putting myself out there and making friends. Too introverted, I suppose."

"We're friends."

"Yeah, well, you kind of forced yourself on me."

He laughs. "God, don't say it like that."

I snort. "I'm glad you told me."

"Yeah?"

I nod. "And I promise I won't tell anyone. It's your secret and it'll stay between you and me."

"Thank you," he says with a smile. After a few seconds he says, "Can I ask you another question?"

"Is it going to scare the living shit out of me again?"

"My question scared you?"

"Are you kidding? I'm in the bed of one of the most popular football players on campus, in a house with even more popular football players, and you ask me if I dated some guy? Of course I was scared."

His fast softens. "I'm sorry. Not for asking, but for not realizing how and why it would be scary for you."

"It's fine. I haven't dealt with much bullying on campus. That was in high school. And probably why I keep everything lowkey. Better to fly under the radar."

"That's kind of sad, too," he says.

I shrug. "What was your other question?"

He bites down on his lip. "It's kind of personal, so definitely tell me to shut the fuck up if you need to."

I laugh. "Okay."

"You've like...been with guys, right? Dated? Hooked up?"

"Yeah."

"Okay, so how did you get to that point?"

"What do you mean?"

"How do you know if someone is...you know, into guys? Or like, into you? Especially if you're not out."

"Ah. Well, I just knew. And as cliché as it is, when someone's into you, you'll know."

"Ugh." He flops onto his back and puts his palms over his eyes.

"What?"

"Nothing."

"Tell me."

"We graduate this year."

"Right," I say, wondering where he's going with this.

"They always say college is for experimenting and having fun, and I've been too afraid to do anything, and now I'm in my senior year, and it's the last chance I have to even try. To have the experience before...before life gets in the way."

"I see. Well, there are apps."

He scrunches up his face. "Then anyone who sees me will know."

The thought of offering myself up comes to mind. Of course it does. But I'm not about to assume he's attracted to me. That's the problem with the heteros. They think if you're gay you're automatically attracted to everyone of the same sex. Also, it doesn't make me feel too good to offer myself up as an experiment. Something for him to try on and discard. If he wants me, that's different.

I bite my lip to keep from saying what's on the tip of my tongue. The thought makes my stomach coil, but he's my friend. Only that.

"I can take you to a club. It's not in town, and it caters to those of us in the alphabet mafia."

He chokes on a laugh. "The what?"

"Alphabet mafia. LGBTQIA. The alphabet."

Adrian laughs and laughs. "That's a good one. I haven't heard of that."

I shake my head, smiling as I watch him. "Anyway. Yeah, you could go there and see if, you know, anyone catches your eye."

He watches me for a while, his eyes assessing. "You'd do that for me?"

With a nod, I say, "I can be a good wingman."

It takes a second for him to respond. "Hmm. Okay. Sure."

"No pressure," I tell him. "You don't have to."

"I know." His eyes scan my face again. "Why not, though?" he says with a shrug.

"Right."

"Wait. I thought you hated social scenes and parties. You go to clubs?"

"I've only been a couple times. It's really not my scene. Loud music, loud people, crowded spaces, but yeah, I've been."

"Okay, so, next weekend?"

"Sure."

"Perfect. You're the best."

I smile and roll to my back where the smile slowly slips from my face.

CHAPTER FIVE
MATÍAS

I'VE SEEN Adrian more than usual this week. Not only in class, but he's opted to eat lunch with me a couple of times, asking me questions about the bar and basically panicking the way I was when he invited me to his party. He's been adorable...if a six-foot-four, two-hundred-and-something-pound football player can be adorable.

I'm seeing a different side of Adrian since he told me his secret. He's opened up even more, and in doing so, allowed me to be more myself around him. I felt like I was carrying my own secret, not wanting him to know because I was afraid he'd not want to be my friend, and now I'm at my most authentic self with him.

He walked to my dorm with me after class one day, simply because we were so caught up in conversation. Once we were at the door, he was like, "Oh. I guess I should leave you alone now."

I wanted to invite him in. I never want our talks to come to an end, but I know that they must, so I simply nodded and said goodbye.

It's now Friday, and I'm in my car heading toward his

house to pick him up. My stomach is in knots, and not for the reason I'd like it to be. Instead of first date nerves, it's *he could potentially find someone to hookup with* nerves.

I'm wearing dark blue chinos and a white Henley with white tennis shoes. My brown hair is a mess of loose curls on top of my head, and I took extra time to trim up the small amount of hair on my face and spritz some cologne on. Maybe he won't be the only one looking for a hookup.

When I park outside the house he shares with his friends, I send him a text to let him know I'm here. He jogs out five minutes later and makes me want to drive off, because I don't want to be the person who delivers him to someone else.

Good god, he looks sexy. He's wearing a long-sleeved, white shirt and a pair of black pants. It's not even the clothes that are special, it's the way he looks in them. He's muscular, and there's no hiding it. The shirt isn't tight, but you can still tell how well-built he is through it. He's got a nice watch on his wrist, his hair is freshly buzzed, and his beard is neat and trim.

When he gets inside, I breathe in his scent. It's a mixture of whatever he uses in the shower, and subtle citrus cologne.

"You—" I almost say *you look good* but quickly change it up. "You cut your hair."

He runs a hand over his head. "Yeah, just wanted a change. It'll grow back."

"I like it," I say, and then immediately feel embarrassed. "Anyway, you ready?"

"I think so." He pats down his legs. "Wallet, phone, and hopefully I find some courage in one of these pockets."

"Oh please," I say with a laugh. "You'll be fine."

The hour-long drive is filled, not with music, but with a lively discussion about which breakfast food is better. Adrian swears you're not eating breakfast if you're not eating eggs, bacon, and sausage, but I say, you need to have some pancakes or waffles. After that, we laugh for about fifteen minutes while simply talking about some TV show we both watched and how funny we thought a particular line was.

Once we park, we find our way inside, get a stamp on the hand, and then go straight for the bar.

Adrian orders a beer, and I get a fancy iced tea, which is basically just an iced tea and lemonade combo.

The bar is crowded with people trying to get drinks, so we quickly move away and find a high-top table to stand near.

There are quite a few people on the dancefloor, plenty of people lingering against the wall, and several people at tables.

"Sooo," I say, looking around. "What's your type?"

He chuckles nervously. "Uhh, well, I don't know. Umm."

"Okay, are we thinking big, like you," I say, eyeing his arms. "Smaller? Feminine? Masculine? Brown hair or blond hair?" I take a sip of my drink.

"I don't want anyone as big as me. I mean, that's a lot of weight."

"Okay," I say with a snort. "So, no bears for you."

"Uhh, no."

"Do you watch porn?"

He looks around like he's nervous someone is going to hear...or care. "Well, yeah."

"What do you typically watch?"

Adrian shifts, his face flushing slightly. "This feels weird to talk about."

"Why? Because it's gay porn? I bet you or your friends have talked about watching porn, or talked about what type of girls you like. Big boobs. Big ass. Etcetera."

"Okay, well, yeah, but I don't tell my friends which porn clip I was watching."

I point out a guy in front of us. He's got a little makeup on, blond hair, and a tank top that shows off his small frame.

"Mmm. Not really."

The next guy I point out has slightly darker hair and pale skin. He's wearing khaki shorts and a maroon shirt. He's also wearing glasses and looks a little older than us.

Adrian gives me a look that screams *why did you even ask?*

"Well, I'm trying to help," I say with a laugh.

"What about that one?" I ask, pointing to a Black guy with a bright smile, wearing jeans and a Polo shirt.

He tilts his head from side to side. "Maybe."

"He's not too big. Not too small."

"Just right? Are we Goldilocks now?"

"Not *we*," I say. "You. I know my type."

"What is it?" he asks.

"Nope. We're here for you."

He grumbles and takes a drink. "Should we dance?"

"I don't dance," I tell him. "Plus they'll think we're together, which won't be helpful. In fact, maybe I should go to the bathroom and see if someone approaches you."

He grabs my arm. "No. Please."

"All right, all right."

We end up just talking at the table for half an hour. When we go to the bar for another beer for Adrian and a water for me, that's when someone approaches.

"Can I buy you guys a shot?"

I look over and find an attractive man on the other side of Adrian. He's wearing a striped T-shirt and blue jeans and has a baseball cap on. His eyes are blue, and his smile is kind.

"Oh. Well, I'm not drinking, but he can have one," I say, putting my hand on Adrian's shoulder.

"Perfect. What do you like?"

"Uhh. Oh, I don't know. Tequila?"

"Tequila, huh?" the guy says with a grin. "I do bad things when I drink tequila."

Adrian's cheeks turn pink, and he looks over at me. I lift my brows and give him an encouraging nod.

"Oh, yeah?" he asks, leaning against the bar. "What kind of bad things?"

The man laughs. "Maybe you'll find out."

As they get their drinks, I decide to slip away and go to the bathroom. On the way back, I'm stopped by a tall and fairly muscular guy in a black button-up.

"Hey."

"Hi," I reply, looking up at him.

"You with anyone?"

"Just my friend."

"Can I buy you a drink?"

"Well, I'm the DD, so it'll have to be a boring drink."

He gives me a crooked smile. "Just because the drink is boring doesn't mean our conversation has to be."

I grin. "Okay."

We end up a few people away from Adrian and the guy he's talking to.

"So, what's your name?" he asks.

"Matías. Yours?"

"Blake. Do you live around here?"

"About an hour away. South River."

"I went to SRU," he says with excitement. "Are you in school there?"

"Yep. I graduate this year."

"Awesome." He takes a sip of his drink, staring at me the whole time. "I really love your eyes."

"Really?" I question. "They're just brown."

"They're a honey-brown. Really pretty."

My smile grows. "Thanks."

"Hey, Cruz. Oh, sorry. Hey, can I talk to you for a second?" Adrian asks, busting in between me and Blake.

"Cruz?" Blake questions.

"My last name," I say.

He looks relieved. "I thought you were trying to give me some fake name there for a second. Hopefully I get your real number by the end of the night."

We watch each other, smiles on our lips.

"Cruz."

"I'll be back," I tell Blake. "What's wrong?" I ask Adrian as he tugs me farther down the bar.

"That guy. His name is Jeremy. He wants to uhh...you know. Like now."

"Oh." My eyes widen.

"Yeah."

"Well, what are you thinking?"

"That I'm definitely not having sex with some random dude in a bathroom or an alley or even at his place. He doesn't know I don't know shit about this. I don't even know what to expect. Like, I was thinking maybe a little flirting. Maybe a kiss. Oh, my god. I sound so ridiculous right now."

"No you don't."

"I just wasn't expecting things to escalate so fast."

"Wanna go?" I ask him.

He looks over my shoulder. "I don't wanna mess up what you have going on."

"It's fine."

"You sure?" he asks, looking in my eyes. I nod. "Okay. Yeah, let's go."

"All right."

I walk over to the table where Blake waits for me. "I have to get my friend home."

"Oh, okay." He looks disappointed at first, but then a slow smile creeps onto his face. "Well, can I get your number?"

I smile at him and glance over at Adrian who's watching the exchange. "Sure. Yeah."

He pulls his phone from his pocket and hands it over to me. I type in my number and hand it back.

"This is the real one, right?" he teases with a grin.

"It is," I reply with a nod.

"Well, it was nice meeting you," he states, coming in for a hug.

"Nice meeting you, too."

When I pull away, I find I can't bring myself to make eye contact with Adrian. I end up at his side, and we walk out and make our way to the car.

"Get a date?" he asks.

"No. We'll see if he calls me. He probably won't."

After a second he says, "He will."

I clear my throat and unlock my silver sedan. "Sorry the night didn't turn out well for you."

He waves it off as he sits down. "It's fine. Baby steps, right?"

Twenty minutes from his house, he speaks up. "I don't really want the night to end, though. It's only a little after eleven."

"Only," I say with a snort.

"Hey, we were up until like five in the morning last weekend."

"What do you wanna do?"

He shrugs. "My roommates are having a party."

"Oh, god."

He laughs. "I didn't say we have to go."

"I only have a dorm, so it's not very spacious."

"That's fine," he says. "We can pick up some food and just watch TV."

"That's what you wanna do?"

"Yeah, why not?"

I shake my head, a laugh escaping me. "I mean, I guess."

"Good. You pick the food. I pick the movie."

CHAPTER SIX

MATÍAS

WE END up with pizza from a late-night diner and Adrian chooses to watch some comedy movie I've never seen.

He starts off at my desk, while I eat on my bed, but once he's done, he kicks off his shoes and makes himself comfortable next to me.

My full-sized bed is pushed against the wall, so he's in the corner with a pillow behind his back while I'm on the other side.

What the hell is my life?

It's almost one in the morning when my phone buzzes against the nightstand. It's a text from Blake.

> Hey. Just wanted to say thanks for giving me your number and ask if you'd be free tomorrow.

"Oh," I say out loud, not meaning to.

"What's wrong?"

"Nothing. It's Blake. From the bar."

"Blake from the bar," he says, deadpan. "He wants to meet up?"

"Tomorrow."

He nods, scratching at his chin, eyes focused on the TV. "Are you going to?"

"Maybe."

"Is that your type?"

"Pretty much."

"Hmm."

"What? You don't think he's cute?"

"I don't have to. If you do, that's fine."

"Well—"

"I guess I should go," he says, scooting off the bed.

"What? Why?"

"You're texting. I don't know."

He seems agitated now and I'm confused. "You don't even have a car and you live half an hour away. More if you're walking."

"It's fine."

"Adrian."

He turns to face me after he gets his shoes on. "What?"

"What's going on?"

He shakes his head like he's annoyed, huffing out a sigh. "Do you like me?"

"What? Of course I do."

"Not like..." He pauses. "I mean, am I not being obvious enough?"

"Obvious?"

He blows out a breath. "Never mind. I'll see you later."

He's out the door, leaving me on the bed in a sea of confusion. When it hits me, my eyes double in size and I leap out of the bed and rush to the door.

"Adrian!"

He's down the hall, but spins around at the sound of his name. He looks frustrated but he stops moving and waits for me to get to him.

"Are you saying..."

His eyes dance over my face, landing on my lips for several seconds before staring deep into my eyes. "That I like you?" he finishes. "Yeah."

"But...when?"

"Since the beginning." He takes a breath and rubs the back of his neck. "I was already secretly crushing, but knew I'd never be able to tell you. When James let it slip that you're gay, I was excited. I thought, well, maybe. Then I was confused at the party with you and Penelope. I thought I was giving you hints. I was touching you a lot. Taking you to my room, inviting you to stay, and then insisting you stay. Once I told you, I thought, well, if he doesn't realize now..."

I shake my head. "No. There's not one time I ever thought you'd be remotely interested."

He sighs. "I guess I'm not good at this."

"Maybe I'm not either."

He laughs. "Well."

"Let's go back to my room."

Once we're inside, I face him. "Why didn't you say anything when I was basically forcing you to meet guys tonight?"

"Well, I thought you definitely weren't interested if you were doing that, so I just went with it."

I pinch my lips together. "Damn. I'm sorry."

He shrugs, putting his hands in his pockets. "I suppose it

doesn't matter if it's only one-sided." His eyes are on the floor, but I can see a hint of pink in his cheeks.

A laugh escapes me. "I guess I've done a good job keeping my feelings close to the vest then."

Adrian looks up, eyes scanning my face. "So..."

"Let's just say the crush is reciprocated."

His face splits with a grin, eyes lighting up in relief. "So, I *am* your type."

I smirk and roll my eyes. "And I guess I'm yours."

He dips his chin, eyes laser-focused on me. The energy shifts around us. The tension is thick, and we're both getting closer to each other.

"I want to kiss you."

"Okay," I say softly, both of us leaning in.

I tilt my head back so his lips can land on mine. It's soft at first. A few pecks to get a feel for each other.

When his lips part, I slide my tongue between them, eliciting a groan from his throat.

My entire body melts on the inside.

Adrian grabs my hip with one hand and cradles my face with the other. Our tongues meet and dance, and our moans come together in harmony.

After several long seconds, we pull away, but keep our foreheads connected. Adrian releases a soft sigh that sounds like it's full of relief, then his hand cups the back of my head and he presses his lips to mine in a firm kiss. And then another.

"God, you have no idea how long I've been wanting to do that," he finally says, head still against mine.

"You're telling me," I say with a shy smile. "I may have fantasized about this a time or two."

He smirks. "Good. Glad I wasn't alone in fantasyland."

Fidgeting with my fingers, I say, "What now?"

"Everything," he replies with a wide smile. "I want to do everything with you."

My stupid, naive heart soars. It skips a beat and makes me skip past asking any questions. Like, do you think you're ever going to come out? Is this just for fun? Will I simply be your dirty little secret? Are you using me?

Instead of laying down rules to protect my pride and dignity, I fall into bed with him where we continue to makeout for the next hour. We don't set boundaries. We don't iron out details. We just pretend like we don't have anything to worry about—and that's problem number one.

Eight Years Later

Matías

CHAPTER SEVEN
MATÍAS

"The new project manager is coming in this week," Mr. Bryant, our HR rep, tells me. "He's new to the area, and he and his wife are moving into their house as we speak. He should be in the office Friday to sign some paperwork."

"Okay. I have three meetings Friday, but I'll try to find time to introduce myself."

Mr. Bryant looks at his watch. "It's almost six-thirty. You heading out soon?"

"Yeah. Soon."

"You work too much, you know. Take it from an old man; get some play time in there, too."

"Coming from the old man who's also still at work ninety minutes after we're supposed to be gone?"

"I'm old," he says with a shrug, running a hand through his white hair. "I'm telling you to learn from my mistakes."

"I play plenty," I say with a smirk. "Don't worry about me."

"Yeah, yeah. I'll see you tomorrow."

"Night, Peter."

"Night, Matt."

It's another thirty minutes before I leave the building, but when I do, I go straight home to shower and then I'm in my car again. I have an appointment I don't want to be late for.

I drive forty-five minutes outside of South River, arriving in Wyndgrove. The Victorian mansion sits on the outskirts of town. I park in a lot half a block away, and walk up to the four story house, past the perfectly landscaped hedges until I round the corner and press the button at the gate.

"Name?"

"Matías Cruz."

"Thank you, Mr. Cruz."

The black wrought iron fence opens up and allows me to step in. At the small guard shack, I hand over my ID to get checked in.

I'm surrounded by lush gardens as I stroll up the pathway that leads to the wraparound porch, then I make my way through the exquisitely restored mansion from the 1800s.

While it definitely holds a lot of the old charm, it's been upgraded with both opulence and lasciviousness. A sex club hidden behind a 19th century facade.

I ignore the people in the drawing room, who are all talking or drinking, and go straight for the stairs that'll lead me to the third floor where I have a room reserved.

I've been a member of Summons House for five years, and I've always had fairly regular visits. Tonight, I'm seeing a guy I've known for several months, and hopefully he's already ready for me.

When I open the door, I find him on his knees, wearing only a pair of briefs.

My lips quirk up into a grin as I close the door behind me.

"Waiting long?" I ask as I make my way around him, taking in his body.

"I'd wait as long as I needed to," he replies, eyes trained on the door.

I give a hum of approval as I find myself back in front of him.

"It was a busy day. I apologize for the delay, but I'm here now."

Christian's eyes flicker up to my face. "Can I make you feel better?"

I step closer. "Let's see."

CHAPTER EIGHT

MATÍAS

I DIDN'T GET HOME until after midnight last night, and after a quick meal, I crawled into bed feeling only partly satisfied.

Christian's a decent guy. He's attractive, he listens, and we typically have a good time together. My problem is that we've met up at least five times now, and I think he's starting to grow an attachment. It's probably my fault. I should've stopped agreeing to meet up after the second time.

My alarm woke me up at six, and I walked into my office at seven-thirty. Since then, I've had two meetings—one here and one at another office. I brought lunch back to my desk so I could eat while I sent out half a dozen emails, and then I quickly met with an engineering team before finding myself behind my desk to work on an employee training PowerPoint.

A knock on the door pulls me out of my work. "Yes?"

Mr. Bryant opens the door. "Sorry to bother you, but the new guy is here now."

"I thought he wasn't coming until Friday?" I ask with a quick glance at the calendar on my desk.

Mr. Bryant shrugs.

I sigh. "Give me a few."

After about ten minutes, I get up and open the door to my office, peering out until I spot Mr. Bryant standing in the doorway of the office across the room. I give him a nod and walk back to my desk.

As I'm finishing writing myself a note, a small knock hits my open door. "Hello."

Footsteps enter my office and I look up.

My breath doesn't hitch, my eyes don't bulge. The sudden reappearance of my past doesn't present itself like it does in the movies. I don't stumble over my words and make an ass out of myself. I simply freeze, my face stoic as my brain tries to comprehend what I'm seeing.

I internally debate with myself if this is who I think it is. It can't possibly be him. He must have a doppelganger, and yet, nobody else could look like this.

"Matías?"

His question is my answer. It is him.

I dip my chin. "Well, everyone here calls me Matt, or actually, Mr. Cruz."

He smiles, putting his hand in the pocket of his gray slacks. "When I saw Matt Cruz on the paperwork, I didn't put it together that it could be you. Nobody ever called you Matt in college."

"Well," I sigh. "They do now."

His lips fall into a frown, but he makes his way to the seat in front of my desk. "Wow, this is crazy. I can't—I can't believe it." When I don't reply, he continues. "So, I guess I'm working for you now."

As reality sinks in, I rub a hand over my forehead, exhaling. "I guess so."

"I've signed all the HR paperwork," he says. "I took a peek inside my office. Looks like I'll need to liven it up a little, but I have things from my old office I can bring over. Do you have any information for me?"

I stare at him, his face just as annoyingly perfect and handsome as it was in college, probably more so. He's got a little bit of a five o'clock shadow happening, but it's lined up nicely. His brown hair is shiny and combed perfectly. Looking into his eyes transports me back into a time where things were much different.

"I'll email you," I say after clearing my throat. "You'll need to meet with the team and get with Mrs. O'Terry. She'll get you caught up on a project that we're about to start on. She's your assistant project manager."

He nods. "Okay.

"I take it you've done this for a little while?" I ask.

Once again, he smiles. "Yes, a little while. I started out in finance, so this will be my first time in IT. I've done my research though, and I've taken an IT project management course."

"Perfect."

He stands but doesn't move to leave. When I glance up at him, I notice his lips are downturned slightly and I already know what he's thinking.

"Don't bother apologizing, Adrian. It's been a long time."

After a few seconds, he sighs. "I wish I would've handled things differently."

I raise my brows before going back to my computer. "Well, you did what you wanted to at the time, and we both need to accept that."

"Matías," he says quietly, seeking my attention.

I exhale through my nose before glancing back at him. "Yes?"

"I'd like to make things right. Especially now that we'll be working together. Let me take you for a drink. Or dinner if you're still not a drinker," he says with a tiny grin.

"Will your wife be joining us?" I ask, tilting my head.

He opens his mouth to say something but no words come out. When they do, they're a chopped up mess.

"Uh...well, I—"

"It's fine. Not necessary."

He lingers for a few seconds before leaving. Once he's gone, I let my shoulders drop as I exhale.

I can't believe he's back in South River, and not only that, working on the same floor as me. I didn't think I'd see him again, and now I'll see him almost every day.

At one point I might've thought this was a blessing, but I can't imagine anything worse right now.

Adrian Kennedy was my first love—and my first heart-break. Even saying that makes it sound minimal. Like it was puppy love and a normal breakup.

It wasn't.

What we had was the deepest connection I had experi-enced up until that point, and I haven't been able to find anything comparable since. Because I've never been in love again, I've yet to experience that soul-crushing pain when it ends. Which is exactly why I don't do relationships.

He's the one and only person to affect me so deeply, and that's why it's terrible that he's here.

It's only going to bring up memories—both good and bad —and considering he's married to a woman, I don't see us getting past what broke us in the first place.

I bury myself in work until seven o'clock, and then I go straight to my favorite restaurant, Alejandra's, and pick up some food to go.

When I approach my house, it's already nearing eight, but

since it's the middle of June, there's still over an hour before the sun goes down completely. And clearly, people are taking advantage of the lingering light, because there are two huge U-Hauls on my street—and one of them is blocking most of my driveway.

Annoyed, I park along the curb in front of my house and march toward the neighbor's. All I want to do is park in my garage, eat some dinner, then have a drink until I forget I have to see Adrian every day at work.

I hear noise in the back of the truck that's in their driveway, so I give it a couple bangs with my hand.

"Excuse me. Can you move your truck?"

"What's that?" a voice calls out, followed by footsteps.

When he comes down the ramp, he's only wearing a pair of blue shorts and some tennis shoes. His shirtless torso is shiny with sweat, and ripped with muscles. Not as much from eight years ago, but definitely still there.

"Are you kidding me?" I say aloud.

"Matías?" Adrian questions, brows knit together. "What are you doing here?"

I huff out a breath and run my hand over my face. With a gesture to the house next door, I say, "I live there."

His jaw drops. "Are you joking?"

"No." With another sigh, I point to the U-Haul blocking my driveway. "Can you move that please?"

He walks closer, patting his pockets for the keys. "Yeah. Sorry, uhh..." I shake my head in disbelief that this is happening. "I might've left them in the truck."

I turn to go back to my car, but his voice stops me.

"Matías." I freeze, still giving him my back until I finally angle my head over my shoulder. He doesn't seem to know what it is he wants to say. Or he's cycling through a million different things. "I—"

Before he can continue, a door bangs shut and then another voice joins us. "Hey, what's going on?"

I stare at my car, biting down on my teeth. I can't deal with this right now. Or ever. I don't want to.

"I just need to move the truck for the neighbor," Adrian says.

Instead of turning around and doing the friendly neighbor thing of introducing myself, I walk straight to my car and hide behind the tinted windows until Adrian moves the truck and I can pull into my garage.

What is happening?

CHAPTER NINE
MATÍAS

Luckily for me, Wednesday and Thursday don't include any sightings of Adrian. At least not at work. He's been home both days, moving stuff into the house and meeting other neighbors. I only know because I've seen him each time I've driven in or out of the garage.

But now it's Friday morning, and the day he was scheduled to initially start, so with every footstep that approaches my door, I expect it to be him coming to talk to me. When I venture out to go to another floor for a meeting, I think I'll run into him.

It isn't until lunch time, when I'm heading toward the elevators, that he finally corners me.

"Hey."

I look over and find him in a nice, black suit. "Hey."

The doors open, and the two of us walk in. I press L and he leans in the corner. "Getting lunch?"

"It *is* lunchtime," I reply.

"Maybe you'll let me join you," he asks, a little timidly. "You can fill me in on all the good places to eat."

"You lived here before."

"It's been eight years."

"I'm aware," I say.

"Some places aren't here anymore, and there's a lot of new businesses."

The doors open and one of the guys waiting outside nods to me. "Mr. Cruz."

I dip my chin and give him a small grin as a greeting. Adrian follows behind me.

"What about that pizza diner?"

I know exactly what he's talking about, and I'm not sure why he'd bring up the place we often went to together. Is he trying to torture me?

"No. It's too far from the business district, and I have to be back in"—I look at my watch for the time—"seventy minutes for a meeting."

He snorts. "Okay, fine. Where are you going?"

"There's a bistro a block and a half away."

"Okay."

He falls into step with me.

"I see you've invited yourself."

"If you really don't want me around, I'll leave," he says, sounding somewhat dejected. "But I really want a chance to talk to you."

I sigh, but don't say anything, and my silence is permission for him to join. We walk without saying a word until we're at the restaurant and ordering our Thai food.

We sit at a two seater table next to a black wall and surrounded by a lot of chattering customers.

While we wait for our food to arrive, he speaks up.

"I'm sorry for how I handled everything back then. I'd like to say I was just young and afraid, but—"

"But you're still an uncaring asshole?"

His head drops to the side as he gives me a look. "It was much more than that, Matías. I told you about my family."

I take a sip of my water. "There are things that are understandable, and there are things that are unforgivable."

"You don't think you can forgive me?" he questions with sadness in his voice.

"You know, people say forgiveness is for the forgiver, but I don't agree. You want my forgiveness so you can move on without guilt, but forgiving you gives me nothing. It doesn't erase my memory. It doesn't fill a void. It doesn't take us back to the past to figure out another way to do things. Forgiveness is for the guilty party, not for the wronged, and I no longer subscribe to catering to those who've hurt me. Like I said, you did exactly what you meant to and wanted, and my feelings were not a concern. I have to live with that and so do you."

The waiter appears with our plates and quickly disappears.

"I understand it was a long time ago. You're married," I say, struggling to keep the disbelief out of my voice. "We've moved on. I can have a working relationship with you because I'm an adult, but if you think we can be friends again, you're wrong. It cannot happen. Lunches like this will not happen again."

He watches me, his expression giving away his shock. He must've expected the Matías from college. Not the Matías I've grown into.

"It won't happen again."

His words aren't a statement of finality, but more a repetition of what I said to see if he heard clearly.

"So, have you talked to Mrs. O—"

He holds up a hand, cutting me off. "You don't want to be friends?"

I hold his gaze as I put my chopsticks down. "I definitely don't want to be friends." My eyes roam his face, neck, and any other available spot I can see. "We could never just be *friends*, and you know that."

He swallows, his cheeks turning the lightest shade of pink. "I thought it was because you were mad."

"Oh, I am," I say, turning my attention back on my food. "I'm not afraid to admit I'm a grudge holder, but what happened between us wasn't some petty, childish drama. It affected me, Adrian. It's the reason I approach relationships the way that I do, but you aren't just anyone, are you? So, we *cannot* be friends, because it wouldn't be just that."

His head dips imperceptibly before he reaches for his water, and the rest of our lunch remains relatively quiet minus a few work-related topics.

When the check is placed on the table, we both reach for it but I get to it first, his fingers landing on mine.

Our eyes meet and my chest grows warm. He pulls away slowly.

The walk back to the building is uncomfortably tense. The elevator ride even more so, because once again, he had to open his mouth.

"What I felt for you was real, Matías. I've never experienced anything like it. I was honest with you about my feelings. I told you things I've never told anyone. You are the keeper of my secrets, and I appreciate that more than you know. Not once in all these years have I forgotten about you. You showed me true happiness, and a love..." His voice shakes and I close my eyes. "A love I didn't deserve. I only hope that even though I broke your heart, you still remember some of the good times we had. And I hope that I gave you a fraction of what you gave me."

The elevator doors part, and he walks past me and into the hall.

CHAPTER TEN

MATÍAS

The first two weeks of Adrian working here goes well enough. We've kept communication via email or quick and concise sentences when discussing the project he's heading. Gina O'Terry is qualified enough to answer most questions he should have, but when I have to communicate a problem with the team, I go to him—via email.

Everyone on the floor seems to love him. He's still more extroverted than me, and everyone is always laughing while talking to him.

Sometimes, I want to be in on it. I want to know what story he's telling, or see his face when he laughs. Do his eyes still close every time? Does his head still fall back like it's the funniest thing he's ever heard? Does he still ask ridiculous icebreaker questions like *what flavor ice cream would you be?* I want to know in what ways he's changed and in what ways he's still the same.

But then I go home, and I see him and his wife outside, working on the garden. I watch as he drapes an arm around her shoulder as they inspect their work. I hear the way she laughs at whatever he has to say, and I realize I'll never be the

58

one listening to his stories—or be a part of his life in any other way besides as his boss. I won't know any new things about him, but what I do have is that I'll be the only one who knows the real him. I know his secrets. I know more than she'll ever know, and somehow that balances things.

On week three, I'm told by the VP of project management that I, as well as a few other project managers, need to make a trip to Grand Rapids, which is about three and a half hours from South River. We'll act as representatives of Galaxy Moon Studios and meet with our outsourcing partner to check on the execution of our projects and determine if there are any challenges.

The meeting itself isn't a new concept. I've traveled often enough to work with our counterparts and clients, but now Adrian works with us, and that means he travels with us as well.

Anytime I have to travel within driving distance, I travel alone. Everyone knows that. I don't want to sit in a car for hours, making conversation. So, when I've gathered everyone in my office to inform them of the plan of business, both Andrea Livingstone and Drew Chavez decide to ride together. They've been friends for quite a while, so it makes sense. After they leave, Adrian lingers.

"Does that mean we're riding together?"

"We both have our own vehicles, right?"

He scratches the back of his neck, his head tilted to the side, and I'm suddenly back in college, watching him do the same exact move whenever he has to say something and he's nervous about how the other person will take it.

"Well, I only have one right now, and…and my wife is using it today. We sold our other—"

"Okay, fine," I say, cutting him off. "Let's go."

I grab everything I need and leave the office. The journey

to the parking garage is long and silent. I hit the button on my key fob to unlock my silver Lexus, and after putting my briefcase in the back, I climb into the driver seat as Adrian settles into the passenger side.

It's not until I've been driving for twenty minutes that Adrian finally breaks the silence.

"I can't sit in this car with you for four hours and not speak at all."

"Do you want to go over what we'll be discussing at the meeting?"

He makes a small noise in his throat. "I'm aware of why we're going. I read the email and listened to your speech."

"Do you have any questions about work in general?"

"Matías."

I glance over at him and my heart squeezes, so I look back at the road.

"The only other conversations we could have would include us reminiscing about the past. It's not really some-thing I want to relive."

With a subtle sigh, he looks out the window. Maybe it's ridiculous to be upset over something that happened so long ago, but it's not an easy thing to get over. Not when it shaped who I am and how I approach relationships. But also, how do we talk about it? How do we talk about *us* without stepping over a line that shouldn't be crossed? Because the truth is, no matter how much my heart still hurts over what happened, it would be easy to jump back in. Just to have a taste of what it used to be like. To remember how good it was between us. But he's married.

"What do you do when you're not at work?" he asks, shifting in his seat to look at me.

My eyes flicker over. "Really?"

"It's not about the past," he says with a small shrug.

"When time allows, I'll take a canoe to Lake Renap. Maybe jog the trail around there."

"Outdoorsy stuff. I take it you're still not big on being around a lot of people then."

I inhale through my nose, my chest expanding. "No, still not a fan of people."

He chuckles. "That's not what I meant, but okay."

"I'm around people for work because it's necessary, but I choose not to spend my free time at bars or clubs if that's what you mean. I prefer solitude."

He's quiet for a while, and when I take a peek, I see him chewing on his bottom lip and running his hand up and down his thigh. He's trying to keep from saying something that's floating around in his head.

My eyes linger too long on his thigh considering I'm driving, so I shake myself out of it and refocus.

"Are you dating anyone?"

The words hang between us, heavy and uncomfortable. When I don't answer, because I'm stuck in my head about how to respond, he continues.

"I mean, do you go out socially to meet anyone?"

"You don't have to go out socially to find someone to date."

"Of course. There are tons of apps. Is that what you do?"

I look at him again and wonder why he's so curious. Would he care? That would be quite hypocritical.

"I'm not dating anyone exclusively," I answer, hoping to leave it at that.

When I think he's done asking questions, he's back with another.

"Are you happy?"

I open my mouth to give the usual response. *Of course,* followed by a tight-lipped smile that hides the truth. But I think contentment and happiness are quite different, and while I've been content with my life for a while, I'm not sure I'd say I was happy. I'm just living. I work, I fuck, I eat, and occasionally, I get out on the lake to contemplate if this is how I want to live my life. But I can't tell him all of that.

"Are you?" I ask instead.

His answer isn't immediate, but when it comes, it's paired with a shrug. "Yeah." I glance at him and he forces a tight-lipped smile.

I nod. "Yeah. Same."

And for the first time in a long time, I think maybe it wouldn't be so bad to go back into the past. To be young and in love. To laugh and find joy in the smallest things. To be naive enough to think the world wouldn't come to fuck you.

"Remember the Halloween party at your house?" I ask.

His smile stretches across his face, and I can't help but smile back at him.

"Of course I do."

The Past

Adrian

CHAPTER ELEVEN

ADRIAN

"Are you serious right now?" I ask through my laughter.

"What?" Matías asks, looking down at his red and white striped sweater.

"Where's Waldo?"

"Right here," he answers with a smile.

I flick the little ball on the top of his beanie. "Yeah, I know."

I let him in the house and go straight to my room. The party doesn't start for another few hours, and my roommates are out getting last minute drinks and supplies.

"What are you gonna be dressed as?"

"You'll see." Once we're in my room, I close and lock the door. "But first." I pull off his beanie and toss it on the dresser.

"Hey," he whines. I run my fingers through his hair, tugging on the strands in the back. "Oh."

I smirk against his lips. "I thought so."

"Shut up."

I press my lips firmly against his, kissing him like I

haven't seen him in months, when it's only been a day. I've found it's getting harder and harder to be away from him.

It's only been two weeks since we made out in his room for over an hour, finally solidifying this thing between us. Nobody knows, of course, but we do, and that's enough for now.

I lift him up to sit on the dresser, and his legs wrap around me as our moans grow into frantic breaths.

"The bed," he breathes.

I carry him over, placing him on his back as I climb over his body. "I don't know how much time we have," I say before kissing along his neck.

"Then don't waste any. Take off your pants."

I grin. "So bossy."

He bites his bottom lip, cheeks flushed.

I quickly undress, and he does the same. We haven't had sex yet. We haven't done much more than kiss and touch. Matías has given me blowjobs, but I've yet to return the favor. Not for any reason other than I feel like I'll be bad at it. I can use my hand no problem, but I don't want him to be disappointed. However, I really want to try.

When Matías moves, ready to push me to my back, I stop him.

"Lie back."

His brows go up. "You sure?"

I nod, bracing myself over him again, kissing his lips, chin, throat, and chest. I kiss a trail down his stomach, until I get to the head of his cock.

When I glance up, he's staring down at me, lust gleaming in his eyes, excitement and impatience bursting at the seams.

I kiss the underside of his head and continue down his shaft.

"Oh god," he moans, head flopping back to the pillow.

I make my way back up and then circle the tip with my tongue before taking the shaft in my hand and putting it in my mouth.

"Oh Jesus," he cries. "Yes."

His words fill me with confidence, so I keep going. I take him deeper into my mouth, and when he moans, my cock twitches. I try to take more, but nearly gag, so I ease back up to the tip.

"Yeah. Lick the head. Oh fuck," he cries.

I obey his command while stroking his shaft, looking up at him. His muscles are flexing as he grips the covers under him, his eyes squeezed closed and bottom lip trapped between his teeth.

"Oh, fuck. Adrian," he gasps, his eyes opening and finding mine. "I'm gonna come."

I keep my pace, my heart racing in my chest. My tongue flickers against the underside of his head, hand moving up and down.

"Oh, god. Oh—" His words are cut off by a roar of pleasure.

Cum shoots out, landing on his stomach, pouring over the sides and sliding through my fingers. My tongue laps up some of it as well, and it's the first taste of a man I've had on my tongue.

I swallow, watching his body spasm as he sucks in gulps of air.

"Holy shit. Oh, my god," he breathes.

I smile. "Good?"

"Very, very good," he says, breathless.

With my other hand cupped under my right, I try to keep the cum from dripping anywhere as I grab a towel from the top of my hamper and wipe my hands.

"It's about to be your turn as soon as I can breathe again," he says.

Then the door downstairs closes, and the voices of my roommates filter in.

He sits up quickly, wide eyes frozen on me until he gets up and snatches the towel from my hand to clean himself up.

Matías plucks up his discarded clothes, putting on his ridiculous sweater and beanie as I step into my boxers.

"I guess I'll have to make it up to you later," he says.

"I look forward to it."

He comes up to me, his hand on my cheek as he kisses me. "That was incredible."

I start laughing, and he backs up, confused. "What? You were."

Shaking my head, I walk over to my closet and pull out my costume.

"Seriously?" he asks, fighting his laugh. "You're dressing up as Mr. Incredible?"

"I mean, it tracks, right?"

"I hate you," he says with a laugh.

"Sure you do."

With another quick peck, he goes to the door. "I'm gonna go to the bathroom."

"I'll meet you in the kitchen."

Once he's gone, I change into my costume and jog downstairs, finding my friends in the kitchen.

"Mr. Incredible is here to help."

They laugh at me. "You're so stupid. You're gonna wear that tight ass shit all night?" Johnson asks.

"Jealous everyone will be staring at me?"

He shakes his head. "Whatever, Mr. Incredible. Get the rest of the beer from the truck, will ya?"

I jog out and grab the two cases of Bud Light from the

backseat of his truck, and walk in just as Matías comes down the stairs.

I smile at him, happy he's agreed to come to another party since I know they aren't really his thing.

He laughs when I do a spin, showing off my costume. His smile never leaves his face. "You're insane."

I shrug. "Matías is here!" I shout to the guys as I walk in the kitchen. "See if you can find him."

"What?"

"Huh?"

Their confusion comes to an end when Matías walks in behind me, and they all start laughing.

"How many drunk people are gonna be playing a game of Where's Waldo tonight?" Barlow asks.

"Hell, I might play," Johnson says.

But I'm gonna win, I think to myself. I hope to find him in my bed.

CHAPTER TWELVE

ADRIAN

When the party is in full swing, once again Matías and I find ourselves at a beer pong table, looking for a win.

I nearly lose the game for us when I lean over to tell him I can't stop thinking about having his dick in my mouth earlier.

His eyes widen before he pushes me away. Okay, so maybe I'm a little drunk, but it's too loud in here for anyone to have heard me.

He was clearly flustered, because he missed his shot.

We eventually win, and afterward, we make our way to the kitchen.

I can't stop staring at him and thinking about everything I want to do to him.

"You need to stop," he says quietly as he grabs a bottle of water from the fridge and hands it to me.

My smile is slow and lascivious. "Stop what?"

"Looking at me that way."

He glances around but nobody's paying attention.

"I can't help it."

"Well, try. Or I'll have to stop coming to these parties."

I pout. "Fine."

"Drink your water."

"Yes, sir."

I take a gulp and then reach into a bag of chips.

"What are you doing tomorrow?" he asks me.

"Besides sleeping until one?"

He shakes his head with a small grin. "Besides that."

"Nothing."

"I want to do something with you."

I grin at him. "Oh yeah?"

"Not that," he chastises, looking around again.

"Okay."

"You don't want to know what it is?"

I shrug. "Doesn't matter. I'll be with you."

His smile stretches across his face and when I look at him, he turns away and pretends to care about a spill on the counter.

"Okay, well, I'll be here to get you at two."

"Are you leaving?" I ask.

He nods. "I'll text you later."

"Okay."

I hate that I can't hug him or kiss him goodbye. I want to walk him to the car and watch as he drives away, but even that would be too much. He's just a guy from class according to everyone else, and we have been nearly inseparable all night.

"Be safe," I say.

"Always."

I grin and he walks away, and suddenly I don't even want to party anymore. I would rather be with him.

I'm so screwed.

I wait the exact amount of time it should take for him to get home and then I text.

I miss you.

You're drunk.

Yes, but I always miss you when I'm not with you.

I think maybe I went too far. We're hardly official. We can't be official when we're a secret. I'm saying I miss him already? What's wrong with me? Twenty minutes goes by and I'm already in my room, resigned to trying to sleep while the party still rages on.

I'm outside. Want to join me?

I grab a T-shirt and some pants and run out the door, down the stairs, and across the yard. I ignore the complaints of people I run into and search for his car.

Go right.

I turn and find his headlights pointing the opposite direction, his car double parked next to someone who's at this party.

I run over and jump in. "Found you."

He smiles. "You did. Let's go, Mr. Incredible."

CHAPTER THIRTEEN

ADRIAN

WE GET into his dorm room undetected, and quickly change out of our costumes. Matías gets into a pair of lounge pants and a T-shirt, while I put on what I quickly grabbed from my room, which is a white T-shirt and black-and-white athletic pants.

I steal a mint from a tin he has on his nightstand so my breath doesn't reek of alcohol, and we lie in his bed and turn the TV on.

"Ah. This is much better," I say, wrapping my arms around him.

He chuckles. "I'm turning you into me, it seems."

"Nah. I've just never known what it was like to be happy with someone. No wonder all my friends disappeared whenever they were dating someone. It's a hell of a lot more fun to be with you than be with a hundred other people."

He's quiet for a while. "What will you tell them?"

"What do you mean?"

"When they inevitably ask where you're disappearing to or what your other plans are?"

I haven't thought about it yet. Matías and I have spent plenty of time together the past couple weeks, but not enough to rouse suspicion. I've still spent time with my friends, plus football's been keeping me busy, but I know it'll likely get to a point where I have to turn down their invitations to things because I've already made plans with Matías. Even if those plans simply consist of us camping out in his room.

"I'm not sure," I answer. "I doubt they'll ask."

He doesn't reply, but I can tell he doesn't believe me. Hell, I hardly believe me. Of course they'll ask.

But I don't let it ruin the night. We cuddle and watch some TV show Matías put on, and then I let my hand slip under his shirt.

He arches his back and wiggles his ass in front of my crotch as we spoon.

I run my hand up his lean torso before traveling back down and dipping into the waistband of his pants.

He lets out a soft moan and my cock stirs to life.

I kiss his neck as my hand finds his shaft.

"I think I owe you an orgasm," he says in a breathy tone.

"You can get another one too. I'm not stingy."

Matías rolls over on his back and removes his pants before facing me. I do the same thing, bringing our erections together when I scoot in close.

"I think…" I pause, staring into his eyes. "I think I want to do more soon."

His brows lift slightly. "Oh."

I kiss his soft lips. "Maybe not tonight, but very soon." My hand curves over his hip and grips his ass.

"Okay," he breathes, body beginning to undulate. "What do you want to do exactly?"

"Well." My hand moves up his back as I nuzzle into his neck. "We could start with dinner."

"No, no," he says, hand on my chest to push me away. I look at him and his hand travels to my cock. "What do you want to do with me? To me?"

"Oh," I say, catching on. "I definitely want to taste you again."

"Mmm." His moan escapes as he digs his teeth into his bottom lip.

"I want more of your cum in my mouth next time."

He nods, eyes low and full of lust. He turns around to reach into his nightstand and brings out a bottle of lube. Squeezing some into his hand, he strokes himself and then me, getting us both slick.

"Fuck," I groan. "I love when you touch me."

His lips twitch. "I love touching you." He brings our cocks together, stroking us as one while rocking his hips. "Keep going," he breathes.

"I've been thinking about what it would be like to be inside you," I say, pausing to gauge his reaction. We haven't discussed what he's used to. I don't know if he typically tops or bottoms or is cool with both. I assumed we'd figure it out when the time came, but it seems like the time is approaching. "Would that be okay?"

He smiles at me. "Yes, that would be okay."

"I want you on your back so I can watch your face when I slip inside. I want to feel how tight you are around me."

His hand moves faster, both of us now grinding against each other, seeking as much friction as possible.

"I can't wait to feel you," he says with a moan.

"Fuck. I want your legs wrapped around me."

He nods, skin flushing. "I want you to come inside me."

"Oh, god." I take over stroking us both since my hand is a little bigger, gripping us as well as I can as I move my fist up and down. "I can't wait to fill you up."

His eyes close like he's picturing it all in his head. I'm imagining it too, but he's too beautiful to not look at, so I watch his face.

"I want to be deep inside you while you stroke yourself. I want to watch your cum shoot out and paint your skin."

"Fuck, Adrian," he moans. The way my name leaves his lips, all whispery and dripping with desire makes my chest warm.

"I want you to paint my skin right now," I say, still stroking. "Come on me, Matías. Mark me as yours and I'll do the same."

"Oh, shit," he cries, his hand gripping the outer edge of my thigh. "I'm about to—"

I look down between us as cum explodes from his tip, landing on my cock and stomach.

"Fuck yeah. Oh, god."

My orgasm hits hard, streams of white shooting out and making a mess everywhere. It's on him, me, and the bed.

Matías moans his pleasure, reaching between us to run his fingers through the liquid. He wipes some of his cum from my stomach and wipes mine from his, then brings his hand to our cocks to give them another leisurely stroke.

"Thoroughly marked."

I grin, leaning forward to kiss him, and I'm suddenly hit with the strongest emotions I've ever had. Why do I like him this much in such a short amount of time? It doesn't seem normal. Shouldn't it take months?

And then it hits me. We were friends for at least two months before we moved into a more intimate relationship. I knew I liked him immediately. I knew I was attracted to him at the same time.

"You okay?" he asks.

I realize he's already standing next to the bed, a cloth in his hand.

"Yeah," I say with a smile. "The happiest."

His lips stretch across his face. "Me too."

Present Day

Adrian

CHAPTER FOURTEEN

ADRIAN

O̲u̲r̲ ̲m̲e̲e̲t̲i̲n̲g̲ with our outsourcing partner takes hours. By the time we're done, it's nearing five-thirty, and none of us have eaten.

Drew is the one who suggests we all eat dinner before getting back in the car for another four hours. Andrea immediately co-signs.

Matías looks at his watch. "Yeah, we should definitely eat."

Andrea, already on her phone, says, "There's a sushi spot two blocks away."

"Adrian doesn't eat sushi," Matías quickly responds.

My head turns to him, and his snaps up from his phone, like he just realized what he said. "Or do you?"

I shake my head. "Nope. Still not a fan."

"There's an Italian place three blocks that way," he says, gesturing to the right. "Or a Mexican spot about two and a half blocks away."

"Mexican," Drew answers immediately.

"A margarita sounds good," Andrea adds.

I shrug. "I'm happy with that."

Drew and Andrea say they're gonna drive there, but Matías wants to walk.

"It doesn't make sense to drive two blocks away and struggle to find parking along the street that you'll have to pay for anyway. We're already parked in the garage here, and it's not a long walk."

I chuckle. "You don't have to explain it to me."

"I am gonna drop off my briefcase though."

On the walk to the car, I debate trying to bring up the Halloween party again. I was surprised he brought it up in the first place, but besides mentioning our costumes, and some argument that happened between Johnson and Barlow, which I didn't even remember, he didn't say anything else.

The Halloween party was a significant moment in my life. The first time I'd given a blowjob, for one. And then later that night at his place when I realized I was falling for him.

"So, you remembered I don't like sushi."

"I shouldn't have assumed. You could've had a change of heart. Sort of hard to keep up with what you like and what you don't."

Well, that didn't go as planned.

"I'm still pretty much the same," I say as we head out of the parking garage and onto the street.

He looks at me, his eyes roaming all the way down my body until they get to the ring on my finger.

"Hmm."

I slip my hand in my pocket, and I don't know why.

I study him as we walk to the restaurant, cataloging everything that's the same, but also the differences as well. He's still got what looks like silky smooth hair, though now he wears it in a more sleek, business style. I remember tugging on those strands many, many times.

He's bigger now, and not just because he got older, but

it's clear he's spent time in the gym, and he used to cringe when I'd invite him to workout with me.

The biggest difference is his personality. He was never one for people. I know he'd choose quiet nights at home versus parties and social events. He's obviously still the same way, but he's quite closed off. He's stiff and serious. That's not the Matías I knew.

When we walk into the restaurant, he peers around, looking for Andrea and Drew but they aren't here yet. We grab a table for four and wait.

A waitress comes by to get our drink orders and to drop off a basket of chips with some salsa.

I expect him to ask for water, but he surprises me when he orders a margarita on the rocks. I order the same thing and wait for the waitress to leave.

"I didn't think you were gonna drink."

"Yeah, well, I've changed a little bit."

"I can see that."

His eyes find me, and it's hard not to look at him like I don't appreciate his beauty. I turn my head and pretend to watch a TV mounted over the bar.

"Who do you root for now?" he asks.

I turn around. "Huh?"

"You moved to Chicago. But you used to live here. I remember you telling me about a rivalry."

I grin, happy that he remembered. "Right. Well, I adapted to life there in Chicago. I was a Bears fan through and through."

"And now that you're here," he questions. "Are you adapting again?"

Something in his tone makes me freeze. He puts an accent on *here* and *adapting*. It feels like he's asking something else, or maybe it's just in my head.

"I'm not sure."

He nods, watching me carefully.

The waitress arrives with our drinks just as Andrea and Drew show up, so she takes their drink orders before disappearing into the kitchen.

"Should've stayed in the parking garage," Matías says with a grin.

"I didn't think the streets would be so packed," Andrea replies. "It's a Tuesday, for crying out loud."

"It's Taco Tuesday" I say, pointing to the table tent with the specials.

"Ooh," she exclaims, picking it up and reading it.

The waitress brings their drinks and takes our food order, and then we're left to make small talk.

"How are you liking the area?" Drew asks me, picking up his glass.

"I like it. I actually went to college in South River, so it's not too new."

"Oh, yeah? How long were you away for?"

"Almost eight years."

"Where did you go?" Andrea asks before biting into a chip.

"Chicago."

"Nice," Drew replies. "I love Chicago. What made you come back?"

I shift in my seat, twisting my margarita glass around. "Work. I uhh, worked with my dad in Chicago. He has his own business there, but I was looking for a change."

"How does he feel about you leaving?"

I force a smile. "Not the happiest, but..." I shrug and leave it at that.

"You went to college in South River too, right?" Drew asks Matías.

"Matías and I were classmates."

"Matías?" Drew questions. "Not Matt?"

"My name is Matías. I just go by Matt at work. People began shortening it when I started there, so I went with it."

"So you two were friends?" Andrea asks.

We both hesitate, but then I reply. "Yeah, but I didn't know he was working at Galaxy Moon, so there were no special favors to get me the job," I say with a laugh.

"We hadn't spoken in quite some time," Matías adds.

The conversation soon shifts, and we do eventually start talking about work, then Drew and I discuss the NBA finals. Andrea excuses herself to make a call to her husband, and then Drew mentions trying some dating app.

"It's hard to meet women. All I do is work and sleep. The apps make it easier to filter through the bullshit."

"Had any luck?"

"Not really. But there's a lot of apps. I'm sure something will work eventually."

"What apps do you use?" I ask Matías.

"You're on dating apps?" Drew asks.

"I don't think our apps would be the same," he tells him with a grin.

"Oh, right. Is it easier? I'd assume all guys are pretty straightforward about what they want or what they're looking for."

"You'd think," Matías answers before taking a sip. "I have a specific type I look for now, so you're right, the apps help filtering. I put in what I'm looking for, and I can go to their profiles to see if they fit before I waste time sending a message."

"What about you?" Drew turns his attention to me.

"Oh." I sit up a little. "I'm married, so no apps for me."

"How'd you meet her?" Drew asks, and suddenly I want him to leave because I don't want to have this conversation right now.

"Through my dad, actually. His business partner had a daughter, and we were introduced."

"Some people just get lucky, I guess," he says.

"Mm," Matías murmurs, nodding his head.

Andrea returns. "I need to start heading back. My kid is sick."

She digs into her purse and pulls out her wallet.

"I'll get it," Matías offers, holding up his hand. "I hope your kid feels better soon."

"Thank you."

Andrea and Drew both shake our hands and leave the restaurant. I check the clock and see that it's a quarter till eight. We won't be home until after midnight, and I haven't even checked in with my wife.

"I'm gonna use the bathroom."

After I do my business and wash my hands, I pull out my phone and find a couple texts and a call from her. I forgot I turned off my ringer during the meetings.

I call her back and listen to it ring.

"Hello?"

"Hey. I didn't get your messages until now. I turned off the ringer for the meeting and forgot to turn it back on."

"That's fine. Are you on your way home?"

"Not yet. We just got done eating dinner. We had missed lunch so we were all starving."

"Oh okay. So you'll be getting in late?"

"Yeah. Don't feel like you have to wait up."

"Okay. Well..." the line goes quiet.

"You there?"

"Yeah. Just be safe."

"Will do. See you in the morning."

"Okay."

The line goes dead, and I huff out a breath.

Our relationship is far from perfect. In fact, I'd say it's a little rocky. I suppose it's both of our faults, but I'm not sure how to make it better. Or if it's possible to do so.

The door swings open and some guy walks in, so I leave and find Matías at the table drinking water.

"Hope you don't have to get back right away. I drank one more margarita than I should've and probably need to give it some time before I drive."

"Oh. That's fine. Can't have you breaking the law."

"If I were alone, I'd probably just get a hotel, but..." His eyes slide over and drink in my body. "Can't do that."

I try not to let my thoughts run away with that line. "And miss work tomorrow?" I question with a little chuckle, trying to joke. "My Matías didn't even want to skip class after we stayed up until three in the morning. There's no way you'd call out of work."

I realize afterward that I said *my Matías*, and I wish I could shovel the words back in my mouth.

He doesn't mention it, but it's clear by the look on his face that he heard it. "Well, I've definitely called out once or twice before. I don't make it a habit."

I begin drinking the water I had abandoned earlier for tequila, and we munch on some leftover chips and salsa.

"Why did you call out before?"

"Just a late night."

"With someone?" I question, not knowing why I needed to ask, because I certainly don't want the answer.

"Yes, I was with someone," he replies easily.

I nod. "Well, I suppose it was worth it."

He grins, like he's remembering the night and is fond of the memories. I want to take back the question and rewind time because I don't want him remembering someone else.

He eats a chip, his eyes on me but not really. He's clearly in his head, but his gaze is in my direction. I watch his eyes roam and his teeth scrape across his bottom lip.

"What are you thinking about?"

His eyes find mine. "You don't want to know," he says with a hint of a smirk.

"This other guy that you had such a late night with?" I ask, mad at myself for sounding jealous, because where do I get off?

One brow raises, and he's thinking the same thing.

"No, actually."

"Then tell me."

He leans forward, a lazy grin on his lips—his eyes giving away his inebriation. "If you ask me again, I'll tell you, but I'm warning you, you probably don't want to know. I'm not *your* Matías anymore. Things have changed slightly since we were together." He wipes his mouth with a napkin. "So, do you want to know what it is that I'm thinking about?"

His expression tells me it's sexual. His eyes and the way they study me let me know where his mind is at. The way his teeth dig into his bottom lip tell me he's imaging or remembering something, and my heart wants to know what it is. However, my brain is begging me not to ask. If I know, I'll never forget it. I won't stop thinking about it. It could be a very big mistake.

Matías is grinning at me, amused by my conundrum. He knows what he just did. He lobbed the ball and now it's in my court. What happens next is up to me.

I swallow, thinking about how my wife is at home waiting for me, but the man I once loved is sitting in front of me baiting me into a question that will no doubt flip my world upside down.

I lick my lips and inhale. "What are you thinking about?"

CHAPTER FIFTEEN

ADRIAN

"I WAS THINKING about how good it might be to have you on your knees, with a collar around your neck, a leash in my hand, and a riding crop in the other." He folds his left arm on the table, the fingers on his right hand brushing against his bottom lip. "I was thinking about whether or not you'd obey me, allowing me to use you for my pleasure before I gave you yours." He drops his other arm, leaning forward slightly as he stares into my eyes. "I was thinking about whether or not you know what it's like to be with a man. Not a college kid still learning what he likes, but a man who knows what he's doing. A man who could open your world to things you haven't thought about." Leaning back, he shrugs. "I was thinking about whether or not you'd turn me down if I decided to pursue you. Or if you love your wife enough to say no to the first person you ever loved, who loved you back more than you know, who hasn't stopped thinking about since you walked away from him eight years ago. That's what I was thinking."

It's hard to regret hearing that answer, but part of me

does regret asking. My brain is misfiring all over the place, trying to figure out which feelings to feel.

The sexual aspect of his thoughts send a thrill of pleasure down my spine. Intrigue and confusion mix together before realizing he's questioned whether I've been with another man since him while stating he now knows exactly what he wants, and apparently it's submission. Then he drops the bomb of questioning my loyalty to my wife by informing me he's at least thought about pursuing me, and what would I do if he tries. Admitting he's not stopped thinking about me while bringing up the fact that he loved me is an arrow to the heart, and I don't know what to focus on. What do I respond to first?

I'll be thinking about his response for a long time, maybe forever.

My lips part and come together, just to part again. "I—" He grins. "I'm not sure how to reply," I answer honestly.

His head dips slightly. "Fair enough."

"But," I start, reaching for a napkin to nervously rip to shreds as I stare at the pieces, "I want you to know I haven't been with another man since—"

"Look at me," he commands.

My eyes meet his and I repeat myself. "I haven't been with another man since you."

He inhales. "So, you're loyal to your wife."

I keep looking into his eyes, my heart galloping in my chest. "We've had our issues."

He nods once. "I imagine so."

I look away, unable to keep eye contact any longer. He was right. We shouldn't be trying to be friends. Or be left alone together.

"I'm sober if you want me to start driving," I tell him.

Matías watches me for a few seconds. "Okay."

~

An hour into the drive, Matías falls asleep, but my brain is wired and I fear I'll never sleep again. When I do, my dreams will be filled with Matías. When I wake, he'll still be there, lingering in the corner of my mind.

Love is a strange thing. It's consuming, yes. Sometimes it's blind and intoxicating. Other times it's freeing. It can make you feel warm and protected. It can make you afraid. It's not ever exactly the same for everyone, but once you love someone, there's a part of your heart carved out only for them. That's why it's hard to move past someone who maybe isn't right for you. You've carved a piece of yourself for them and you don't want to let it go. You don't want it to have been for nothing.

I loved Matías. I loved him more than I thought possible. He's right. He's the first person I ever fell in love with. I told him so back then. I haven't seen him in years, and we've definitely gone through our own changes, but being in his life now brings everything back. With all the memories, the feelings also come rushing to the forefront. My heart recognizes that he's the piece that's been gone. It would be easy to fall in love with him all over again, if the circumstances were right.

But I'm married. I love her. Not in the same way, unfortunately. Not even remotely. But I care about her.

There's a lot Matías and I have to talk about, but he's still getting his anger out. He's not over what I did, and I don't blame him. We can't be friends though. He's right about that. But he should know the truth, even if nothing comes from it.

I drive us all the way home before waking him. I'm in the driveway when I reach over and rest my hand on his shoulder. Even just touching him there has my mind running away from me.

"Matías," I say softly, watching his face for movement. For no reason other than wanting to, I suppose, I move my hand to his thigh, giving him a little shake. "Matías."

His hand comes down on mine as he startles awake. He meets my gaze, and my hand burns under the heat of his.

His fingers curl under mine, and for a moment, we're holding hands.

"We're home," I say.

He looks through the windshield, and then lets go of my hand to press a button that opens the garage.

"You can pull in."

Begrudgingly, I pull my hand from his thigh and put the car in drive.

He opens his door and steps out, so I do the same, both of us stretching as soon as we close the doors.

"Thanks for driving," he says.

"Sure."

"You've gotten better over time."

My lips quirk. "I wasn't bad before."

He snorts. "Okay. We got pulled over twice while you were driving."

"But I didn't actually get a ticket so it doesn't count."

Matías smiles at me and my chest warms. "Not sure it works that way."

With a small shake of his head, he reaches into the back seat to grab his briefcase. After closing the door, he looks at me over the top of the car.

"Goodnight, Adrian."

I nod my head. "Goodnight, Matías."

And then I walk out of the garage, through the grass, and straight into my house.

CHAPTER SIXTEEN

ADRIAN

I SLEPT LIKE SHIT. I tossed and turned, thinking about Matías. The Matías I knew back then, and the one that's now my neighbor. Living next to him and working with him is going to drive me to the brink of insanity.

I like to think of myself as a good person who tries to do the right things. I'm far from perfect and I make mistakes, but I feel like my proximity to Matías is going to be the end of me.

Charlotte walks up to me as I'm pouring my coffee into my tumbler.

"Morning." She kisses my cheek before opening the fridge.

"Morning."

"You must've got in late. I didn't even hear you come into the room."

"It was after midnight," I say, rubbing my eyes.

"Was it a good trip?" she asks, pulling a carton of eggs out and placing them on the counter.

"Uhh, as good as a work trip can be, I guess," I say with a slight chuckle.

"Dad called," she says, making my spine stiffen.

"Oh?"

"He wants to visit as soon as we're settled."

"Why?"

She huffs. "To check on me? To make sure we're okay?"

"We're not children anymore. I left Chicago to get out from under our parents, and now your dad is already wanting to visit?"

"Well, you don't have to see him then," she says, getting upset. "It'll spark questions, but I guess I'll deal with that."

"We'll talk about it later. I gotta get to work."

"Okay."

I lean over her shoulder and kiss her temple but she just stares down at the bowl of cracked eggs.

I try not to think about her dad coming to visit, because it only makes me mad. If he's coming, I don't doubt he'll send information back to my own father. I don't need them spying on us. But those two have been friends for decades, and they care too much about what Charlotte and I have going on.

In the office, I go straight to my desk to get to work, but when I look up, I see Matías strutting past my window and all thoughts of work fly out of my head.

He stands in the middle of the room, talking to someone. He smiles and slips one hand in his pocket. My eyes trace every part of him, wanting to know what he looks like under the clothes. I wonder how his body looks now with the changes age and the gym have made.

Then I remember what he said at the restaurant. He wants me in a collar. On a leash. *A leash?!* He wants to use a riding crop. He wants to use me.

My stomach flips and my dick twitches.

Don't think about this now.

In college, he was definitely more experienced than I was.

He did teach me things. He had to take the lead several times, so him being in control now isn't too surprising. I would've never thought of him in this kinky sort of way. When we had sex, we just did what felt good. We were figuring things out about each other. Learning what the other person liked. Now he knows. He's definitely still more experienced than I am. He could teach me even more now.

I shake my head. This isn't something I should be imagining, so I put my head down and get to work.

I manage to avoid a face-to-face encounter with him while at work. I send him two work-related emails, and then I go home at the end of the day.

But even at home, there are several times throughout the evening where I zone out and imagine what it would be like to be with Matías in the way he mentioned. To be with him in any way.

He's the only man I've ever had sex with, and while we started off slow back then, we got to know each other in ways I never thought would happen for me. And now he's on a whole other level, and I can't help but be bothered by the fact that, for the last eight years, I've been on a playing field for a sport I have no interest in. I can't learn, advance, or grow into myself when I'm doing something I couldn't care less about.

It's hard not to wonder *what if.*

The Past

Matías

MATÍAS

IT's the middle of November, and we're having our first official date. Well, at least that's how we're referring to it. We've had several nights alone here in my room, and we've been to a couple of parties, but we haven't had what felt like a date.

We go to a movie, and it's safe because college guys go to movies together all the time. It doesn't outwardly look like we're a couple. As long as we don't hold hands, kiss, or stare longingly into each other's eyes, then Adrian's secret is safe.

But in the back of the dark theater, he rubs his leg against mine and I grin. His fingers dance over my thigh at the darkest moments in the movie and my pulse races.

By the time the movie is over, we're both starving, so we stop by Nicola's pizza parlor, and decide to eat inside.

The air is a biting thirty-nine degrees in windy conditions, so the warmth of the restaurant is inviting. We sit at a booth in the back, blowing our breath into our hands to warm them up.

We order a large pizza and some drinks, but before it's even out, Adrian's roommates show up.

"Hey!" Tyrell says, spotting us as soon as he walks in.

"Did y'all already order?" Frankie asks, scooting in next to Adrian.

"We did. What're y'all up to?" he questions.

Tyrell sits next to me. "Just came to pick up some pizza before we head to this party. You guys wanna come?"

I would rather die, I think to myself. Tonight is our date night, which will hopefully be ending in us having sex for the first time, so I definitely don't want to go to a party. I try to get the message across with my eyes.

"Whose party?" Adrian asks.

"Thatcher's."

"Gene Thatcher?" he questions.

"Yep," Frankie replies.

"Nah. I don't really like that guy."

"Why?" Tyrell asks.

Adrian shrugs. "We had some beef last year. I'd rather not."

Tyrell shrugs. "So what are y'all gonna do?"

The pizza gets dropped off at that moment, and then Adrian says, "Eat. Probably convince Matías to tutor me so I don't fail the exam coming up in project management," he says with a grin.

I roll my eyes.

Frankie chuckles while standing up. "Well, I'm gonna go check on the pizzas. I'll see y'all later."

"Bye," I say as they both get up.

"See ya," Adrian says, grabbing a piece of pizza. "Well, at least they didn't stay."

"Do you really not like the guy who's hosting?

He wipes his mouth with a napkin and grins. "I hardly know him, but tonight is our night. I want you all to myself."

I smile and take another bite.

~

When we get to my room, I excuse myself to the bathroom to prepare for tonight. Adrian wants to be inside me, and while I also want to be inside him, I know that's a conversation to have later. I've been both top and bottom before, so this isn't new to me. Everything is new to him, and I want him to feel at his most comfortable for our first time.

In the room, I find him sprawled out on my bed, his legs spread, one dangling off the side while his fingers are locked behind his head as he watches TV.

"You look comfortable," I say.

"I'd be more comfortable with you next to me," he replies, moving to the side and patting the free space next to him.

"Who knew you'd be such a cuddler?" I ask with a laugh.

"I haven't been. I mean, not really."

I climb in next to him and give him my back. "We've never talked about your dating history."

He laughs. "I don't have one to speak about."

"Come on. You've dated people. Have you seen you?"

"In high school, I dated two girls."

"And you didn't cuddle?"

"No. I was sneaking around," he says with a laugh. "We didn't have time to hang out in bed. If my parents ever caught me, I'd be killed. Sex is for married people only."

"Oh."

"Yeah. So, I didn't do a lot of cuddling. We'd meet at the mall or go to a movie because I could say I was just out with friends. I never wanted anyone to meet my family anyway."

"What about your first few years here?"

"There's been moments."

"Moments?"

"Drunk moments. One drunk moment stretched into a couple of months."

"Wow. That long?"

He playfully squeezes my side. "Shut up."

"Are you..." I pause, not sure how to word this or if I even should. "Are you really into women?"

He goes quiet behind me and I regret asking. I spin around to face him. "I'm sorry. I shouldn't have asked."

His fingers run through my hair. "It's fine. I've been asking myself the same thing, actually."

"Really?"

"I've been with women. Not a lot. Not what people would assume, probably, but you know, I've given it the good ol' college try."

I snort.

"I always thought it was fine. Nothing to write home about. I figured it wasn't great because we were either too young and inexperienced, or didn't really know or like each other. Just drunk hookups, you know? Or..." he trails off. "I don't know. I've been interested in guys for a while. Intrigued, I guess I should say. I've found myself attracted to a few, and the porn was always better for me."

"So, you think you might be gay? Not bi?"

"Probably."

I kiss his lips and the conversation stops there. Our hands start roaming, and I wrap my leg around his, grinding into him with a moan.

He turns, pushing me onto my back while he braces himself over me. He kisses my jaw and neck, sucking at the flesh before gently biting down.

"Oh, yeah," I cry, my hand flying to the back of his head to hold him in place. "Lube's in the drawer." My voice is low and husky.

He leans over to get it, settling himself on his knees between my legs. I watch as he pours it into his hand before pressing his lubed up fingers against my hole. He holds eye contact as he slips one fingertip inside.

I bite my lip and give him a nod to let him know to keep going. His finger travels deeper into me, thrusting in and out at a cautious and leisurely pace.

"You okay?" he asks, his face showing a hint of concern.

"I'm fine. More."

His tongue swipes across his bottom lip before another finger slides in next to the first.

"Oh, god," I moan, eyes closing as my back arches.

"You like it?" he questions.

"Yes," I answer with a slight chuckle. "Yes, Adrian, I love it."

There's a low rumble in his throat before he really begins moving his fingers. He leans over me, kissing and licking my neck while stretching me out.

After a while, he pulls away, but keeps his fingers inside, watching his actions and moaning his pleasure.

"Mm. My god, Matías."

My name has never sounded so good before.

"I'm ready," I tell him frantically. Desperately. "Please."

Slowly extracting his fingers, he pours more lube into his palm and rubs more into me. Leaning over, he snatches the condom he placed on the nightstand, and I watch enraptured as he slides the latex over his length.

With more lube in his hand, he strokes himself before taking a deep breath and meeting my gaze.

"Ready?" he questions.

"Yes. Are you?"

He gives me a nervous smile. "Yes."

He begins to push in, his eyes focused on where he's

disappearing inside me before they flicker to my face to see if I'm okay.

I nod and he goes in a little deeper, his head fully inside now.

"Fuck," he groans. "Oh, my god."

He braces himself on either side of me, his hips pushing forward until he's all the way in. We both cry out at the same time.

"Holy shit," he says. "So fucking tight."

I moan. "You're so big."

"Is it okay?" he asks, concern coating his voice.

I manage to let out a chuckle. "Yes. Big is good."

He smiles and begins rocking his hips again. He's full of praise for me, and I'm hardly doing anything.

"God, you're so good," he says. "You feel so good."

His forehead rests against mine as he rotates his hips while he's deep inside.

"Holy shit," I say on a gasp. "Adrian. Fuck." I dig my nails into his back.

Easing away, he kisses my cheekbone before resting on his knees. He holds my legs apart, pushing them up slightly as he fucks me.

"Oh my god," he moans, eyes focused on where our bodies meet. "This…" He thrusts deep, closing his eyes, a rumble in his throat. "This is so good."

I watch his body move, every muscle rippling. He's built like a god, and right now he's mine. I praise him, telling him how much I love his body, his cock, and how good he makes me feel. He moans, my words making him move faster and go deeper.

I reach for my dick, stroking myself as I watch him. He holds the undersides of my thighs, slowly pulling out just to watch himself slide back in.

His cheeks are red, and his lip is taking abuse from his teeth as he keeps biting down on it.

"So fucking good," I tell him. "You're so fucking good."

He looks at me and holds eye contact, something whirring in his brain. There's something in his eyes that tells me he wants to say something, but he doesn't. Instead, he leans over me again, pressing a kiss to my lips before his tongue twirls with mine.

Leaning on one arm, his other reaches down and grabs the side of my ass, squeezing the flesh.

His thrusts change, now short and staccato.

My hands find their home on his lower back, sliding over the curves of his ass. "Yes, yes," I chant. "Give it to me."

"Oh, god," he grunts. "Oh, god. Matías. Fuck."

"Come for me," I whisper.

"Oh, yes. I'm coming. I'm coming. I'm co—"

His words are cut off by an animalistic roar. His back bows, and he thrusts deep before going back to the shorter thrusts, moaning in my ear. Another deep thrust and that's where he holds, and I feel his cock twitching and throbbing inside me.

"Oh, yes," I cry, running my hands up his back. "Yes."

He's sucking in air like he's struggling to breathe, his sweat mixing with mine as his head rests in the crook of my neck.

Then he eases away, back on his knees, and keeps thrusting.

"Stroke yourself," he says through labored breaths. "I need to see you come with me inside you."

Need. Not want.

I flatten my tongue and lick my palm before wrapping my fingers around my dick. My fist moves up and down my shaft as I watch him—his face full of bliss.

It's never been like this before. I've never felt this way while having sex. The pleasure is amazing, but it's not just physical. What I feel is also internal. It makes the physicality part of sex even more enjoyable.

I'm not closing my eyes and focusing on what his dick is doing and the sensations it's providing. I'm staring into his eyes, watching his lips, and the way his Adam's apple bobs when he swallows. I'm enraptured by how he's looking at me, and suddenly, I'm coming.

"Oh, god," I cry out, eyes finally closing as I throw my head back.

I grunt and suck in deep breaths as cum shoots up in the air before landing on me.

"Oh, yes," he murmurs. "Holy shit."

I keep stroking, my movements slowing as I watch the rest of my release drip onto my stomach.

Adrian stops moving, both of us only capable of sucking in all the oxygen in the room.

I let my hand flop to the side, my entire body spent.

"Oh, my god," Adrian says, the words filled with reverence.

He pulls out slowly, holding onto the condom as he eases back. He steps off the bed and discards the latex in my trashcan.

Kneeling on the floor next to the bed, he brushes the wet strands of my hair out of my eyes and kisses me softly on the lips. He pulls away to meet my gaze and then kisses my forehead. Something about the gentle moment after having such incredible sex makes my heart thump and my eyes burn.

"It's not the best time to say this," he begins, making my lungs seize. "I've thought about it a dozen times already but I've been too scared. It's not just because of this. What we just did."

My eyes feel like they're bulging out of my head, waiting to hear what he's about to say. "Okay," I manage to get out.

"I love you, Matías."

The air whooshes out of me, and I stare at him for several seconds before saying, "I love you, too."

CHAPTER EIGHTEEN

MATÍAS

WE ARE DISGUSTINGLY IN LOVE. If we were able to be ourselves around others, we'd be the ones they'd groan about. Anytime we're alone together, we're touching and kissing, smiling and laughing. We can hardly keep from touching each other, even if it's just simply to feel connected.

It's been an incredible couple months. The sneaking and lying hasn't been a problem. His friends seem oblivious, but likely caught up in their own lives and relationships to notice that he's hardly around.

"What are you doing for Thanksgiving?" I ask Adrian as I take a fry out of the bag and pop it into my mouth.

He's in the passenger seat of my car, unwrapping his burger. "Uh, I think my dad is expecting me home."

We haven't talked about his parents much, but anytime they're brought up, it's with a negative connotation. It's clear they aren't close, but it's also obvious that there's a fear there. He's afraid of them, whether it's a fear of disappointing them or angering them, I'm not sure. Possibly a mix of both.

I also know his family has a lot of money. His dad has a lucrative business that he owns, and he expects Adrian to work there and eventually take the reins, though Adrian doesn't seem to have much interest in that.

"Well, Chicago's not too far away. What's that? A five hour drive?"

He nods, and everything in his face tells me it's not anything he wants to talk about, so I drop it.

"I'm going to see my mom. She's only three hours away."

"That's nice," he replies. "What about Christmas? Are you going there for that, too?"

I shrug, chewing another fry. "Not sure. Sometimes she goes to visit her sister. I'll have to see what her plans are."

"If you stay here, I'll try my best to stay here too. We can spend the holiday together."

"That would be nice," I say. "I've never spent a holiday with a boyfriend before.

"Me either."

I laugh. "Considering I'm your first, I'd assume not."

He wipes his mouth with a napkin. "Not with a girlfriend either. Any short-lived relationships I had seemed to always fall at a time where I never had to buy anyone a gift. Probably a good thing. I'm a bad gift-giver. Just fair warning."

"I'm sure you're fine," I say with a chuckle.

"Yeah, get back to me after Christmas."

After we finish eating in the parking lot, I get out to throw away the trash and run into a familiar face walking out of the building with his own bag.

"Matías?"

I tilt my head, squinting at him until it hits me. The guy from the bar. The one I never replied to when he texted me.

"Hey," I say in a voice too high and screechy. "How are you?"

He smiles. "I'm good. How are you?

"I'm good," I say with a nod.

He licks his lips, shoving one hand into the pocket of his hoodie. "I texted you, and either you gave me a wrong number or you decided you weren't interested. Not sure which I'd prefer, to be honest," he says with a small grin.

"Sorry," I say, my lips drawing down on the ends. "It was my number, but it was a weird night, and my friend was with me, and—"

"That friend?" he questions, pointing his chin at my car behind me.

I turn and find Adrian watching the interaction from the passenger seat.

"Yes. That friend."

"Based on how he's looking at me right now, I'm assuming not just a friend anymore."

I chew on my bottom lip, unsure how to reply. Adrian's not out, but disagreeing with his assessment feels wrong too.

"Uh. It's complicated."

He nods. "Well, I can give you my card, and if you're ever *not* in a complicated situation, you can call me. My cell is on there."

Blake hands it over and smiles at me before walking to his car.

I make my way back to Adrian, the card in my fingers.

"Is that the guy from the bar?" he asks as soon as I close the door.

"Yeah."

"Thought so. What's that?" he questions, gesturing to my hand.

"His card," I say, looking down at it.

Blake Morisson. Personal trainer.

I hand it to Adrian and then reach for my seatbelt.

"Do guys hit on you often?"

"Not often."

"But they do."

"Sometimes. It depends."

Adrian's mood shifts as we drive. I take the card from his hand and throw it out the window before rolling it back up.

"You don't have anything to worry about."

"The problem is, I think I have a lot to worry about."

He doesn't elaborate, but I know he needs to stew in his feelings for a while first before he'll be ready to talk about what's bothering him.

We ride to his house in silence, and when I park, he reaches over and puts his hand on my thigh.

"I love you."

My lips quirk up. "I love *you*."

When he departs, I head back to my door with a head full of questions.

We've been wrapped up in our own personal bubble, but we haven't talked about a few important things. Will he ever come out? What does that mean for us if he doesn't? Are we expected to be a secret forever, or is forever not even an option for him?

I tell myself I'll wait for him to bring it up, but really, I'm afraid of hearing his answers.

Matías

<h1 style="text-align:center">CHAPTER NINETEEN
MATÍAS</h1>

WHEN I WOKE up the morning after our work trip, I almost regretted telling Adrian what I did—about my little fantasy. But at the same time, he asked, and I wanted to tell him. I can't regret something I wanted to do, right?

But it's not going to get me anything. It didn't bring me comfort or make me feel any better about the situation we're in. He's still married. It doesn't matter what I want to do to him or with him. It doesn't matter that I want him bent over so I can spank him and flog him—punishing him for the past while simultaneously quenching the thirst I have.

I ignored him for the next couple of days, as best as I could, anyway, while remaining a professional at work. The truth of the matter is...it's becoming harder to act like I'm not affected by his presence. I'm still upset about how he broke my heart, but he's here now. He's back in my life, and really, that's all I ever wanted. I just want him to be single.

His marriage means nothing to me. It's bullshit. It's a facade and a lie, and he and I both know it. Why he's with her, I don't know, but it's not because he believes she's his soulmate. It's not possible.

My phone rings as I stare out of my office window, watching Adrian talk with one of his team members.

"Hello?"

"Mr. Cruz, I'm just checking in regarding the upcoming conference."

It's the VP of our department—Mr. Wright.

"Yes, sir. We've made our travel arrangements already. Tom Nelson is stepping into my role while I'm gone, so we won't get behind."

"Perfect. Please make sure our new project manager is aware he'll be attending. A few new analysts will join as well. In total, we'll have thirteen people from our office attending."

"Oh, okay. Yes, sir."

"Talk later."

The call ends and I huff out a breath. Why is the universe testing my strength?

I walk over to my door and open it up. "Mr. Kennedy? Can I speak to you for a minute?"

Adrian looks up and then says a few words to the guy he's talking to before heading over.

I'm at my desk when he walks in, so he closes the door and lingers in front of it, putting his hands in his pockets.

"What's up?"

I rub the section of skin between my eyebrows. "We have a conference next week. We've known about it for a while, but Mr. Wright just called and said to ensure you know you'll be attending."

"Okay," he says a little slowly. "Where?"

"Las Vegas."

"Oh. Okay," he replies.

"I can send you an email with the dates and hotel information, however, this close to the conference, I worry they won't have rooms available on site."

"Well, I guess we'll see."

A moment passes between us where we're silent, just looking at each other. I nod and pretend to focus on my computer.

"I'll wait for your email," he says, opening the door.

Then he's gone.

An hour later, his response pops into my inbox.

Mr. Cruz,

You were right. The hotel the conference is being held in is completely booked. As are the nearest two. I will likely be a few hotels down the strip. Do you have an itinerary so I can plan to get there on time?

Adrian Kennedy

I hit reply and attach the itinerary, ready to send it with only that, but I hesitate. The devil on my shoulder whispers in my ear, and there's no angel on the other side to counter the thoughts.

It's reckless, wrong, and a terrible idea.

He's married. I'm his boss. It's a disaster waiting to happen.

I begin typing.

Mr. Kennedy,

. . .

I might have an idea. If you'd like to meet me in my office, we can discuss.

Mr. Cruz
Director of Project Management

I hit send and wait. I don't know if he's read it already and is hesitating or downright refusing to come in here, or if he's simply busy and not had time to read it.

Ten minutes. Fifteen minutes. Thirty minutes later, and I know he's had to have seen it. I look at the clock and realize it's almost time to go home for the weekend.

Maybe it's for the best.

As I grab my things and turn off my computer, there's a knock at the door.

"Come in."

I stand at the side of my desk, my keys in one hand and briefcase in the other.

"You asked me to come speak with you," Adrian says, eyes filled with curiosity and a hint of concern.

Now that time has passed, I'm backing down on my idea. I probably shouldn't bring it up. I can just make up something else.

The door clicks behind Adrian, and he leans against it, his eyes traveling the length of my body.

I inhale through my nose, my mind lost in filthy thoughts and sinful desires.

"I booked a suite. There's two bedrooms."

His head lifts marginally, eyes widening only a little bit. "Oh."

"It's pretty spacious."

He stands up straight, hands coming out of his pockets so he can cross his arms over his chest.

"Okay."

"There are early speeches, and if you want breakfast, you'll need to be up even earlier. It's easier to stay on location."

"Right," he says, not giving me any indication about what he's thinking.

"And like I said, we'd have our own rooms. Separated by a living room."

"Right," he says again. "Okay. Yeah. Can I let you know?"

I nod. "Sure."

I start walking toward him and he moves away from the door, eyes on me.

"Matías?"

I stop, angling my head over my shoulder. We're so close. Inches separate his face from mine.

"Yes?"

"It's not a good idea, is it?"

My tongue wets my bottom lip as I stare at him. "Probably not."

He nods once and I leave.

CHAPTER TWENTY

MATÍAS

THE DAY before we're scheduled to fly out to Vegas, I'm in my backyard, ripping up weeds from the garden and mowing the grass. Once I'm done in the back, I remove my sweat-soaked shirt and wipe my face with it before tossing it on the patio table and then moving to the front yard.

I'm halfway into cutting the grass when Adrian's wife pulls into their driveway. I keep my head down and try to ignore her, but she's clearly ready to introduce herself, and I can't ignore her when she walks over, waving her hand in the air.

I stop the lawn mower and pull out one of my earbuds. "Hi," I say with a small smile.

"Hi. Sorry to interrupt, but I just wanted to introduce myself. I'm Charlotte."

"I'm Matt," I reply, giving her my hand. "Sorry. Sweaty."

She grins as she carefully wipes her palm on the side of her jeans. "No worries. My husband and I have lived here for over a month and haven't even said hello yet. But it's just been busy."

My brows dip. He hasn't told her I'm his boss.

The front door to their house closes and Adrian struts over with a nervous look on his face. His eyes drink in my half naked torso before they find his wife.

"Hey."

"I was just introducing myself to the neighbor," she says with a smile, gesturing toward me. "This is Matt."

I look at him, waiting to see what he says. Why wouldn't he tell her I work with him? I'd assume she doesn't know about our past, but to not say his boss is his neighbor seems weird.

"Oh, yeah. We work together," he says, giving me a forced smile. "Small world."

"Indeed," I reply, my eyes on him.

"Really?" Charlotte questions, her expression confused. "You never told me."

He hasn't told her a lot, I'm sure.

Adrian shrugs, his hand going to the back of his neck as he tilts his head. "I don't know. Not a big deal, I guess."

Charlotte gives him a look but quickly covers it up. "Well, okay." She faces me. "Matt, you should come over for dinner sometime."

"That's probably not appropriate," Adrian says quickly.

My brow arches slightly.

"What do you mean?" Charlotte asks.

"No fraternizing," he offers.

She laughs. "Isn't that for romantic relationships?"

"Not always," he says. "But he's my superior."

Charlotte looks at me. "Oh."

I smile at her and then look at Adrian. "I won't tell if you won't."

He stares at me while his wife giggles. "Well, I need to get the groceries inside. It was nice meeting you, Matt."

"You too," I reply with a small nod.

When she's gone, he speaks. "Why do you have everyone call you Matt?"

That's definitely not the first thing I thought he'd say, and I'm not quite ready to tell him I don't want his wife calling me by the same name he does. I've always preferred the way my name falls from his lips. Especially when he was gasping and moaning.

"It's a shortened version of my name," I say instead.

He's trying to keep from looking at my torso, but he's failing. "Is it weird that I didn't tell her you and I work together?"

"Kind of."

He snorts. "Thanks."

"Why didn't you?"

He crosses his arms. "I'm not sure. It just felt like something I wanted to keep to myself."

"Hmm."

"Would you ever come over for dinner?" he asks, looking down at the ground.

"Do you think I should?"

It takes him a few seconds to answer. "No."

I nod.

"Sometimes what we want and what's right are not the same thing, and we're forced to choose between the two," he says.

"Right for who?" I question.

He dips his head in acknowledgment. "I'll see you tomorrow?"

"You will."

He gazes past me, eyes toward the sky for a few seconds before he speaks. "Can I still stay in your suite?"

It's the first time he's brought it up since I asked. I figured he'd stay at a different hotel and suffer the commute.

"Is that the *right* thing to do or what you *want* to do?"

His lips twitch slightly. "See you tomorrow, Matías."

"See you."

CHAPTER TWENTY-ONE

MATÍAS

As I'm waiting for my luggage at the airport in Las Vegas, Adrian struts toward me, already pulling his suitcase behind him.

"Morning," he says with a grin, bringing a cup of coffee to his lips. "My flight got in a couple hours ago." His brows knit. "Why are you looking at me like that?"

"I need coffee."

He looks at the cup in his hand and smirks, handing it over. "Here. I've already had one. I guess I don't need another."

"It's fine," I say.

"Just take it."

My fingers brush his when I grab the cup. "Thanks." I take a sip and then another. "Ah."

Adrian laughs. "Feeling a little more human?"

"Almost." I watch as the luggage starts coming around on the conveyor belt. "You've just been wandering around the airport?"

"Waiting for you."

"Is that right?"

"We're roommates."

I snort before it turns into a full belly laugh.

"What?" he says, laughing along with me. "I can't get into the room without you."

"So, we're roommates," I state, looking him up and down.

"With our own rooms."

"Mmhmm," I murmur.

When I spot my luggage, I hand him the coffee and grab it before it passes me. I take back the drink when I'm next to him, and we start heading toward the exit.

"It's just for convenience," he says. "Being close to the conferences and other events."

"Right."

"I don't want to have to walk back and forth every day, or struggle to get a cab just to drive for a few minutes."

"Yeah. That makes sense."

"Plus, what if I need to change for an event? Then I'd have to go all the way to my hotel and rush back."

"Are you trying to convince me of something?" I ask as we come to a line waiting for cabs. "Or yourself?"

He exhales. "I'm just saying."

"Okay."

"I don't have ulterior motives."

I face him. "That's a shame."

He swallows, and then it's our turn to get into a cab.

After we check in, we go straight to the room to get unpacked. We'll be here for four nights. Four long, excruciatingly tortuous nights, because how am I supposed to stay away from him when I invited him to stay in my suite?

I believe it's called thinking with your dick, which is

ridiculous, because my dick has no right to be near him. Even if he were single, I should make him beg me to even get close to it again.

The thought of him on his knees, begging me to give it to him...

No.

"The room's nice," he says, taking me out of my thoughts.

"Yeah."

"Oh, the view is too."

He walks over to the floor-to-ceiling window, his hands pressed against the glass like a child. I imagine having him pressed against the same window, naked, taking my cock in his ass while he stares down at the people walking the streets.

"Jesus Christ," I mutter to myself.

"You okay?" he asks, turning around.

"Yep. Gonna check out the rooms."

In the first room I go to, I put my luggage on the bed and start unzipping it.

"You don't wanna check out the other one? What if it's better?" Adrian asks, walking around my room.

"It doesn't matter. As long as there's a bed, I'm good. And they both have their own bathrooms."

"Okay. Well, I guess I'm gonna go unpack."

"Wanna get something to eat after? I'm starving."

"Sure."

Thirty minutes later, we're downstairs eating at a buffet restaurant.

"I've never been to Vegas before, have you?" Adrian asks between bites of his food.

"A couple times."

"Think we'll have time to sightsee?" he asks with a boyish grin.

"Starting tomorrow, the itinerary is full of conferences, workshops, and keynote speakers."

"Fun."

I smirk. "We have today, and we can extend an extra day. It'll be a Saturday anyway, so it's not like we have to go back to work right away."

His smile is wide and beaming. "I think that's a great idea."

After we're done eating, we go back to the room to change into clothes better suited for the scorching heat, and then make our way down into the lobby.

"Where to?" I ask him.

"Let's just wander around here first. I heard they have a huge aquarium."

I pay for us to go into the shark reef aquarium, where we walk through the tunnel and watch as the sharks, fish, and turtles swim above and around us.

After that, we hotel hop, making our way down the strip, and doing everything from riding gondolas, walking through a shopping area built to look like a street in ancient Rome, and riding the big apple coaster, which admittedly took some convincing from Adrian.

We stop inside The Excalibur to cool down and find something to drink and snack on. At a sports bar, we see signage for the Thunder from Down Under show that takes place in this resort.

"Interested?" I ask Adrian with a lifted brow when I notice him reading the information on the sign.

His cheeks redden slightly and he gives me a sheepish smile. "No." When I just grin, he says, "Unless you want to."

I laugh, taking a sip of my water. "I wasn't thinking about it."

He looks at the photo again—a shot of six shirtless men, all of them chiseled beyond belief.

"Can I ask you a personal question?" I ask, wiping my mouth after taking a bite of salad.

Adrian meets my gaze before picking up one of his buffalo wings. "I'm kind of nervous, but okay."

"Why are you married?" I pause. "To a woman."

He tenses up, pausing mid-way to taking a bite. He puts the wing down on his plate and licks his fingers.

"Well, okay. I suppose I expected this question."

"I'm just confused. You said you were gay."

His shifty eyes let me know he's still very nervous about anyone finding out.

"It's a complicated story and one you probably wouldn't understand."

"I can understand quite a lot."

"I've gone over it a hundred times, especially recently. I knew there would be a time where we'd have to have this talk, and I've practiced my speech, and even to me it sounds ridiculous."

A group of four are seated next to us, and I know this isn't the place to have this sort of conversation.

"Are you?" I ask him. "Just tell me that."

He stares at me for several seconds before nodding his head. "What I told you in college is true. Everything I ever said to you is true, Matías."

My shoulders sag. It's weird to feel a sense of relief over the fact that he's gay, but that means he can't possibly be a hundred percent in love with his wife. He's pretending. His life is a lie, and my heart breaks for him.

I sit up straight and reach for my water. "You said a lot back then."

Memories of his whispered *I love yous* come back to me. I

remember him telling me he'd never been that happy before. He told me I was the best thing to happen to him. He told me he'd never want anyone the way he wanted me.

He watches me like he knows what I'm thinking. Like he's remembering the same words.

"I've missed you," I tell him, the words coming out of my mouth before I can think better of it.

Adrian's face lights up and I'm suddenly back in my dorm room, seeing his face light up the same way when I told him I loved him for the first time.

He was kneeling on the floor after we had sex, telling me he loved me. That he had thought to say it before but was afraid. I was grateful to have already been laying down, because I might've gone weak-kneed at his confession.

After I told him I loved him, his face lit up just like it is now. His smile stretches across his face, his eyes twinkling.

"I've missed you, too."

CHAPTER TWENTY-TWO

MATÍAS

AFTER WALKING through the hotel for a little bit, we make our way back outside to find it a little cooler now that the sun is going down.

We stop to watch the water show at the Bellagio, our arms touching as we lean against a railing. Adrian naively takes a card from one of the many card slappers on the streets.

"Oh," he says when he looks down at it.

"Yep. That's what we've been walking on. Look down."

He shows it to me, and there's a blonde woman pulling down her underwear, with the name *Alexis* written down the side, and the request to call her on the right.

"Not into blondes," I say with a grin.

He drops it with the rest on the ground. "What are you into?"

"I thought I told you."

"When?"

"At dinner, after Andrea and Drew left us."

"Oh." We walk in silence for a little while longer. "How did that come about?"

"That's a conversation for another time. Complicated, like your own story."

"I see."

We continue talking, conversations about people from our past, and whether we know what happened to them or not. Before long, we're in the hallway, leading to our suite.

"I'm gonna shower," I tell him as soon as we walk in.

"Me too. I've sweated gallons today."

I snort. "I'll probably be back out in the living area afterward."

"Okay."

I don't know why I told him that. To warn him I'll be in a shared space? To hopefully have him join me?

The shower is refreshing, and once I'm out, I dry myself off and rub in some lotion. In my room, I grab a pair of boxer-briefs and step inside them before pulling up a pair of dark heather joggers, finishing with a plain white T-shirt.

I run a hand through my wet hair and head into the living room. Adrian's already on the couch, nestled into the corner of the sectional, his legs stretched across the cushions. He lounges in a loose tank top and basketball shorts. He's got the TV on, but he's on his phone.

"Hey," he says, looking over at me and then doing a double take. He sits up, putting his feet on the floor. "Wasn't sure what to put on."

"I'm not worried about it," I say, heading to the fridge to grab a bottle of water. I hold it up. "Want one?"

"Yeah. Feeling a little dehydrated."

I walk over and toss him one before settling into the cushion on the opposite side. Uncapping the bottle, I look to my left to stare at the view of the Strip below us.

"Well, look at us," I say after swallowing down a gulp. "Who would've thought we'd be here together?"

He gives me an uncomfortable smile. "There was a time when I thought we'd go everywhere together."

"Me too, but we can't change the past, can we?"

After a few seconds he says, "No, we can't change anything. Not the past, not our previous choices—"

"Not who we are," I add with a pointed stare.

He swallows. "There are lots of things we can't change, but we can learn to make smarter choices. We can strive to be better."

I nod once, my eyes trained on him.

He looks so good. His arms are toned and muscular, his thighs peek out from under his shorts when he moves, and his lips hypnotize me, making me remember every place they've been on my body.

"Well, in keeping with making smart and better decisions, I guess I should go to my room," I say, standing up.

Adrian looks up at me, and my god, I can only imagine the look on his face if he were on the floor, at my feet, not a scrap of clothing on either one of us.

"Oh." He stands. "I guess we have an early morning."

I nod. "Yeah."

"Would it..." he pauses, chewing on his lip as he scratches the back of his neck. "Is it weird to ask for a hug?"

My chest expands and warms, my stupid heart thumping against my ribs. It's not weird. Not at all. I've been around him again for months and we've yet to hug. I can't say I haven't also thought about what it would feel like to have him in my arms again.

"No," I say, tossing my water bottle on the couch. "It's not weird."

We each take two steps to get to one another, and then we're embracing.

It's not a typical friendly hug—one that's brief and

without any feelings. It's not an awkward, one-armed side hug either. We're body to body, not worried about keeping our hips pushed back to keep from touching.

His arms are under mine, wrapped around my back, while I snake mine around his shoulders. Our faces touch as we each nestle into the other person's neck. He inhales my scent as my lips brush against his skin. It takes everything in me to keep from actually kissing him.

I move my hands, rubbing his back softly, filled with an emotion I didn't expect.

I missed him. I knew that. I was mad at him. I was happy he returned. I was confused and frustrated to find he was married. But I was glad to see him again. It's been a roller coaster of feelings, but here, in this moment, having him in my arms is something I didn't know I needed.

I don't hug many people. Not like this. This is good for my soul. It breaks me open and fills me with warmth and comfort.

I feel both elated and heartbroken.

I never want to let him go, but he's not mine.

I want to cry, and I don't know if it's because I'm so happy or terribly sad.

Adrian squeezes me and makes a quiet noise in his throat. His hands run up and down my back, and then the fingers of my left hand dance across his shoulders, finding place at the nape of his neck. I comb them through the strands of his hair, and his body shivers.

"This isn't weird," I whisper next to his ear.

"No," he says in a quiet voice. "It feels like home."

My heart cracks open, bleeding into my chest. Kill me now.

"It's not smart, either."

We both begin to ease away, our cheeks rubbing against each other.

He turns into my face like he wants to kiss me. "Probably not."

His breath ghosts across my skin he speaks, and I close my eyes and tug on the strands of his hair.

My cock stirs to life, pressed against his hip. I know when he feels it, because his body freezes. His hands stop moving up and down my back, and besides his chest moving with each breath, he's just still.

His arms slowly unwrap from around my body, and I take a tiny step back, but keep my hands locked around the back of his neck.

He grabs my hips, our foreheads touching as we try to bring ourselves to release one another.

I force myself to let him go, letting my hand curve around his jaw, where he nuzzles into my palm. With a small grin, I push his hair off his forehead and plant a small kiss at his hairline.

Adrian inhales deeply before looking at me. The seconds feel like they stretch into hours as we stare at each other.

He has more of a reason not to do this than I do. Sure, he's my subordinate, but I don't give a fuck about the rules. Not when it comes to him. His marriage is inconsequential. It's built on lies and untruths anyway. What's another? Especially when it means he could finally be himself.

"Goodnight, Adrian," I finally say, taking another step back and stripping us of any contact.

"Goodnight," he says after a few seconds.

My eyes drink in his body one more time, and I notice his growing erection pressing against the thin material of his shorts.

"Good god," I mutter before rushing into my room to lock myself in.

The Past

Adrian

CHAPTER TWENTY-THREE

ADRIAN

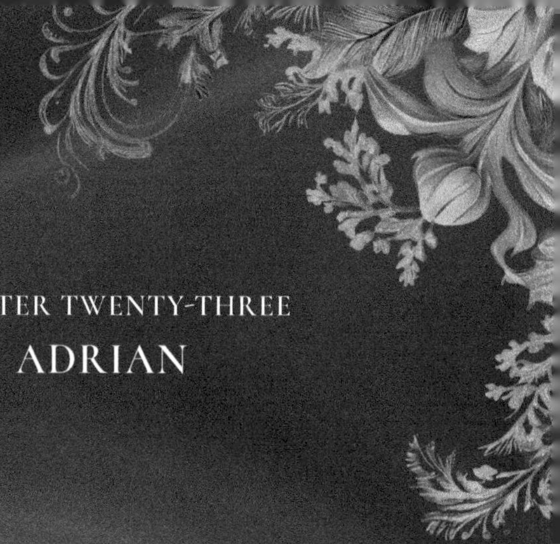

I TUG at the collar of my button-up as I sit at the dining room table, surrounded by my family and their close friends, Mr. and Mrs. Thistle.

"We're so glad you two could join us," my mom says, smiling at my sister and me.

I nod my head, a forced grin on my face.

"Of course, Mom," Amelia replies.

Mom quickly turns to talk to Leanna Thistle at her left, and Amelia leans over to whisper out of the side of her mouth. "Like we had a choice."

I snort, rolling my eyes.

"How's school going?" my father asks from the other side of the table, eyes trained on me.

"Good." I clear my throat, straightening up. "I'm passing all of my classes, and football—"

"Well, I'd hope so," he says, cutting me off. "There's no other alternative but to pass them." He smiles for the sake of his friends, like he's joking, but he's not. I either pass each class with flying colors, or I'm cut off financially. "And football is of no importance," he says dismissively. "I'm afraid you'll only damage your brain playing that game."

"Anybody special in your life, Adrian?" Leanna asks me, reaching for her wine.

My mind instantly goes to Matías, but hell would freeze over before I'd confess that here and now.

"No, not really," I answer with a smile. "I'm too busy with school anyway."

The last part is added in the hopes that it appeases my father. He only wants me to succeed, so if I mention I'm only focused on classes, maybe he'll be happy.

"Well, if you didn't play football, you'd probably have more free time," he says. "College is the perfect place to find a partner. You'll know they're also pursuing a degree and have hopes and plans for the future. Then you can leave college together with an idea to build your future together."

I inhale and nod. Nothing I say will ever be good enough for my father.

"How about you, Amelia?" Mom asks, turning the attention to my sister.

"I've started to see someone," she says with a small smile. "It's in the beginning stages, but he's a good guy."

"What's his major?" Dad asks.

"Uh, animal science."

Dad scrunches his face slightly. "Well, it's something. How did you meet him?"

"Stacy introduced us."

Mom grabs her glass of wine and takes a drink while Dad sits up straighter in his seat. His eyes flicker to his friends, but it's not like they don't know how he is. "I thought we discussed her."

Amelia shifts uncomfortably. "She's in two of my classes. I can't ignore her completely."

"We don't need the way she chooses to live her life to rub off on you."

With a small scoff, disguised as a chuckle, Amelia says, "I don't think that's how that works."

"It's a mental illness, Amelia," Dad says sternly, his eyes moving to me. "It's not natural and it will not be tolerated in this family."

"I know, Dad," Amelia says.

I nod at him, feeling sweat break out all over my body.

Amelia's friend Stacy is a lesbian, and our parents only found out because they overheard a conversation Amelia and I were having where she mentioned Stacy and her girlfriend.

Thanksgiving dinner stretches for hours, and Amelia and I know we're not excused until our parents get up. We have quiet and uninteresting conversations until Dad stands, signaling dinner is officially over.

"We'll be in the study," he says to Amelia and I. "Help the staff take the dishes into the kitchen."

We nod our obedience. Once they leave, two women who've worked for our family for years emerge into the formal dining room, and begin gathering plates.

Amelia and I join in, but Mary stops us. "We got it. It's okay."

"He could come back," I say simply.

Mary nods and all four of us clear the table and get the dishes into the kitchen.

"Go have some fun," Mary says with a hand on my shoulder.

"Thank you."

"Bye, Mary. Linda," Amelia says, hugging them. "Thanks for everything."

Amelia and I head through the expansive house until we get to the staircase that'll lead us to our rooms.

"Same place?" she asks before going into her room.

"Yeah."

I quickly change out of the formal clothing we're required to wear for dinner, and get into a pair of sweats and a hoodie. I make my way up to the third floor that holds an expanded loft, then open the French doors that lead to the deck.

I'm outside for a few minutes before Amelia appears, wearing fuzzy socks, fleece pants, and a thick robe tied tight around her body.

"What a fucking bore," she says, dropping into the chair next to me. "I hate coming here."

"I'm thinking of not coming for Christmas."

Her head snaps in my direction, eyes wide. "Do you have a death wish?"

I shrug. "I'll blame school or something. I can't keep coming out here. They're awful to be around."

She nods. "I know. It's never fun."

"So, you have a boyfriend?" I ask.

She scoffs. "No. I just figured I'd say that considering how he reacted to you not having a girlfriend."

"Nice."

"I messed it up by bringing up Stacy."

"Yeah," I say with a nod.

Amelia takes a scrunchie off her wrist and ties her long, brown hair up into a messy bun. "So, nothing new with you?"

I haven't told Amelia about Matías, because I haven't told her that I'm gay. I know I can trust her more than my parents, and I don't think she'd spill the news to them, but I'm still struggling to say the words out loud to anyone.

Speaking them out loud means there's no more hiding, and I'm not sure I'm ready to be out from the cover of secrecy. Secrecy is my safe blanket, and once it's off, I'm visible and vulnerable to the world.

"Not really," I say.

She watches me for a few seconds but doesn't push it. We spend the next few hours outside until we think we might actually freeze to death, then we hug and go to our individual rooms.

In the morning, I'm sitting in the library because nobody ever comes in here. Matías is sending me pictures of him with his mom's new dog. The dog is a small little thing and sits on his shoulder as he's on the couch.

I laugh and tell him to try to smuggle it back to school.

He sends me a video of the dog barking while simultaneously running in a circle, head in the air like he's barking at the clouds.

Okay, maybe don't bring him. He's loud for such a small dog.

He's crazy. He's not barking at anything. Just mad at the air, I guess.

When are you gonna be back?

Miss me or something?

More than you know. I'll be leaving in a few hours.

I miss you too! I'll be back in South River this evening. It's not a far drive.

Can't wait to see you.

Me either. I love you.

Love you more.

I look up, a smile still on my face, and find my father in the doorway.

My smile drops immediately, and I take my feet off the coffee table and put them on the floor. "Hey."

He doesn't say anything, only quietly makes his way into the room where he goes to the window and peeks out.

After an uncomfortable amount of time, he finally speaks. "You're due to come work for me once you graduate. I've built this company and made it into what it is. You are in position to take the reins when I'm ready to retire, which won't be any time soon, but you still have plenty to learn." He faces me. "You and your sister have never needed to get a job or pay for your own phone bills or anything like that. You are my children, and I'm aware that I'm responsible for you, however, because I do pay for everything, I believe I'm entitled to some information."

I begin sweating, because I have no idea what he's getting at. Talking to my father is never a relaxing situation. We're never able to talk or joke with each other. He's only capable of lecturing me.

"I know kids tend to think their parents are oblivious, but I am not. I know you better than you think I do. Likely better than you know yourself. I watched you grow up. Hell, I raised you. You've had the world at your fingertips. Born into money, blessed with good looks, and given the best tutors money could buy. You're a smart boy, Adrian. I know you are. You are my legacy—what lives on after I die, and what you do with my company is important to me. I want it to remain in the family. I want it to grow and be bigger than ever, and I think you can do that."

I nod, swallowing. "Yes, sir."

"A few years ago, you were here visiting for Christmas. You remember?"

I dip my chin, not sure where this is heading. My brain works overtime trying to remember what happened three years ago.

"Just eighteen," he says. "So young, so stupid."

"Sir?"

He huffs and walks over, his jaw tense. "I've been hoping that your little internet searches were simply curiosity. Dumb, childish curiosity. You had just started college, and you're surrounded by a plethora of individuals who were not raised the way you were. You start getting ideas or information from kids whose parents didn't teach them right from wrong. With the internet at your fingertips, I understand you can type in anything to seek answers. In the last few years, you've yet to bring a girl home, let alone even mention one. You've never had interest in dating, and I can respect keeping yourself focused on more important things, but I hope it's only that."

My heart races in my chest. What the hell is going on? What did I look up three years ago and how does he know?

"My company will not go to a deviant, and no child of mine will be gay and still be my child."

He stares me down, waiting. For what? For me to deny it? To question it? No matter what I do or say, it won't be the right thing.

I simply nod my head once, tears brimming in my eyes. After a few more seconds of watching me, he walks out of the room.

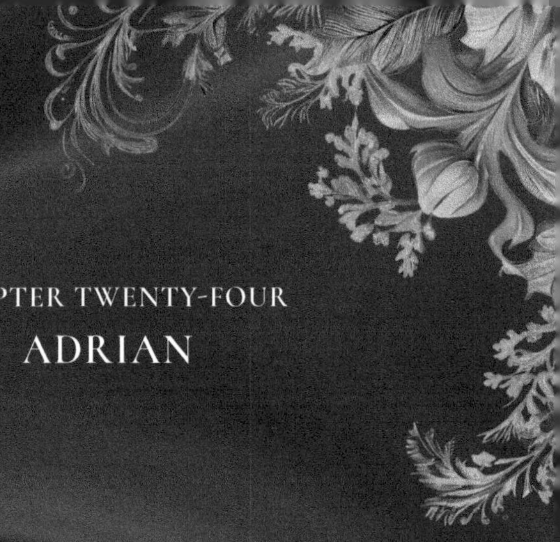

CHAPTER TWENTY-FOUR
ADRIAN

ON THE WAY BACK HOME, I rack my brain trying to remember what I did three years ago, but then a memory flashes through my mind, and I hit the brakes in the middle of the road. Luckily, nobody is behind me.

It was my first year of college, which was when I was really questioning myself and the thoughts and feelings I was having. I found myself attracted to a guy in one of my classes. I had always been able to admit when a guy was attractive. That didn't make anyone gay. But this guy in particular made me nervous. I got excited to be around him. I was hanging on every word and movement, and I started to think about other things. What it would be like to touch him and kiss him.

It freaked me out. I was already well aware of my parents and their viewpoints. How did I go eighteen years without feeling this way? Was I just suppressing it? Was I afraid to see it because I knew it wouldn't be accepted?

I went home for Christmas break and started to Google things on my phone.

How to know if you're gay.

Can you be attracted to guys and girls?

I thought those searches were safe behind the screen of my own phone, but I remember now my father coming to me and slamming my phone down in front of me as I was sitting at the breakfast counter. He gave me a stern look, but it wasn't out of the norm for him to give us looks like that. He was easily agitated. I figured he was mad that I left my phone somewhere he wanted to sit.

But now—now I'm thinking he must've picked it up believing it was his. I probably did leave it on the couch where he sits. He thought it was his, opened it up, and saw my searches.

My searches were questions. It wasn't gay porn or gay hook-up sites. He knew I was trying to figure it out. I was curious. Maybe he's gone this whole time hoping it was just a phase. That it never came to fruition.

Fuck.

My phone rings, the sound blaring over the speakers. I click a button and say, "Hello?"

"Hey. I'm leaving my mom's house now, and I'm bringing leftovers she's forced upon me. How far out are you?"

"About three hours."

"Okay, I'll be there shortly after. Wanna meet in my room?"

"Of course."

He laughs. "Good. See you soon."

"See you."

What I have with Matías doesn't feel wrong. I'm not mentally ill for loving him. I'm not a deviant or anything else my father likes to say. But I'm still trapped under my father's thumb. Without him, I have no money. My job and future aren't secured. I don't know what I'm supposed to do, but right now, after not seeing Matías for a few days, I don't want to worry about it.

I want him. I want him right now in this moment, and that's what I'll focus on. I can't worry about the fact that I want him in the future as well, and what that'll mean.

❧

Halfway into eating his leftovers, he asks, "How was your Thanksgiving?"

I swallow down the turkey and the majority of the truth. "It was fine."

He nods, but I feel his gaze on me. He doesn't push, which is one of the reasons why I appreciate him. He's aware of my family dynamic, and he won't force me to talk about them.

"Still think you can stay here for Christmas?"

"I'm gonna try like hell," I say, looking at him with a grin. "I'd prefer being here with you."

He smiles and it warms my heart.

We finish eating and throw everything away before climbing into his bed. Wrapped in each other's arms, we kiss and cuddle before our exhaustion takes over.

Matías falls asleep first, and I spend thirty minutes running my hand through his hair and kissing his forehead, wondering how it'll be possible for me to keep him when I have the father that I do.

He'll never accept me if I tell him I'm gay, and therefore he'll never accept Matías. I can't ever bring him home. I can't talk about him to anyone. He'll forever be my secret, and I doubt he'll be okay with that.

I tighten my grip on him like I'm afraid someone's going to come take him from me now, and I eventually fall asleep. But the thoughts and fears never leave.

Present Day

Adrian

CHAPTER TWENTY-FIVE

ADRIAN

I SHOULDN'T HAVE ASKED for that hug. It was a selfish move. I wanted to feel him again. I wanted the connection. To see if hugging him was the same as it was all those years ago.

It wasn't. It was different but not in a worse way. He's bigger now, muscular where he didn't used to be. Grip tighter and stronger, but maybe that's just because it's been so long since we've embraced. Perhaps he needed and longed for the hug as much as I did.

Now I can't stop thinking about it. My mind rewinds the moment over and over again, remembering how I felt when he tugged on my hair, or when I touched his neck with my lips—so desperate to bite into him and then lick and kiss it better. His cock hardening against me almost did me in. I was afraid he'd soon see or feel my own arousal. I remember it all, but mostly, I want it again. I want more.

I attempt to put all those thoughts aside as I get ready. When I walk into the living room, I see him standing in front of the floor-to-ceiling window, his white button-up tucked into slacks that accentuate his ass. His hair is slicked back, the waves visible from here.

He turns when he hears my steps, giving me a thorough look up and down before a small smile touches his lips.

"Morning."

"Good morning," I say, making my way next to him. "What a view."

I feel his gaze on the side of my face. "Yes." He turns to peer out the window again. "It's quite nice."

"Do we have time for coffee?"

He looks at his watch. "Yeah, but we should leave now. The coffee shop in the lobby will probably be busy, but it's better than the coffee they have in here."

Matías puts on his suit jacket, and then we both pull our lanyards over our heads before heading into the hall.

The tension is thick between us. We're both probably thinking about last night, so the elevator ride is silent.

As we're in line, waiting for our coffee, my phone vibrates in my pocket. I pull it out and read the screen.

Charlotte

Good morning. I hope you have a good day.
Sorry I missed your call last night. I fell
asleep early.

My eyes flicker to Matías, but he's just staring straight ahead.

No worries. Thank you. I hope you have a
good day too. Talk later.

. . .

I slip the phone back into my pocket as we approach the counter. After we get our coffees, we begin walking to the conference room where we run into the people from our office. For the next hour and a half, I sit next to Matías, trying to focus on the speech, but only thinking about his leg touching mine, and how good his thighs look through the navy blue pants.

Jesus, what's wrong with me?

We stay busy until one when we can finally break for lunch. I find myself irrationally frustrated when Matías invites a couple of the people from the office to eat with us.

During the entire lunch, he barely acknowledges me. He engages in conversation with others, and when I join in, he'll glance in my direction before focusing on his food.

I try to make eye contact with him, but it's like he's actively avoiding me.

After lunch, he continues talking to a man named Mike, and we make our way to a panel filled with experts about project management. There's some Q & A time at the end, and then we break until it's time for networking.

"I'll be back," Matías tells me with barely a look before strutting across the room to talk to some guy he clearly knows.

They hug, smiling and laughing before pulling away and engaging in what seems to be a very lively conversation.

I find myself feeling jealous and angry, which is ridiculous. I don't have any right.

Fueled by those irrational thoughts, I pull out my phone and call Charlotte, finding my way into a corner.

"Hello?"

"Hey."

"Hey!" she says with some excitement in her voice. "How's it going? How's Vegas?"

"Well, I'm in a room with a bunch of suits as we all talk about work, so it's about as fun as it sounds."

She laughs. "Well, maybe you'll get time to explore a little."

I don't tell her about my first day with Matías. She doesn't even know we're sharing a room. I know how that looks. I know it's not the best idea to keep that a secret, but it's nothing compared to the biggest secret I'm keeping from her. And I bet even if she knew we were sharing a room, it would be fine. We're co-workers. It's a business trip. She'd have nothing to fear.

A tingling sensation at the back of my head tells me I'm wrong. She does have something to fear, and it's probably worse because she'd never see it coming.

"Matías is here," I blurt out, hoping that by being honest about this, I'll feel better about the things I'm keeping from her.

"Oh, yeah?"

I nod. "Yeah." Silence stretches. "You know, we actually knew each other in school."

"College?"

"Yeah."

"Wow. Were you close friends?"

I scratch the back of my neck. "No...not really. We had a class together. He helped me out because I was notoriously late or absent."

She chuckles a little. "Well, small world. Why didn't you tell me before?"

I shrug like she can see me. "Didn't really think about it. It's not a big deal, you know? He's just my boss now."

She goes quiet for a minute. "Well, Dad wants to come out next month. The second week. Is that okay?"

I fail to hold in my sigh. "Do I have a choice?"

"Adrian, what do you expect me to do? Ignore my father for the rest of my life because he's friends with yours? You know they only want the best for us."

"Best," I say with a sardonic laugh. "Sure. They want what's best for them. My father doesn't give a shit about what's best for me."

Her exasperation is released through a loud sigh. "Adrian, I know we didn't come together on the best circumstances, but you can't keep—"

"I don't want to talk about this right now. I have to go anyway. I'll call you later."

"Fine." She exhales again. "Okay, fine. Bye."

The rest of the day goes by at a snail's pace. I'm frustrated over my call with Charlotte and the impending date of her father's arrival. I'm annoyed that Matías suddenly started to ignore me, but seems to lament his attention on everyone else.

I want to go to the room, but I share it with the man I want and can't have.

"You good?"

My head snaps up to find Matías at my side. "Oh. Yeah, mmhmm."

He gives me a weird look. "Okay, well, it's over, so I'm gonna head to the room now. You ready?"

"Yeah."

Once again, the journey is silent and uncomfortable.

Inside the room, he speaks.

"I was planning on just ordering in for dinner tonight."

"That's fine."

I go to my room to shower and change before flopping onto my bed. After a while, Matías knocks on the door.

"Yeah?"

"Can I come in?"

"Sure."

He stands in the doorway. "You ready to order?"

"Is there a menu?"

Strutting in, he goes to the dresser and picks up a folder, pulling out a menu. "I'm ordering from here."

After handing it to me, he stands near my bed as I look it over. I'm too focused on his presence to actually read it the first time, so I look it over again, this time paying attention.

I relay my order to him and he walks out. I hear his voice on the phone in the other room, and then silence.

When there's a knock on the main door, I get out of bed and make my way to the living area.

We gather our food, and I take mine to the small table in between the living room and kitchen. Matías looks like he's gonna join me, but then stops himself.

"I'll probably eat in my room."

I snort, shaking my head. "Of course."

"What?" he questions.

"I knew I shouldn't have asked for a hug. You've gone all weird on me."

He steps forward. "What do you mean?"

"All day today you've avoided looking at me. You didn't speak to me. You acted as though I wasn't around."

"What do you want me to do, Adrian?" he exclaims, coming forward to drop his food on the table. "You're married!"

"I know!" I yell, putting my fork down. "I fucking know that. The words *I'm married* run through my head over and over every time I look at you."

"I ignored you because the alternative is to touch you. To hold you. To steal you away and bring you up here so I can have my way with you. I had to ignore you, because my thoughts were running away with fantasies and ideas I'm not welcome to. I ignored you to keep from making you do something you might regret."

I exhale and look up at him. "I could never regret you. I've never regretted any moment with you, Matías."

He begins to shake his head. "Don't. Don't open the door. Don't make me think there's a chance."

I stand, running a hand through my hair. With a sigh, I say, "I don't know what's possible between us. At times I feel like maybe nothing, but at others, I hope for the most incredible future. The two thoughts have been at war in my mind for a long time."

Matías chews on the inside of his bottom lip, watching me for what feels like forever before he speaks.

"You're still hiding who you are. You've somehow painted yourself into a life that you will never find happiness in. Tell me, have you ever been happy?"

"I was at my happiest with you."

His shoulders sag a little, and his head tilts. "But you're not happy now."

I exhale, throwing my hands up. "I'm fine. I'm...content, I guess. My life could be worse."

"That's not a way to live, Adrian."

"I know," I say a little too sharply. "I know," I repeat, my tone quieter. "But I don't know what to do."

"I think the problem is that you know exactly what you have to do, and it frightens you."

With a sigh, I rub my forehead, looking down at the ground. "The things that I do know, do terrify me. You're right." I look at him. "I know I want you. Right now. I want to kiss you and touch you. I want what we had before, and I want more. That is terrifying for many reasons.

"I've always tried to be a good guy, and Charlotte doesn't deserve the lies and deceit, but I struggle with who to care about more. Her or myself? For years, she's been the focus. I've never allowed myself to be authentic—to be happy, and now here we are. You stand before me, the embodiment of happiness. Every meaningful and joyous memory I have is wrapped up in you. Tell me how I walk away from that. Tell me how I can look at you and remember the only time I've felt happy and loved, and be strong enough to deny myself those feelings again. It's hard not to feel selfish, Matías. Not when I've gone my whole life living for other people."

He rubs his hand over his chest, right over his heart. "You can't ask me to tell you to walk away, because I remember what it feels like to be the one left behind, and I've been waiting for you to come back to me for a long time. If you want me. Truly. Without reservation or fear, come to me and tell me, and I'll be waiting."

CHAPTER TWENTY-SIX

ADRIAN

HE WALKS AWAY FROM ME, and I'm forced to feel a tiny bit of what it must've felt like for him when I walked away all those years ago. This is nowhere near the same. I'm aware I blindsided him and hurt him in the worst way. And now, he's just trying to be cautious. He wants me to be sure, but being with Matías is the only sure thing I've ever known. Walking away from him split me apart. My heart has been living without a piece of it for years, because that piece resides in him.

I'm married. I'm married.

It's not a real marriage. It never felt real to me. But that doesn't mean Charlotte doesn't believe it to be real. But to gain the courage to tell her the truth about me isn't something that'll come quick. I can't call her right now and tell her over the phone so I can rush into his room and be with him. But I also don't think I'll be able to wait much longer.

The need I feel to be with him gets stronger every minute. Retaining any sense of good morals grows precarious every moment I'm close to him.

I'm still at the table, barely picking at my food as he sits in his room. When his phone rings, it filters through the door, as does his voice when he talks.

"Hello? Hi. No, I'm not home right now. I'm in Vegas on a work trip." A pause, and then he laughs. "Oh, really?" Does he sound flirtatious? When he speaks again, it's a bit quieter, and I find myself holding still to try to hear better. "Tell me what exactly." Another chuckle, and I find myself getting upset that anyone else is making him laugh. Is this the guy from earlier today? The one he spent so much time talking to? "Well, I'm not sure. I'll let you know."

A couple minutes after he ends the call, he walks back into the main living area to get rid of his trash, eyes flashing to me briefly.

He puts his phone on the counter as he pulls open the cabinet that houses the trash can and drops everything in there.

I walk over to dump mine as well, and once again his phone rings. The screen lights up and the name Christian shows up across the top. We both look down at it before meeting each other's gaze.

"Is that someone you aren't exclusively dating?" I ask.

"Maybe. Does it matter?"

"You're not gonna answer it?"

"Would you like me to?"

I shrug, feigning indifference as I walk back to the table.

The phone stops ringing. "Yes?" Matías answers.

"Hi. I was wondering if you're going to be free next week-end," a voice says from the phone. Matías put it on speaker.

I turn around and find him watching me. "What do you have in mind?" he asks.

"Another visit to Summons House."

"Hmm. Well, let me get back to you. I need to make sure I won't have other plans."

"Yes, sir."

"Talk to you later."

"Okay."

Matías presses the end button on the screen and waits for me to have a response. It's clear in the way he was speaking to Christian, that whoever was on the phone earlier was someone different. He didn't speak to him with much emotion.

"What's Summons House?" I ask.

He smirks. "Look it up. And let me know if I'll have plans next weekend."

I'm in my room, tossing and turning as I contemplate what I want to do. I know cheating is wrong. More often than not, it's categorized as a *mistake* when people get caught. They're either drunk and not thinking, they were mad at their partner and went off and cheated. It hardly ever *means* anything. There are tons of excuses, and none of them justify the action. I'm smart enough to know that, no matter what, it's wrong.

My dwelling on it, and thinking about it takes away the excuse of a mistake. The fact that I'm turning it over in my head so much probably makes it worse. I'm deciding if I want to break my marriage vows and disrespect someone I'm supposed to love and cherish. If I do it, I've made the conscious decision to hurt her.

But then there's this other voice telling me that I'm hurting myself. I've *been* hurting myself. I've also subconsciously hurt Charlotte by not being honest in the beginning. Not that I felt I had a choice. She was forced on me by my father. Our relationship was never authentic. We didn't have a meet-cute and fall in love. We were a carefully constructed partnership in order to help her—something I hate my father for forcing me into. And now, I feel trapped.

Being with Matías wouldn't be a mistake, and it would mean everything to me. I could never discount it as something cheap, or just for sex.

I shove the covers off me with an exhale. I can't sleep with all these thoughts in my head.

Maybe it's time to tell my parents the truth. To tell everyone the truth. I switched jobs to get out from under my father. I couldn't work there anymore. I've saved up enough money to be okay for a while. If he cuts me off, at least I have a steady job. I might have to downgrade or change the way I've been able to spend on a whim, but I'd be happier. And even the richest people don't have the richest lives. I want my life to be full, not my wallet.

I plant my feet on the ground and get up to get some water, bringing my phone with me. Sitting on the couch, I stare out at the view and zone out. When I hear a bed creak, I'm brought back into the present. I look at Matías's door and hear him moving around some more. Guess it makes sense that he can't sleep either, though not for the same reasons. He doesn't have to stress over as much. He's not committed to anyone. He's out to everyone who knows him.

I get on my phone and scroll through a couple pages of apps before I find the one that's titled *Excel Sheets*, though it's not that at all. It's a glimpse of the past. A time capsule I've never been able to get rid of, even when I went years without looking at it.

When I click it, it opens up to a site that holds all the photos I've taken since having this phone. Hundreds of backed up photos that live on even if I don't have them saved to my phone.

Starting from the beginning, I swipe through a lot of my early college days, before finally landing on images of Matías at one of my parties. There's some of the two of us, and us with my roommates. Nothing scandalous, just memories of a time when life was a little easier.

The more I swipe, the riskier they get. Selfies of him and I together in my room or his. Faces close, shirts removed as we lounge in bed. One of him kissing my cheek. One of him just lying in my bed, smiling up at me.

My lips turn up on the ends as I look at them.

Every photo of just us together is us hidden behind the four walls of our bedrooms. There are not any pictures of us being a couple out in public, and it breaks my heart to know that I kept him hidden the entire time. What we had was amazing, but it could've been even better if I hadn't been so afraid. I let my father come between us and it ruined everything.

I shift a little when the next photos come up, my eyes flickering to his door like I'm afraid he'll catch me and know what I'm looking at.

These were photos and videos he sent me when I was traveling with the football team, or really any time we weren't together for more than twenty-four hours.

I turn my volume down before I play the first video, and when it begins, my heart pounds in my chest. He's on his bed with the phone propped on the nightstand. It gets everything from the stomach down, and he's jerking himself with slow strokes before the pace picks up.

Though I'm only wearing a pair of boxers, my entire body warms like I'm wrapped in a thick fleece blanket while sitting next to a fire.

I swallow and get out of it only to be intrigued by the other videos. Clicking through them, I watch several seconds of each—one of them starts, and within only five seconds, he's coming.

My cock is already hardening, finding its way through the slit in my boxers, ready to escape and be handled.

I reach down to tuck it back in, but when I touch myself as I watch the rest of the video, I can't find it in me to pull my hand away.

Stroking slowly, I watch as Matías's fist continues to move up and down his shaft, his cum covering his fingers and stomach. Then I start it over.

My chest heaves as I watch, then the need to hear him takes over. I only put the volume up the tiniest amount, then hold the phone to my ear to hear the noises he makes.

When he comes, the sound sends goosebumps traveling down my arms, and heat licking up my back. I close my eyes, just listening to him as I stroke.

Something gets my attention. I don't know what the noise was exactly since I was so focused on listening to the video, but I open my eyes and find Matías in his doorway. He's frozen in place, watching me with a look of surprise on his features.

"Oh." I scramble to put the phone down and tuck my erection back into my boxers. Embarrassment fills my cheeks with even more heat, and my cock throbs, desperate for the release that was so close.

"Continue," Matías says, expression shifting from shock to lust.

My dick twitches its excitement at the permission to keep going, but I can't.

"I should go to my room," I say, turning to put my feet on the ground so I can stand.

Matías walks over, sitting on the other side of the couch, facing me. "Continue."

My chest expands with a deep breath. He's wearing a pair of lounge pants and nothing else. His body has changed and no longer looks like it did in the videos I was just watching, but I find myself more entranced by him. He's got a dusting of hair on his torso, and defined muscles, and my hands long to rub up and down his body to feel the roughness of what he has to offer. I want the scratch of hair against my skin. I want to feel the strength of his body below or above mine.

"Matías," I start.

His head inclines slightly and he scoots to the edge of the cushion. "I won't even touch you. Just let me watch."

I wet my lips, wanting to give him what he wants. I lean back slightly in the seat and reach into my boxers.

"What are you gonna watch?" he asks.

"Nothing. Just you."

His nostrils flare slightly as he mimics my pose, leaning back into the cushion, legs spread. He pulls his pants down to his knees, revealing his white boxer-briefs that leave little to the imagination.

My eyes stay focused on his cock, watching as it strains against the material as it gets harder. I trace the lines of his abs and replay his voice when he came in the video. I imagine him doing now what he did then, wondering how different he might sound. Wanting to see his cum paint his skin.

I release a moan as my hand moves up and down, my eyes closing.

"Look at me," he says.

I obey, biting into my lip as he runs his palm over his crotch. My gaze moves to his face, and we watch each other for a little while before he reaches into his underwear and my attention is stolen.

He doesn't take it out, but he leisurely strokes himself.

The look on his face is enough to do me in. He's so

fucking sexy. My eyes bounce around—face, cock, torso. Cock, lips, thighs. Face, cock.

Oh god, his cock is visible now. Just the tip peeking out above his fingers.

"Fuck," I moan, gaze locked in, the memory of his voice in my ears. "Oh, my god."

He gets up, yanking his pants to his hips. "Get to the edge," he tells me, walking closer.

"Wha—what?" I ask through a breath, my orgasm ready to explode out of me.

Matías drops to his knees. Oh, shit. He's on his knees in front of me.

He gestures with his fingers, calling me forward. I scoot to the edge, stroking myself right in front of his face. He's so close. Close enough to wrap his lips around me if he wanted.

He's got a close-up view now, but he doesn't say anything. He doesn't touch me. He just waits.

"Oh, fuck," I exclaim, focused on his lips, thinking about what it would feel like to be in his mouth again. "Matías."

His shoulders roll back as his chin lifts to look at me, a pleasure-filled moan deep in his throat. He had a physical reaction to me using his name.

"I'm gonna come."

Instead of aiming my cock at myself, I point it straight ahead, ready to shoot my load on the floor in front of him. I assume that's what he wants since he wanted me on the edge.

The first burst of cum shoots out, nearly landing on his chest. I close my eyes and keep stroking, my muscles tense as pleasure takes over.

My eyes flicker open, ready to close again, but I spot Matías in front of me, his mouth open as he catches more of my cum in his mouth.

"Oh, shit," I exclaim, nearly choking on my gasp.

The way he looks up at me is intoxicating. He's sensual, sinful desire wrapped into a package and presented to me at my feet. My arousal glistens on his chin.

I stand up, my cum leaving my cock in drips rather than ribbons now, and he peers up at me and opens his mouth, so I aim it as best as I can to land on his tongue.

"Holy shit," I gasp.

When my body is spent, I stumble back to the couch and sit.

Matías wipes his hand across his chin, cleaning up any mess. His eyes never leave my face, and I'm unsure of what to say.

He gives me a small grin as he stands. "Still so good."

Before I can bring myself to say anything, he's walking away and disappearing into his room.

CHAPTER TWENTY-SEVEN

ADRIAN

I SPENT all of last night convincing myself that what happened between Matías and I wasn't even a big deal. It wasn't cheating, right? We didn't even touch. I masturbated, and masturbation is not cheating.

Okay, so I had a small audience. Is that cheating?

I came into his mouth. All right, that's probably crossing a line, but our bodies never touched. Do I get some sort of grace?

Running late, I get out of bed and rush to the shower, confusing thoughts swirling in my head like a tornado, wreaking havoc on my brain.

I know that it's still wrong, and anybody would be upset to learn their significant other masturbated in front of someone, but it could be worse, right?

God. I'm so screwed. I'm officially one of those douchey men who come up with any sort of excuse to make themselves feel better over what they did.

How can I possibly stay another night in this hotel room with him, when that was the last thing we did? When I want to do it again. When I want more to happen.

Once I'm dressed, I rush out into the living room prepared to apologize for my tardiness, but I don't see Matías. The suite is quiet. I find a tented piece of paper on the table with my name scrawled across the front. When I open it up, I read his note.

I heard you in the shower, but I had to leave early since I have my panel this morning. I'll see you later.

Don't be weird.

I scoff, but there's a small smile on my lips when I place the note back on the table. *Don't be weird.* Please. How can I act like he wasn't on his knees in front of me, giving me commands, and swallowing my cum?

With a glance at the time, I rush out the door and down into the lobby. I'm only a few minutes late, but luckily nobody notices when I slip inside the conference room while Matías is mid-speech.

He spots me immediately, however—his gaze looking me up and down as he continues to talk.

Unfortunately, I learn nothing from his Q & A because my mind is revisiting the events of last night, and I wonder how I'll ever move past that.

While someone asks him a question, his eyes find me as I sit in the back at the end of the row. His finger rubs along the underside of his bottom lip, the hint of a smirk on his mouth before he refocuses and answers the question.

There's no hiding what he was thinking. He and I are both living in the same moment from eight hours ago.

When he's done, he gets caught up talking to people, so I

slip out of the room and head to the next event. It isn't until eleven o'clock that we see each other again.

"Morning." His voice is smooth as silk as he comes around from behind me. "Running late this morning?"

"Didn't sleep well," I say before clearing my throat, avoiding his gaze.

"Hmm."

I fill up my paper cup at the water jug in the hall, taking a sip as I chance a glance at him over the rim. "You? How'd you sleep?"

He grins. "Fine." There's a brief pause. "Want to get lunch?"

I bring the cup down and nod once. "Yeah. Sure."

As I follow his lead, he says hi to a handful of people as we walk, smiling and laughing, not a worry or stressful thought in his head. Must be nice.

It isn't until we're near the elevators that I snap into the present and start asking questions.

"Where are we eating?"

"In the room," he says simply, stretching his arm into the elevator to hold the doors for a few people exiting.

He steps inside as I wait in the hall. Crossing one foot over the other while he slips his hands in his pockets, he doesn't seem to care one way or the other if I join him.

The doors begin to close and I rush in.

Maybe he knew I was coming all along.

"Are you being weird?" he asks without looking at me.

"No."

He laughs. "Okay."

It's silent for a while, then he says, "You didn't do anything wrong."

"My wife might disagree."

His jaw tenses but he doesn't say anything. The doors open, and we walk out and head to the room.

Once inside, he tosses the key on the counter and removes his tie. "I don't want to talk about your wife anymore."

"When have we ever?"

"I don't want to hear it. That word. That title."

I swallow, taking in his anger. "It's easy to do when you don't have one. When you have no one to answer to. No one to hurt."

He lets out a mocking laugh. "Well, you know all about hurting people. Glad to see you've gotten to a point where you actually care. You didn't used to."

Matías stands at the window, looking out.

"I did care about hurting you, Matías."

He spins around. "You did it anyway, and yet now you're so morally conscious. Afraid to cheat on a wife you're not even attracted to. A wife you can never love in a way she deserves. However, you didn't seem to think twice when it came to hurting me—the one and only person to love you for exactly who you are."

"Marriage is different. There were vows."

He scoffs. "Don't even get me started, Adrian. Those vows were tainted the moment you uttered them. Don't kid yourself."

"You used to care about obeying the rules and you were always worried about someone's feelings being hurt."

"Yeah, look what that got me."

The words are like an arrow to the heart.

I step closer to him. "I wanted to be with you. I never wanted it to end."

"But?"

"My father controlled my life. He knew. He confronted me

about it on Thanksgiving weekend, threatening that I'd have nothing if he ever found out his son was gay. He was ready to disown me, and I'd have no money or job security. I lived off his wealth through college, not concerned with having to save or work for my own. I was always aware he'd give me a job when I graduated.

"I went back to school trying not to think about it. I still had half a year, and I wanted to spend every second of it with you. I hoped I'd come up with a plan. I hoped it would work its way out one way or another, but the job was in Chicago. I was always going to leave. I spent too much time living in the present that I wasn't thinking about the future. But the present was perfect. The present had you, and that's all I wanted to think about. I knew you weren't gonna go to Chicago. You had your own plans."

He stares at me for a while, exhaling his frustration. "You could've told me. We could've talked about this and came up with a plan."

I shake my head. "That's because you don't know what happened during Christmas break."

"What happened?"

The Past

Adrian

CHAPTER TWENTY-EIGHT
ADRIAN

THIS CHRISTMAS WAS the best Christmas I've had in probably forever. I told my parents I had to stick around campus for tutoring. It didn't go over without a fight, but I was adamant on staying in South River.

Matías and I spent Christmas Eve in his dorm room, and we even had our own mini tree that we decorated with twinkle lights and tiny baubles. We put lights around his window and hung stockings from his dresser.

We got each other a few gifts, and though the wrapping was terrible, we woke up Christmas morning and dug into them like we were children again.

After having what we deemed would be traditional morning Christmas sex, we headed over to my house where my roommates and I had planned to come together to make dinner. They weren't going home for the holiday either, so we figured we'd do the best we could.

It wasn't the best food I've had, but it was edible, and with a few extra friends around the table, we all had the best time.

Now it's the twenty-eighth, and I have to force myself to

stay home. My roommates are getting curious. They've made little sly remarks from time to time, but they don't seem to be near the truth at all.

"Where do you go all the time?" Barlow asks.

"What do you mean?"

"You're always gone, and we don't have class or practice, so you must have a secret girlfriend or something."

"You afraid I'm gonna steal her if you bring her over?" Johnson asks with a laugh.

I laugh. "Uhh no."

"So you do have a girl?" Barlow questions.

"No!"

They both watch me with expressions that tell me I'm not convincing them.

"It's nothing serious," I say. "Just messing around."

"Mmhmm," Johnson murmurs, throwing a mini basketball in the hoop he has hanging on the back of the front door.

"You've been messing around for a while though," Barlow adds.

"Why don't you mind your business?" I say with a chuckle. "What's up with you and Cherisse?"

He rolls his eyes. "Nothing."

We end up talking about whatever they got going on, and I make up small lies about this make-believe girl I'm hooking up with, and then I disappear into my room and text Matías.

Had to tell the guys I'm hooking up with some girl. So, if they mention that, don't panic.

Getting suspicious?

Questioning where I go all the time.

Ah. Well, okay.

I miss you though.

My door flies open and Barlow stands there. "New Year's Eve party. Invite that girl." He throws a ball at me before closing the door.

I sigh.

"She said she couldn't come," I say when my roommates ask where the girl I'm hooking up with is.

"Dude. Maybe she's got another guy. Like a boyfriend. You're probably just the side-piece," Johnson says.

I shrug. "Fine by me."

They laugh and leave it alone, because worrying about my personal life is the last thing they're gonna be thinking about in a house full of girls and beer.

A little before midnight, I sneak away with Matías, heading out back so we can have a moment on the patio while everyone crowds the living room as they countdown to the new year.

"Happy New Year," I murmur drunkenly.

"It's not midnight yet," Matías says with a laugh.

"Close enough. We get to start a new year together."

He grabs my hand. "What about finishing it?"

"I want nothing more than to spend the whole year with you," I say honestly.

It's the truth, but deep down I worry it won't happen, and that's a conversation we need to have soon. But not tonight.

He smiles, and the muffled voices of dozens of drunken college students filter outside. When they get to one, we lean in and kiss, a backdrop of fireworks going off to the side of us as people cheer inside.

"I love you, Adrian," he says quietly.

"I love you. More than you'll know."

It's six in the morning when I sneak Matías out of my room and through the living room where a few people sprawl across the couch and floor.

We step onto the front porch, the sky not yet awake.

"I'll see you tomorrow?" he questions.

"Definitely. Drive safely to your mom's."

"I will," he says with a small grin. "I'll text you when I'm there."

"Okay." A full body shiver takes over my body since I'm only wearing pajamas.

"Get inside," he says, running his hands up and down my upper arms. "I love you."

"I love you, too."

I lean in and give him a kiss. He pulls away quickly, but I know nobody's awake, so I bring him in for another, then playfully kiss him all over his face.

His laugh is magical as he pushes me away. "Stop."
"Never."

He rolls his eyes, but the smile on his lips is permanent. He walks away and gives me a little wave from his car on the street.

I watch until he's gone, and then headlights flash me. My heart hammers in my chest at the knowledge that someone saw, but when I take in the vehicle, my stomach clenches so tight I'm afraid I might throw up right on the porch.

It's my dad.

CHAPTER TWENTY-NINE

ADRIAN

He doesn't get out, forcing me to make the slow and dreadful walk to his SUV, all the while my stomach twists and turns until it's in knots. My heart races in my chest, nearing an explosion.

His window is already down, and his jaw is clenched, nostrils flaring with barely controlled rage.

"What the fuck do you think you're doing, huh?" he seethes. "Out in the open. Where anyone can see."

"Dad, I—"

"No. I warned you. I told you what would happen, and now I find out you skip spending Christmas with your family so you can be out here doing God knows what. You disgust me."

My heart cracks in my chest. "I—"

He doesn't let me finish. "What's his name? Who is he?"

"No," I say, shaking my head, suddenly afraid. "Nobody."

"He's nobody? And yet you risk your future to be with him?" He huffs. "It's fine. I got his license plate number down."

I stand there, my feet frozen to the ground beneath me. My body trembles, fear flowing through my veins.

"It's just college," I say, lying through my teeth. "Isn't it the time to make bad decisions?"

"There are bad decisions and there's life decisions. You've been thinking this way for a while now, and I'm starting to wonder just how doomed you are."

"I'm not doomed. I've been with women. I can be with women again. It's nothing. He...he means nothing to me," I say, feeling the quiver in my voice as the lie spills out.

Dad scoffs, reaching for the gear shift. "I'll be back in a couple hours. Be dressed and ready to leave."

He drives away, leaving me standing there like a statue, wondering what the hell to expect. When I finally move, it's like a zombie, unaware of anything around me until I get to my room. I hardly feel the cold that's seeped into my bones. My father knows now. Unequivocally. I can still try to lie and downplay the truth, but is that what I want?

Maybe now's the perfect time to be honest and tell him everything. He'll be mad, but wouldn't he get over it? He can't actually mean to disown me. Who would do that to their own flesh and blood?

I text Matías, thinking maybe I can tell him. I only say *hi*, but he never replies. He's driving, and he never texts and drives. His phone is probably on silent.

Before I know it, two hours goes by, and I'm standing outside like a trained dog, waiting for my Dad to show up.

I climb into the passenger seat and sit in the sweltering silence. In my head, I go over potential conversations I could have with my dad. The honest one, where I tell him the truth and force him to look me in the eye and tell me I'm not his son anymore, hoping he'd never actually do that. And, I go over the lies I can spew to make the situation better for myself. I come up with things I know he'd say and try to come up with an argument or a defense.

Dad remains stoic, forcing me to continue to live in my head with made up scenarios.

We come to a stop in the parking lot of an office building. With a sigh, he finally speaks.

"Matías Cruz."

My lungs shrink, squeezing all the air from them. "Wh-what?"

"Business and project management major. Attends South River on an academic scholarship. Seems smart, but doesn't come from much."

"Why are you saying all of this?" I ask.

"I know all the important people at South River University. The Dean. The chair of Business Management. You get the idea. I can find out almost anything. On top of that, I created a company that makes a lot of money. It employs thousands. And we're expanding. There are plenty of people willing to listen to me. People who want to make me happy for the chance at a job, or for support in one of their ventures, or for some sort of financial aid. Plain and simple, money rules the world, and I have a lot of it. You benefited from my money, from my connections.

"You graduate in five months. You're set to start working for me after that. You'll go from being dependent on my finances to making your own under my company. I will set you up in an apartment nearby, and it'll be paid for a year until you take over the rent. By then, it shouldn't be a problem. You'll have a steady paycheck. You can keep the car I bought for you, until you can buy another one. You will be able to earn promotion after promotion until you prove you can take my spot as CEO. Then you're set for life."

He sighs. "Or, if you'd rather galivant with that boy and

pretend like anything can come of it, then I take the car, money, and job opportunity from you. He doesn't come from money. He has no connections. He can't get you a job or take care of you, because he'll be struggling to take care of himself. I can make it harder by talking to the companies I know he's applying to. A whispered word from me about his lack of motivation could put an end to his chances at that place of business."

"He doesn't la—" I start, immediately trying to defend him.

My father lifts a brow. "Two struggling kids out of college. Doesn't seem like it'll work. You'll fight. You'll get frustrated with each other. And you won't have a family waiting to help you. It's up to you."

He says the last part like it's actually a fair decision. Like I have a choice at all. Not only has he threatened to make sure I don't have anything, he said just enough to let me know he can ruin Matías's chances at a future too.

I grind my teeth, wanting nothing more than to fight against this, but I can't allow my dad to be responsible for Matías not getting a job he wants. I swallow down my pride, along with my hopes and dreams, and push out a bitter and ugly lie.

"I told you. He means nothing to me. It was just an experiment. Of course I want a future at the company."

Adrian

MATÍAS

My eyes are wide with shock. I've always been aware there are parents who don't accept their kids if they're gay. As wrong as that is, it was never a secret. I've known too many gay people who had that same issue. Disowning your queer kid isn't new either. Unfortunately, it's happened too many times to be a rarity. Threatening the future of a kid you don't know simply because your own child is interested in him is crazy.

I find my way to the couch as I attempt to find words. Adrian follows suit, sitting across from me.

"He has a lot of money and can pull a lot of strings. Not only did he start and grow his own financial advisory company, but he also has a startup funding firm. Unfortunately, when you're rich, you can own and manipulate almost anyone. He had my future wrapped up, but I wasn't going to allow him to ruin yours."

"I wish you would've told me."

"It's embarrassing to admit how awful your parents are. I told you plenty back then, but to tell you the details—the things he's said..." He shakes his head, leaving off the details once again.

"Is your marriage—"

"Another string he pulled?" He sighs. "Yeah."

"Why?" I ask, baffled and confused.

"His business partner. My wife is his daughter. She got into some trouble a few years back. She struggled to stay sober and would disappear for days. Her dad was trying his best to keep her on track and not have any stories make the news. They were in the process of a big business deal, and she was off getting arrested every other month. One day, after being gone for a while, she showed up to her dad's house with a positive pregnancy test and a promise to get better.

"My dad encouraged me to spend time with her, at first as a friend, to spy for her dad. They wanted to know her real thoughts on getting sober. Then he encouraged us to hang out more. When they found out that the baby's father was a drug addict with a rap sheet a mile long, the panic seeped in. They didn't want him to get his claws into their money. I was pushed to do the 'right thing' and say the baby was mine. Charlotte fought like hell. She was against her father almost as much as I was against mine. She didn't want to be with me like I didn't want to be with her. She ran off but came back a few days later, sick as hell.

"By that time, I liked her. We got along okay, and our friendship was starting to feel real, but that was it. I took care of her when she came back, listened to her cry and rant about her father. I did the same thing. She knew the biological father was never going to be a presence in her life. She knew she needed to get better, but she was dead set on defying her father. We secluded ourselves from our parents for the next month, mainly because we could hardly stand to be around them, and in that time I told myself I could probably do it. I could be with her. I could help her. She told me often that she didn't know what she'd do without me. I was the most stable friend she had, and she was terrified of having a baby alone. And it wasn't that she was afraid people would learn she was a single mom because the father was a drug addict in jail. That was her father's concern. He held all the power and she knew if she ran off again to try to do this alone, she'd fail. She'd fail the baby. She didn't have money, and she was an addict barely on the tip of recovery. She needed her father's money. She needed to go to rehab. And she needed someone she could rely on."

I shake my head, completely shocked. "Adrian."

"We eloped, because we didn't want our families to be involved at all. We thought if we had to do what they wanted, we'd at least do it our way. We weren't in love. We hadn't even kissed. It was just a job to do. But after we were married, of course, we started to make our relationship real. Two months later, she lost the baby. She blamed herself and went into a depression and started drinking. I tried everything I could to keep her safe, to keep her from slipping farther into her addiction." He shakes his head. "Anyway, it took a while, but eventually she agreed to go to rehab. When she came out, she was different. I swear there was some sort of brainwashing going on, because she's on her dad's side about everything. She's ready to obey his every wish, and quick to argue with me if I'm not on board with what our parents want us to do.

"I decided I wanted to move. I didn't want to be around my father anymore. I didn't want to work with him. I wanted a clean slate. She didn't want to leave initially. I told her she could stay there. It's not like we had an amazing relationship. It's forced and strained on the best days. My father and I started arguing, and she'd take his side. When I actually quit my job and told her I found a house, she sighed and said she'd come."

I sit back with a sigh. "This is...a lot. I don't even know where to start."

He huffs out a humorless laugh. "Yeah, that's my life."

While I still have questions, it doesn't seem to be the time to ask them. He's just revealed a whole lot to me, and at least now I know what prompted him to cut our relationship off. It doesn't make the hurt go away, but it helps. It also makes me sad to know how he's lived all this time with a father like that, and having no control over almost anything.

"Tell me what you want," I say. "Don't think about your marriage, your father, any future outcomes or fallouts. In this moment, right now, what do *you* want?"

He stares at me for several seconds, and I can tell he's thinking about everything I told him not to think about.

"Adrian," I say in a stern voice. "Don't think about anything else but what would make you happy. What do you want that would make *you* happy? Not anybody else."

"To be with you," he says swiftly. He begins second-guessing himself, his cheeks turning pink as he ducks his chin to avoid eye contact.

My heart begins to gallop, and I stand up and make my way over to him. Sitting on his left, our bodies touching, I say, "You're with me. What else?"

His eyes study every inch of my face. "I want to kiss you."

I wet my lips. "So, kiss me."

"But—"

"No. Do something for you. For once. I won't tell anyone."

I hardly get the last word out before his hand is cupping my cheek and his lips are on mine.

It steals my breath. I'm frozen in place but my mind has

fluttered away, and my heart seems to be on a mission to get out of my chest.

His fingers press on the back of my head, bringing me closer as his tongue swipes against my lips, forcing them apart so he can gain access to my mouth.

Together, our tongues twirl and glide over one another, and my body unfreezes. I grab a hold of both sides of his face, my breaths coming in frantic and heavy. Eight years. It's been eight years since I've tasted him. Since I've felt the softness of his lips.

Everything inside me warms, but as his tongue continues to explore my mouth, and our bodies get closer, the warmth in my veins begins to boil. I want to push him down on the couch and strip him naked. I want his cock in my mouth. I want to bury myself inside him. I want so much, but he deserves to have a choice. He should make the decision.

I pull away slightly, my hands falling to his shirt, where I grip the material and try to catch my breath as my forehead rests against his.

"Fuck," he murmurs. "I've been dying to do that since I saw you in your office."

I smirk, easing back. "Hope it lived up to the desire."

"Definitely."

I stand up and reach into my pants to adjust my very obvious erection, fixing my clothes after the fact. Adrian's eyes watch everything, and then they're finally on my face.

"I guess we have to go back downstairs, huh?"

"Probably," I say. "Or we could sign our names on the registration paper and then sneak away."

He grins. "Such a rule breaker now."

"We didn't get to eat."

"I'm not thinking about eating."

"What are you thinking about?" I ask with a mischievous smile.

"Only what I want."

His eyes slide down my body.

CHAPTER THIRTY-ONE

MATÍAS

Downstairs, we sign our names on the registration form, walk inside and chat for a few minutes with some people, then slip out the side before it gets started. Like children, we laugh as we make our way through the hall, rounding the corner to a set of escalators, then find ourselves on the main floor.

We're surrounded by lots of chatter and the sound of slot machines. I wonder if maybe the moment we had earlier was ruined by having to leave the room. Has he had time to rethink everything? Does he have any sort of regret? Maybe the kiss was enough. Something we've both been thinking about and wanting to do, and now it's done.

"So, do you want to eat or?" I ask, leaving the last half of the sentence dangling between us. I'm giving him an out and holding my breath in the process.

He looks me over before glancing around. When he meets my gaze again, he says, "I think we should go upstairs."

I nod, and we hurry to the elevators.

We aren't lucky enough to get into one alone, joined by a

family of four. We squish into the back where our hands brush against each other.

I let my finger rub against the side of his thigh and watch as he pulls in a deep breath. We only go up a few floors before the family gets off, leaving us alone.

He turns slightly, looking at me as the elevator begins to move. His hand goes to my stomach where two fingers slip between two of the buttons on my shirt.

"I—"

The elevator dings, letting us know we're coming to a stop. He pulls away and faces forward as a couple walk in. They're hand-in-hand, giggling about something.

"Hey, how are ya?" the guy asks with a small nod and a smile.

I smile back. "Good. How about you?"

He looks at the girl. "Can't complain."

"We're on our honeymoon," she says, looking up at her husband with a twinkle in her eyes.

"Congratulations," Adrian says.

"Thanks," they say at the same time.

They get off a few floors later, and just as I'm thinking the mood might've been ruined again, thanks to the reminder of a married couple that might have Adrian in his head about his own marriage, he reaches over and slips his hand in mine.

Our fingers interlock, and we both stare down at the connection.

I realize now that he's never had this. Public displays of affection with someone he's attracted to. In college, we never held hands or kissed or hugged. Not when other people were around. Not in restaurants or movie theaters. He's never had what that couple has—the ability to show love and affection toward someone without a worry in the world. In plain sight.

I bring his hand up to my mouth where I plant a kiss on the back of his palm.

The doors open up on our floor, and our hands fall apart as we walk down the hall. I slide the key card into the slit and wait for the light to turn green. When I push open the door, I walk inside, but don't get three steps in before I feel Adrian's hand clasping around my wrist.

I turn and face him, and we only look at each other for a second before we clash together. We wrap our arms around one another, lips seeking lips. His tongue darts into my mouth, and I suck on it, eliciting a moan from his throat.

His hands run up my back while mine travel lower, touching his ass before I haul him into me.

This kiss isn't like the other one. It's not soft or sweet. It's passionate but in a different way. We're like two volcanoes on the cusp of eruption. Our bodies vibrate, pleasure rumbling in our throats. We're volatile—charged with explosive desire that's been building for years. Everything we've ever wanted is right at the surface.

His teeth cut into my lip, and I yank his hair back, exposing his throat. I kiss and lick a path to his ear and his fingers press hard into my back.

I unbutton his shirt while he tries to undo mine, but once I'm finished with his, I yank on the two sides of the dress shirt, making the rest of the buttons pop off and skitter across the floor.

We frantically undress, kicking off shoes and throwing clothes until we're down to our underwear.

"Come," I say, taking his hand and rushing to my bedroom.

We come to a stop at the side of the mattress and I take in his mostly naked form. "Your body is still so incredible," I say, tracing a finger down the center of his abs.

"Yours has changed a bit," he says with a smirk, his hand curving around my hip.

"I've worked out some."

His smile grows. "Yes, I can see that."

He comes closer, kissing across my collarbone and down my chest. I put my head back as I thread my fingers in his hair.

Suddenly, he lifts me off the ground, like he used to in college. I was smaller then, but it doesn't seem to matter now. Without much effort, he has me in his arms before laying me down on the bed.

Adrian is above me, legs on either side of my body as he kisses and touches every piece of exposed flesh.

He's quiet in his reverence, finally doing something I'm sure he's thought about millions of times. Not just with me, either, but probably any man. It doesn't even bother me to know he's had to have thoughts and fantasies of other men. He's been suppressing himself for so long, unable to do what he knows would bring him pleasure.

This is different for me. I've gotten used to being the aggressor, the doer, the one in charge and in control. It's what I've wanted. I've kept my emotional distance from people, and part of that is to not allow moments like this. I don't lay back and let people kiss and do what they want to me. I don't cuddle and hold hands. I don't do the things that open the door for emotions and feelings.

But Adrian isn't just anybody. He's Adrian. My first love. My first heartbreak. Mine.

The doors have never been closed. Just cracked.

CHAPTER THIRTY-TWO

ADRIAN

I TAKE MY TIME, enjoying being able to touch his body again. I place my hand over the trail of hair on his stomach as I kiss around his hip. My lips stop above the waistband of his boxer-briefs, knowing that's where I want to go and explore, but a small amount of apprehension has me hesitating.

I want to do it, even though I shouldn't.

To anyone else, what I'm doing now, what I'm about to do, what I've been wanting to do, is wrong. Plain and simple. There are no excuses, reasons, or justifications good enough for the line I'm crossing.

But being with Matías? That's not wrong. It can't be. It never was. Not when my dad tried to convince me that that was the case, and not now even though I'm married. He has a part of me still, and probably always will.

My fingers slip into the waistband as I glance up at him. He's watching me like he's waiting for me to bolt—to put a stop and walk away.

I tug them down, and he lifts up so I can free them from his hips.

His cock slaps against his stomach, thick and hard. I lick

my lips, ready and yet still nervous. I realize he's been awfully quiet, which wasn't the norm for him.

Before I touch him again, I ask, "Are you okay?"

His chin dips slightly as he looks down at me. "Yes."

"You're quiet. I thought you liked to tell people what to do. You know, use collars and leashes and whatnot."

His lips twitch before he's biting down on a smile. "Been thinking about that, huh?"

My cheeks feel warm. "Not really."

He laughs. "I'm letting you make the decisions," he says. "What we do is whatever *you* want to do. I don't want you to feel like I'm forcing you into anything." He pauses. "And I'm waiting for you to change your mind."

I drop lower, settling into my place between his legs. "I'm not going to." And then I take his cock in my hand and lift it from his body before I open my mouth and close my lips around him.

"Oh. fuck," he groans, hands fisting the covers.

I moan as I slide him in deeper, getting his shaft wet so I can stroke. I curl my fingers around him, tugging on him with a firm grip at a leisurely pace.

"Oh, yeah," he moans, eyes closing briefly.

I twirl my tongue around the tip before once again taking him further into my mouth. After a few minutes of getting back into the swing of things, I bob up and down on his shaft, slurping and moaning like a porn star.

My dick grows impossibly harder inside my boxers, dying to be touched.

"Adrian," Matías moans, sending a jolt of excitement up my spine. "Fuck. It's so good."

His fingers run through my hair, tugging on the strands while also pushing my head down. I can tell he's trying to control himself, but he fucks my face from his position, his hips moving up and down.

I nearly gag when he goes too deep, making a choking sound, so he stops moving. But I don't want that. I want all of him. I want this new side of him. I want to experience things the way he does them now.

I grab his hand and put it back on my head, moaning around his dick as I take him deeper. He gets the hint and continues moving his hips.

"That's it," he says in a sinful voice. "Take it." He inhales. "Yeah, just like that."

Everything inside me melts. His voice elevates the entire experience, and I never want him to be quiet again.

I pull away. "You like it?" I ask. I know he does, but I need to hear his words.

"I love it." His fingers gently run through my hair. "Now try to take me deep again. Slowly. Breathe through your nose."

I listen, only so happy to do so. He encourages and praises me the entire time.

"Oh, yeah. That's good. Oh, god. You can do it. Ahh."

Pinpricks of heat cover my body. I'm no longer satisfied with just this. I want more. Everything inside of me is begging and pleading for more of him.

"I'm so fucking hard," I say, reaching into my boxers to give my cock some attention.

"Let me see."

I move to the side and shove my boxers down my thighs before stroking my dick again. He opens his mouth then closes it.

"What do you want me to do?"

I know that's not what he was going to say initially, but I get why he's allowing me to make the decisions. It's just not necessary. Decision has been made. Right or wrong, there's no going back, and there's definitely no stopping.

If I'm condemning myself; I might as well have the best fucking time doing it.

"Whatever you want," I answer.

He hesitates for only a second before getting up. "Lie down."

I listen, kicking off my boxers the rest of the way before reaching for my erection.

"No," he says, getting between my parted legs. "Let me."

His hand takes over, his palm warm against my skin. I suck in a shuddering breath as he tightens his grip and moves it slowly up and down.

"You're right. You're so fucking hard." A quick pause, his eyes flickering up to meet my gaze. "For me."

I moan. "Yes."

"Can I taste you?" he asks, his voice low and sultry. "Is that what you want?"

"Fuck." I suck in a breath as he continues to stroke me gently. "Yes. Yes, I want it."

There's a low growl in his throat before he lowers himself, and I watch with bated breath as his lips part, his pink tongue dancing across his bottom lip before he takes me inside his mouth.

My cock slides across his tongue, reaching for the back of his throat before he eases back up. His mouth is magical, and as he coats me with his saliva, his free hand comes up to massage my balls.

"*Lordhavemercy*," I mutter, the words strung together as I push my palms into my eyes. "Holy shit."

Matías moans, continuing his actions before pulling away. My cock slips free from his mouth, but his hand keeps stroking. I watch as he drops onto his stomach and then I feel his tongue twirl around my balls before sucking one into his mouth.

"Holy fuck," I say with a gasp. "Oh, god. Oh, god. Yes. Yes."

He moves to the other one, his hand still keeping up pace on my cock. My brain doesn't know how to work properly anymore. I utter words that don't form proper sentences. I reach for his head, then I grab the covers before changing my mind and tugging on my own hair.

"Matías," I moan, my voice breathy and desperate. "Oh, my god."

His tongue dips slightly lower, teasing the idea of licking another spot on my body that's gone ignored for years.

"Jesus fuck," I cry.

He does it once more before coming back up and taking my dick in his mouth.

His fingers continue to play with my balls, sometimes sliding between my cheeks. He doesn't push, but just gently glides over the hole. Meanwhile, his mouth works me over. I'm near combustion, but there's no way we can stop now. I feel like I haven't done enough. I haven't had my fill of him yet.

"Matías," I breathe. "I'm close. I can't—"

"You ready to come for me?" he asks.

I shake my head.

"No?" he questions.

"I don't want to be done." I look at his face. "I don't want it to end."

Understanding blankets his expressions. "I want you to come," he says. "It doesn't mean it's the end."

I bite into my bottom lip and nod once. "Okay."

"Come in my mouth, Adrian," he says before enveloping me between his lips.

It only takes a couple more minutes before I feel it coming. "Oh, god."

Matías moans, sucking and stroking simultaneously.

"Oh, oh. Yes. I'm...I'm..." I release a roar that the entire floor can probably hear right before my body tenses up and my orgasm explodes out of me and into his mouth.

As I grunt and suck in deep gulps of air, Matías lets out sounds of pleasure as he tastes and swallows every drop.

He continues to lick around my head, taking me gently into his mouth as my body jerks with aftershocks.

After he pulls away, I feel him move up and lay next to me. My eyes are still closed, but I reach out with my hand until I find his, holding two of his fingers in my fist.

"Oh, my god," I breathe.

"Yeah," he says with his own exhale.

I roll to my side and face him, finding him already looking at me.

"You're so handsome," I tell him, the words flying out on their own accord.

He chuckles, a small amount of color filling his cheeks. "Thank you."

I let out a quiet laugh, slightly embarrassed. "You've always been attractive. Obviously."

"Obviously," he teases.

"You've just grown up so much and you...you look very distinguished."

His lips curl up on the ends. "No longer the skinny, nerdy kid?"

"Probably still nerdy," I joke.

He reaches out and runs his knuckles along my jaw. And then, as if he realized he shouldn't, he pulls his hand back and turns to get up.

"I'm gonna use the bathroom," he says, his naked body on full display.

"Oh. What about—"

I don't get the rest of the thought out before he speaks.

"This was about you," he says, glancing over his shoulder with a small smile.

"Okay," I reply after a few seconds, hoping I get to repay him soon.

I get up to find my underwear once he closes the door.

I think about waiting around for him to get out, but doing that seems awkward. And then, as if sensing my sinful behavior, my phone rings from my pants in the main part of the suite, and I find it's my dad calling me.

CHAPTER THIRTY-THREE

ADRIAN

AFTER IGNORING THE CALL, I go to my room to use the bathroom and get cleaned up. My stomach rumbles with hunger, reminding me I haven't eaten anything today. I throw on a pair of black basketball shorts and a white T-shirt with a black Nike swoosh, and head into the kitchen area.

Matías is at the window, seemingly zoned out, wearing a pair of navy blue chino shorts and a button-up shirt with a leaf print that matches his shorts.

"You look like you belong on a beach," I say.

He turns and looks at me. "You look like you belong on a basketball court."

I snort. "So, I'm starving."

"Me too." Something in his gaze tells me he's not only talking about food. "Wanna head out?"

"Sure. Got a place in mind?"

"We'll find something, but it can't be here. I'll probably run into someone I know who'll talk my ear off about work."

"True."

I run back to my room to grab my wallet and phone, and then we make our way to the elevator.

Something about the silence of the elevator makes the tension grow. I think about how Matías quickly got out of bed earlier and what that could mean. I think about what we did, and the weight of that decision. And I wonder if we're going to do it again.

"So, you okay?" I ask.

His dark eyes find mine, a small hint of a smile on his lips. "Yeah. You?"

I nod. "Yeah."

"Good."

The silence goes away when we stop on a floor where two teenage girls get on, talking non-stop about some boy. When we get to the main floor, we make our way to the street and turn right.

I follow Matías's lead as he removes the pair of sunglasses that were hanging on his shirt and puts them on his face.

We end up walking for twenty minutes before we get to the New York-New York Hotel & Casino. Inside, Matías leads me to Nathan's Famous.

"This good?" he asks.

"Yeah."

Once we order and get our food, we find a booth to sit at. The vibe is like a 1950s diner, with the black and white checkered floor, and the red and white tables and chairs.

While we eat, I feel Matías's leg against mine. We both look up at the same time, but neither of us moves away.

"How's your mom?" I ask him.

He smiles. "She's good. Remarried now. She and her husband moved about an hour closer to me."

"That's nice."

"Yeah, it is." He finishes chewing some fries. "How's your sister?"

"She's living in Indianapolis now. She's a corporate lawyer down there."

"Wow. You talk often?"

"As often as we can," I say.

We fall into a comfortable silence as we continue to eat, and when we're done, I find myself unable to keep from looking at him.

He catches me, his lips twitching. "What's up?"

"Nothing."

His smile grows and he folds his arms on the table and leans forward. "What are you thinking about?"

My teeth dig into my bottom lip briefly. "Just...you know, wondering what our plans are."

He inclines his head slightly. "Ah. Well, I thought you wanted to see Vegas? Be a tourist and all that."

I nod. "Yeah, yeah. I thought that was more of a tomorrow thing."

Matías grins. "I suppose it can be. It'll be our free day without any work." He rests his chin in his hand as he looks at me with amusement. "But what could we do for the rest of today then?"

I shrug, feigning nonchalance. "Don't know." My knee brushes against his under the table.

"Hmm," he murmurs, rubbing his hand over his jaw. He looks away, mulling something over in his head as he chews on his bottom lip. When he turns his attention back to me, he questions, "We're doing this?" When I don't reply right away, he continues. "Because I feel like I'm walking on eggshells, waiting for you to change your mind. But if you wanna do this, then I won't restrain myself from doing and saying the things I want to do. So, one more time, and then I won't ask again—is this what you want?"

I stare at him and absorb his question. It's understandable, and I get where he's coming from. I've already made the decision to cheat on my wife. It's done and can't be taken back. Sure, I could stop now, confess to my wife and say it was a one-time thing. A mistake never to be repeated, but when I look across the table, I know that's not true. It will never be a mistake, and it could never be a one-time thing.

I know this is the beginning of something bigger—a life decision that needs to be made. That will come later, but until then...

"Yes. This is what I want."

He visibly relaxes, and then says, "Let's go."

CHAPTER THIRTY-FOUR
MATÍAS

WHAT TOOK twenty minutes to get here feels like an hour on the way back. Almost the entire time, I'm thinking about what I want to do to Adrian. What this means going forward. We're neighbors. We work together. The amount of time we'll have with each other is more than I can ask for.

He's married.

But he doesn't belong with her.

His phone rings and he takes it from his pocket, sighs, and declines the call. I don't ask about it. It's not my business, and I truly don't want to know if it's his wife calling him.

When it goes off the second and third time, we're in our own hotel, traveling up the elevator.

"Did you need to get that?" I ask.

"No," he says simply, and I accept that.

When we get inside the suite, I say, "Leave the phone in your room and meet me in mine."

I take some time to freshen up in the bathroom—the Las Vegas sun is unforgiving, and it takes less than a minute to start sweating when you're outside. Regardless of what we're about to do, I'm going to be clean and prepared.

When I come out of the bathroom, I emerge with only a towel around my waist, and find Adrian in new clothes standing in front of my window.

He looks over his shoulder and sees me, eyes taking me in before he swallows. The fresh scent of soap radiates off of him, letting me know he had the same idea. At least we're still on the same page about something happening between us.

I wasn't lying when I said I wasn't going to ask him if he was sure anymore. From this moment on, I'm going forward with the assumption that he wants this as much as I do.

Strutting forward, I don't stop until I'm touching him, turning him around and trapping him between the window and my body.

My lips find the side of his neck, kissing and gently biting the soft flesh. "Why do you have clothes on?" I ask against his skin.

"Mm. I thought it might be weird to have you come out to me naked."

From behind, I push down the baby blue basketball shorts he has on until they're crumpled at his bare feet.

"It's only weird that you thought I wouldn't like that."

I lick a path up his neck until I get to his ear. He moans, a shiver taking over his body. "Noted," he says breathlessly.

From the hem, I lift the white tank top he has on, and he raises his arms to help me remove it.

"You like the view?" I question, kissing the back of his neck and across his shoulders as my hands run down his sides until they're inside the waistband of his boxers.

"Hm. Yeah," he says, distracted.

I shove the material down and he steps out of them, all the while, I kiss down the middle of his back.

"Good," I say. "Enjoy the view while I taste you."

I kiss lower and lower until I'm on my knees behind him, my lips pressing kisses on his cheeks.

"Oh, god," he says, voice shaking.

I squeeze each cheek in one hand before spreading him apart. He bends forward, hands slapping against the glass, and I let my tongue run up the seam.

He gasps. "Oh, fuck."

I moan as I continue, tasting him thoroughly. My tongue prods at his hole without trying to penetrate completely.

Adrian whimpers and mewls between words of praise and chants for more. When he reaches back and holds my head in place, I nearly explode. A growl of appreciation rumbles in my throat as I continue to devour him.

After a few more minutes, I stand, the towel dropping. I wipe my mouth with my hand and press my body against his, my arms wrapping around his middle. He leans his head against my shoulder, completely out of breath.

"Oh, my god, Matías," he pants.

"Turn around." He faces me, his skin flushed. "Now get on your knees."

Pure lust shines in his eyes, and without a word he obeys, staring at my cock. He peers up at me, his muscular body a work of art at my feet.

"I'm gonna fuck that pretty mouth of yours," I tell him.

He licks his lips, dipping his chin slightly.

I step forward, my erection in my hand as I aim it toward his lips. He parts them, opening wide for me to slide in over his tongue.

"Oh, yeah," I say with a groan.

With my forearm against the glass, I rock my hips,

pushing in and out of his wet mouth. His hands move from my thighs to my ass, touching me wherever he can while I attempt to reach the back of his throat.

I stand straight and run a hand through his hair, tugging on the strands hard enough that he looks up at me while my dick is still in his mouth.

"Oh, fuck. You look so good."

He swirls his tongue along the bottom of my shaft and I slowly push in a little further.

While I watch, I move leisurely in and out of his mouth, watching his saliva drip down his chin.

"So fucking good," I moan. "Come here."

I step back, reaching down for his hand to pull him to his feet. With his back to the window, I close the distance between us and kiss along his cheek while my hands find the curve of his hips.

"I want to fuck you," I tell him, giving him a kiss below his earlobe. "I want nothing more than to be inside you right now."

His breath hitches and he grinds against me. "Oh."

"I'll be so careful with you. You know that," I say, looking him in the eye.

"I know." He swallows. "Maybe you can start that way. And then..."

I bite down on my lip, grinning. "Then you don't want careful?"

His cheeks turn a darker shade of red. "I just mean I don't want you to treat me like I'm delicate. I want all of you."

I nod. "Get on the bed. I'll be back."

I go into the bathroom where I grab a small bottle of lube and a condom that are in my toiletry bag.

Back in the room, I find Adrian lying on the bed, one arm behind his head, his other hand on his cock.

I toss the items on the bed next to him, and his eyes watch them land.

"I know you said you haven't been with any other guy, but have you used any toys all these years?"

Adrian, sprawled naked and fully aware that I just had my tongue in his ass, has the nerve to blush like he can't talk to me about his masturbation techniques.

"Well...uhh..."

I move in between his legs, my knees touching the insides of his thighs. With my right hand, I reach for his cock and begin stroking.

"Tell me," I say in a husky tone.

"Yes," he replies, sucking in a deep breath. "I...I have things that I keep hidden. That I use from time to time when I'm alone."

That statement breaks my heart a little. What brings him pleasure has to be kept hidden, like a dark and dirty secret.

"Okay. Good. So this won't be a complete shock to your body."

He shakes his head slightly, watching my hand work him over. "Probably nothing as big as..." he nods toward my cock.

I grin. "You'll stretch for me."

His teeth dig into his lip. "God," he moans.

"Lie down," I say, moving to allow him more space while I grab the lube.

I cover my fingers with the liquid as he gets situated, and then I pour a little more in my hand to massage into his hole.

With one hand on his cock, giving him the distraction and friction he needs, I slowly start pushing one finger inside.

"Oh, yeah," he groans when I get it all the way in.

After a couple minutes of using just one finger, I slip a second one inside him, eliciting a sinful sound from his throat.

He grips the covers, his muscles flexing as I attempt to prepare him for my cock.

"Matías," he cries out in that sexy way of his—the yearning and ache evident in his tone.

"Does it feel good?" I ask, curling my fingers a little as I move them.

"Yes. So good."

"You ready for another?"

He sucks in a breath. "Yeah."

With more lube, I slide a third finger alongside the others, rotating my wrist and doing my best to loosen him up.

Doing this is the best sort of torture for me. I'm beyond turned on, ready to fuck him into oblivion, edging myself as I get him ready.

When Adrian begins rocking his hips, matching my thrusts with his own, I know he's ready.

I remove my fingers and reach for the condom, covering my length before pouring more lube on my shaft.

I hook one of his legs over my forearm and put the tip at his entrance. We stare at each other until I push in, breaching the ring of muscle. He closes his eyes, pushing his head deeper into the pillow as he lets out a hiss.

"You got it," I tell him. "You can take it."

Slowly, I keep moving forward, making sure to allow him time to adapt to the size of me as best as possible.

Halfway in, and his ass is strangling my cock. "My god," I say through a breath. "You're so fucking tight."

He grunts, muscles flexed and tense. With one hand, I touch his stomach, moving up to his chest.

"You're okay. Relax. Breathe."

Adrian inhales deeply through his nose, and I slip the rest of the way in.

"Oh, fuck."

"Fuck," I say, joining the rest of his exclamation.

I pull back a little, push forward, and repeat, taking longer strokes each time.

"You feel so good," I say softly.

He simply whimpers.

"Are you okay?" I ask, stopping my movements.

Adrian nods, meeting my gaze. "I'm okay. More than okay. Please keep going."

"Mm," I say with a grin. "I like hearing you beg."

"Please," he says again, voice like sin. "Please fuck me."

"Oh, god," I groan, completely done for.

I drop his leg and lay my body over his, my face buried in his neck as I fuck him. His grunts and moans are in my ear—the music to my workout, keeping me motivated to keep going.

"Your dick feels so good," he says in a soft tone.

The compliment rolls over my shoulders and down my back, giving me goosebumps.

"You like having me inside you?" I ask.

He moans. "Yes. You're so fucking hard."

"For you."

"God, Matías."

"I love when you say my name like that."

I pull away, getting on my knees as I spread him wider, watching my cock disappear into his ass.

"Stroke yourself for me," I tell him. "I wanna watch you."

His fingers wrap around his shaft, and he begins moving his fist up and down, his eyes on my body the entire time.

I thrust deeper, not moving too fast, but making sure he feels every inch of me.

"Yes, yes," he chants, eyes closing.

My orgasm builds, teasing its appearance. His cock is so

engorged, the tip a dark pink. His hand moves quicker, seeking the release.

"Yeah," I breathe. "Your ass is so fucking perfect. Keep stroking. Make yourself come."

He whimpers, sweat glistening along his hairline. "Matías."

"Yes. Come for me. Let me see the mess you make."

"Oh, god."

My hips piston back and forth, my release inching closer and closer.

"I'm gonna come," he says. "Oh, god. I'm come—"

His words cut off when his orgasm hits and jets of white cum shoot out of him, pouring over his hand.

"Oh, fuck yes," I groan, the visual bringing my orgasm forward. "Yes, yes. Ah. Fuck."

I slam deep, the first spurt of cum filling the condom, then I pull out and rip it off, jerking myself so I can finish coming on him. Our releases mixing together on his skin.

"Oh, yes. Yes," he cries, watching it happen. "Give it to me."

When I'm done, I collapse next to him, trying to catch my breath as he does the same.

For the next couple minutes, we're nothing but heavy breaths and curse words. When I think I can finally move again, I roll out of bed and head to the bathroom. After I pee and wipe myself off, I bring another wet rag to the room, taking the time to wipe the mess off his hand first, then his stomach and his cock.

He gives me a lazy smile. "That was...incredible."

"I thought so, too."

I toss the washcloth and lay next to him. He attempts to turn to his side, makes a face, then slowly continues.

"Ouch."

I snort. "Sorry."

"I'm not."

This time I allow myself to run my hand over his cheek. "I'm glad." Leaning forward, I plant a kiss on his lips.

"I'm gonna use the bathroom, then I'll be back."

I nod. "Okay. I'll try not to fall asleep."

He chuckles before getting out of the bed. Next thing I know, the bed dips next to me, and his arm wraps around my body.

My spine stiffens, not used to the post-coital cuddling. Cuddling in general, really. But then I open my eyes and see him snuggling in close, and I drape my arm over his as he rests his head on my shoulder.

I smile, and then I fall asleep.

CHAPTER THIRTY-FIVE

ADRIAN

WHEN I WAKE UP, it's to an empty bed and the sun shining in my face. I squint as I look around the room, but when I don't see any sign of Matías, I throw the covers off of me and get out of bed.

When I walk into the living room, I spot him pacing back and forth in front of the main door with the phone against his ear. He turns and sees me, giving me a quick grin before speaking again.

"No, that's not right. The project is due November 15th."

I keep making my way to my bathroom where I brush my teeth and think about the events of last night.

Everything that happened was incredible. My heart feels full for the first time in a while. It was almost like I had been cut off from any sort of familiarity, and then finally came home.

I rinse out my mouth before taking a piss, then I turn the hot water on in the shower and head to my room. It's our last day here, so I find something casual to put on, and then check my discarded phone.

It's almost dead since I never plugged it in last night, but it has several missed calls and text messages. Mostly from my dad and Charlotte.

Charlotte's are just check-ins and wanting to know when my flight gets in. My father's are demands to call him back.

I click on the thread of messages between Charlotte and I, my heart feeling heavy in my chest.

> Hey, I'm fine. Late night last night. It's my final day here, and I'll be on a plane tomorrow at eleven-fifteen. That should put me home around four when you add in the drive.

I drop the phone back on the bed and make my way into the shower. As the water rains over me, I try to come up with a plan.

Charlotte and I aren't meant to be together. I think she knows that, too, but now she's relying on me. I think we both have the underlying fear that without me, she'll slip into her old ways. We've had good times together. We've laughed and enjoyed nights out, but it's always felt like it was just a friendship. And don't get me wrong, friendship is important in a relationship, but I've never been romantically attracted to her. I've done my best to fake it. To force the affection that doesn't do anything for me. The kisses and touches that make me cringe.

It's all a constant reminder of who I truly am, and it makes me live in this constant state of discomfort.

I don't know if she's ever noticed, but if she has, she's never questioned it. I almost wish she would, that way maybe it would force me to be honest.

"Want some company?" Matías's voice asks from the other side of the steam-covered shower door.

Everything in my head melts away when I see the blurry version of his naked body on the other side.

"Yes."

The door opens, and Matías walks in, a perfectly sculptured god with wavy brown hair.

"Morning," he says with a crooked grin, walking me backward into the wall where we're out of the spray of the water.

I smile. "Morning."

His hands land on my hips before his mouth is on mine. As his tongue slides over mine, his hands curve around my cheeks, cupping and squeezing the flesh.

"How's this?" he asks, a finger dancing delicately through the crease.

I suck in a breath. "Fine."

"Good."

He kisses along my jaw until he gets to my neck. My cock hardens against his leg, desperate for his attention.

Matías reaches between us, his fingers wrapping around my length, giving me a slow stroke.

I release a moan and thrust into his hand.

"You want me?" he asks.

"Yes," I breathe.

"How badly do you want me?" he questions, mouth against my ear.

I thrust again. "I want you so much."

He growls, nipping at my ear. "I want to devour you."

A whimpery moan leaves my lips. "Yes."

"You like that idea?"

His fingers dance across my shaft, reaching my balls.

I nod frantically.

"Tell me."

"I want—" I swallow. "I want you to devour me."

Matías steps back and gives me a wicked grin. "Stand over there," he says, stepping under the spray to allow me to get to the back.

When I get into place, he comes forward, pushing his wet hair back and dropping to his knees.

With my cock pointing at his mouth, he leans forward and licks the underside of my shaft before briefly sucking on the tip.

"Turn around." I listen, and face the wall. "Now bend over."

I grab a hold of the bar along the left side and bend, spreading my legs as much as possible.

His hands run up the backs of my thighs, pushing my ass cheeks up before squeezing and spreading them.

When his tongue runs up my crease, I squeeze the bar and suck in a breath before releasing a moan.

"Oh, god."

His tongue swipes up and down, large hands squeezing my cheeks as he licks me. The tip of his tongue begins prodding at my sensitive hole, but it feels so good.

"Yes," I pant. "Please. Oh, god."

He takes my words as permission to do more, so he does. His tongue pushes into my hole, his fingers gripping me tightly.

"Matías," I breathe. "So good."

He turns into an animal, his tongue devouring every part of me. It dips low, licking my balls, before he sucks each one into his mouth, one at a time. Then he's back in my crease, tonguing me down until I'm seeing spots.

With his hands on my waist, he spins me around, and

once again, I grip the bar. He takes my cock into his hand, pulling me into his mouth.

I watch as water hits his back, cascading over every dip and curve of his muscles, dripping down his ass.

I think about what it would be like to be inside him again. To feel how tight he would be around me.

He takes me deep into his mouth, continuing his mission of devouring me. His fingers find my balls, massaging and gently squeezing them before one finger slips between my cheeks.

"Oh," I moan, the word coming out shuddery.

Matías gently pushes one fingertip inside me, but it's enough. I've already been edged with his tongue. My orgasm was already teetering, and now, with just the hint of penetration while his mouth works wonders on my cock, my release explodes out of me.

"Oh, god. Matías."

He moans and jerks my cock into his mouth, taking every drop of my cum.

His swallow is audible, punctuated by a small groan. I watch as his tongue dances around the head, lapping up any last drops.

My body shivers, weak and hardly willing to hold me up.

Matías grabs the bar and pulls himself up, leaning forward to kiss me with my taste still on his tongue.

When he pulls away, he grins. "Get clean. I'll see you out there."

"What about you?" I manage to say through my heavy breaths.

"I showered earlier. I just need to dry off now."

"I mean…" I look down at his cock.

"We can do something about that later."

He opens the shower door and closes it behind him, and I

muster up enough energy to cleanse my body before I walk out and flop to my bed.

My phone vibrates next to me, and out of habit, I pick it up to read the screen.

Charlotte

> Okay. Let me know if you need a ride.

Another message from earlier is right below it.

Dad

> You didn't tell me you were leaving to work for Matías Cruz. Call me back now and explain to me what you think you're doing.

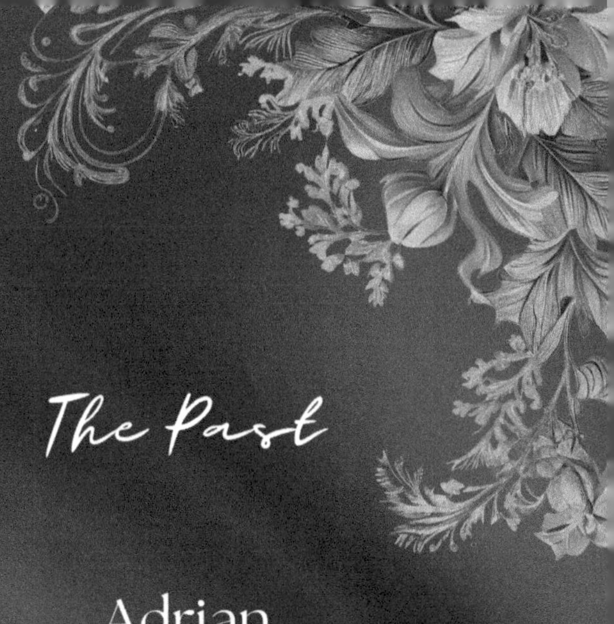

The Past

Adrian

CHAPTER THIRTY-SIX

ADRIAN

I HAVE to see him one last time. I should tell him what happened. Tell him my father saw us and has threatened to ruin everything. But it's embarrassing to be twenty-two years old and tell the person you love that you can't be with them because your dad said so.

Matías is stubborn. He'll fight this. He'll fight this like I want to, but he doesn't know my dad. He doesn't understand what he's capable of, and he won't have to deal with him ever again. I have years to endure my father.

I'm not sure how I could possibly end this, because nothing will feel right. I have no reason to break up with him. We're both so happy. We don't fight. We have no issues. So how do I make him believe there is one?

I wait two days after my father caught us before I see him. I told him I was sick, but I needed to make sure my dad was back home and not lingering in the shadows.

We only have a couple more days of Christmas break left, so that's the deadline I give myself.

I pull up to Matías's dorm, take a deep breath, and try to keep from looking as miserable as I feel.

He opens the door with a wide smile. "Got rid of all your germs?" he asks.

I snort. "I think so."

He yanks me inside. "At this point, I don't care. We can share them." Then he wraps his arms around me and kisses me like it's been years since he saw me last.

We quickly fall into the bed, strip out of our clothes, and have sex for what will likely be the last time.

Matías tries to get on top of me, but I keep him on his back, wanting to take my time, looking into his eyes as I slide in and out of him. At one point, I bury my face in his neck just to discreetly wipe a tear threatening to fall from my eye.

"I want you to be inside me," I tell him quietly in his ear.

"Okay," he says after a brief hesitation.

I've only bottomed a couple times, but if this is the last time, I want to experience it all. So after a few minutes, we change positions and I feel him inside of me one final time.

He stares down at me as thrusts, his orgasm inching closer. My hand moves up and down my shaft, and I try not to think about the sadness of this moment. I focus on the pleasure. On how it feels to have him inside me. To have this moment where our bodies come together to act on the love we feel for each other.

But when I come, my orgasm roaring out of me, it's tinged with a cry of sadness.

Luckily, he doesn't seem to notice, too caught up in his own release.

Afterward, we lie together, cuddled up under his blanket, watching some movie he put on. I'm hardly paying attention, focused more on tracing the veins in his arms, or memorizing every curve of his face. I play with his hair and commit to memory how soft and wavy it is.

"What are you doing tomorrow?" he asks. "Wanna have dinner?"

I open my mouth to immediately say yes, but stop myself. "I'm not sure. The guys have been real suspicious lately."

"Still?" he asks. "I thought you gave them a fake story about some girl."

"Yeah, well, they don't believe me because she's never come around. And I'm always with you. So I worry they might start to think..." I trail off, hating myself for saying the words.

He stiffens. "I see."

"I should probably be around the house more often. Maybe they need to see me talk to some girls or something."

My stomach coils and I want to squash any worries he might have, but I can't.

He spins around to face me, determination in his eyes. "You know I love you, right?"

My heart cracks. "Yes."

"I'm okay with waiting for you. Waiting until you're comfortable. Until you think you'll be ready to come out. This secretive stuff is fine with me. I love our quiet moments here. I love our sneaky moments at your place. I'm willing to wait." He pauses. "As long as I know there will be a time that the secrecy comes to an end."

My fractured heart now shatters. I don't deserve him. He's been amazing during our entire relationship. He's so understanding, and still willing to wait for me. How can I possibly tell him that the time he's waiting for will likely never come?

I get up, struggling to get out from under the covers. I kick them down and finally plant my feet on the floor.

"I-I don't know what to tell you. I can't promise something I can't see," I tell him. "I'm afraid, Matías. I love you and I'm afraid."

He sits up, confusion etched in his features. "What—"

"You don't know what I'm going through. I'm struggling. I'm…I'm…my father. He can't. I can't be gay. I just can't."

"But you are."

"You don't understand," I say, pulling my jeans off the floor and stepping into them. "I don't know that I can promise you the future you want. The one you deserve. We're probably wasting our time."

I watch him blanch at the words, and then I turn my back and put my shoes on. My stomach twists and turns, threatening to throw up everything inside it.

Though I don't want to say these things, it is true. I would just never speak to him this way.

"What's happening here?" he asks, his voice quiet.

"I don't know. I need to go. We need space, I guess. I need to think."

"Adrian, don't do this."

My feet freeze at his tone. I angle my head over my shoulder and get a glimpse at his heartbroken face.

"I'm sorry."

His shoulders fall, like he knows that's it. This is goodbye.

I walk out and make it all the way to my car before I start crying.

CHAPTER THIRTY-SEVEN
MATÍAS

I DON'T KNOW what happened to Adrian in such a short amount of time, but he's changed. It's been just over a week since he fled from my room, telling me he needs a break. He hardly texts me back, and when he does it's with short messages. I've only seen him in passing twice on campus. Both times, he was surrounded by a group of at least seven, and I didn't want to shove my way through and cause a scene.

We're not in any classes together, so my chances to see him are even lower.

He's still saying he needs time, but I think it's clear he's made a decision. After deep sadness for the first few days, all I could feel was anger. And now I'm just confused.

I wasn't forcing him to come out. I told him I was willing to wait—that I was okay with the secrecy and sneaking around. I've been so happy with him, I didn't care that I was a secret. I'd continue to be his secret, but I hoped there'd be a future where that wasn't necessary.

One day, I see him with a girl, his arm wrapped around

her shoulders as his friends hang around. The next day, I see him with the same girl, their positioning close as they speak. She's all giggles and he's nothing but smiles.

I text him from class.

> What are you doing? Are you trying to hurt me on purpose?

His response doesn't come for another hour. Something else that's new. He'd always be quick to respond to me.

> What are you talking about?

> Who's the girl you keep hanging out with? Is this the person you're pretending to date now?

Again, almost forty minutes goes by before he replies.

> I told you I needed to do this.

I don't bother replying again. He's on a mission to end this, so I should just let him. But part of me hopes he'll come to his senses. That he'll miss me.

A month goes by, and with me no longer reaching out, he's stopped texting me altogether. I have to watch from a distance when he leans in to kiss some girl on the forehead. I have to nearly bump into him and said girl when I exit the coffee shop on campus one day. And maybe worst of all, I have to endure the moment he looked at me and pretended he didn't know who I was. He uttered a "My bad, man," like I was a random student. Not someone he's cuddled with. Not someone he's kissed or fucked. Not someone he's loved. I was spared a passing glance before he walked away, arm around a girl who doesn't know the real him.

I've been used and discarded. He wanted to experiment. He told me that in the beginning—when we were just friends. *College is for experimenting and having fun.* I just never thought what we had was only that. But now he's gotten it out of his system, and I'll just be that thing he tried in college.

I become morose. I was never very social to begin with, but I feel even less so now. I go to class, I eat, I go to my room. I no longer have that friendship group I had when I was with Adrian. I hardly even see his friends now, and it's a stark reminder that they were always *his* friends. They tolerated me because I was friends with Adrian. But I had a taste of what it was like to be *normal*. To have people to hang out with, parties to go to, and dinners to share with friends. Now it's been stripped away and now that I know what it's like to have those things, the absence of it is worse.

The remaining months of the school year are awful. Even though I see him with his friends and girls from time to time, I never think to find someone else. I don't have it in me, and it hurts that he seems to be just fine.

So I decide, from here on out, I'll be detached. Maybe it'll save me from future heartbreak. I won't allow this to happen again. I clearly can't trust anyone. Love means nothing.

Apparently you can say you love someone and still hurt them beyond repair. The pain is worse coming from someone who isn't supposed to hurt you. If I never love anyone or let them love me, then if it falls apart, it won't be as bad.

I'll be the one in control now.

Matías

CHAPTER THIRTY-EIGHT

MATÍAS

When I knock on Adrian's door, he doesn't say anything. It's mostly open, so I push it the rest of the way, and find him entrenched in his phone.

"Everything okay?"

"Uh. Yeah."

The pause between the two words makes me believe that's likely not true. It's probably his wife, so it's nothing I want to talk about.

"What do you want to do today?" I ask, leaning against the door jamb.

He tosses his phone and runs a hand over his face before letting out a deep exhale. "I'm open to anything."

I arch a brow. "Is that so?"

Adrian's head goes back slightly. "Uh-oh. Should I be afraid?"

Walking toward his bed, I continue to grin at him. "Not *afraid*. Maybe *excited*."

I crawl onto the bed and between his legs, forcing him to lie back as I hover over him.

"I feel very excited right now, but it's only been fifteen minutes since I came, so."

I laugh. "Don't worry. I won't try to get anything else out of you right now."

"But I do owe *you* something," he says, hands landing on my sides.

"Later."

He pouts. "What if I wanted to do it now?" His hands move toward the waistband of my lounge pants.

"I said later," I say in a stronger tone with space between each word.

His eyes widen briefly before narrowing with lust. "Oh."

"Mm. Now kiss me."

He does so quickly, his hands reaching for my face as he presses his lips against mine. When I pull away, I get on my knees between his legs.

"Tonight, we're going out. Don't wear anything super casual. No jeans or T-shirts. No shorts."

Adrian gets up on his elbows. "Where are we going exactly?"

I run my hands down his thighs. "I think you have an idea."

"What happens in Vegas stays in Vegas?" he questions.

"I hope not."

We go out and eat at a hotel nearby, taking some time to be tourists inside the resort. We walk to other resorts before deciding to head back to our own.

"It's so fucking hot out here," Adrian complains.

"I have a cabana reserved at one of the pools," I tell him. "If you're interested."

He faces me. "A cabana?"

"We'll have our own little area to sit and relax. They have curtains on each side, so we can draw them closed. The pool is twenty-one and older, and much more private and quiet than the beach one they have."

"Did you reserve this before you knew I'd be here?"

I swallow. "Yes."

"Did you plan on bringing someone with you?"

I hesitate. "I wasn't going to bring anyone, no."

"You were gonna meet someone then."

We walk into the elevator with a few others. "Probably."

Adrian doesn't say anything, and I can't tell if it's because he's bothered, or simply because we have an audience now.

Once we get to our floor, he speaks. "And tonight?" he questions. "You were always gonna go, weren't you?"

I stop and face him in the middle of the hall. "Yes. You weren't in my life when I made the reservations. When I made plans. Now you are."

He licks his lips and nods once. "Okay."

Inside the room, I ask, "So, do you wanna go to the pool?"

"Yeah. I'll change."

Both of us meet back in the living room a few minutes later, dressed in our swim trunks, plain T-shirts, and slides.

When we get outside, I find the numbered cabana I reserved, and put my things inside.

"This is nice," Adrian says.

"Yeah, and there's only a few people here. Even better."

Adrian snorts. "Your aversion to people is hilarious."

I close the curtains on the sides, since the back is already closed, leaving only the front one that faces the pool open.

I walk over to Adrian, knowing nobody can see us, and I pull him into me. "I don't have an aversion to you."

He swallows, his hand resting on my hip. "That's good."

"In fact, I quite desire your presence."

"Is that right?"

I lean forward and kiss along his cheekbone. "Mmhmm. That's why I endured all the tourists. Because I was with you."

He runs his fingers through my hair. "Thank you."

I kiss his lips. "You'll thank me later."

His teeth scrape across his bottom lip, then I turn around and take off my shirt. I reach for the sunscreen that sits in the small basket on the coffee table and hand it to Adrian.

He takes it without a word and squirts some into his hand before massaging it into my shoulders and across my back.

I turn around. "Now my front."

He smirks. "Yes, sir."

I bite down on my teeth, jaw clenching. He seems to notice the effect.

As he massages the lotion into my chest, he chews on his lip, like he's mulling over a thought.

He rubs more onto my stomach and says, "Do you only have these types of relationships? With the power exchange? Or have you been in what they'd say is a vanilla relationship?"

"Who's *they*?" I ask with a grin.

"You know. Media."

He rubs more of the sunscreen onto my arms.

"I don't have *relationships* so to speak. My sex life usually consists of people in the lifestyle. I prefer to be in control. There are rules set in place, so everyone knows what they're getting into at the start. It's sex. That's it."

His eyes meet mine. "When did you start that?"

"A couple years after college. I met a guy who was a Dominant. I was intrigued and learned quite a bit."

"When you say *met.*"

"I had sex with him. Yes."

He nods, but there's a hurt expression on his face. He doesn't have the right to be mad or jealous, but I understand it. It's the same way I feel when I think about him being married.

"So, no regular vanilla relation—sexual experiences?"

"Sure, I've had them."

"But you prefer it the other way."

It's not a question. It's like he already knows.

"Yes. It helps me keep emotions from getting involved. I hardly have repeats. If I do, we're both aware it's for the experience, not because we're in love."

"And the guy that called?" he asks, stepping back when he's done covering me in the sunscreen.

"Christian."

"Let's not give him a name," he says with a nose scrunch.

"Take off your shirt and turn around," I tell him, grabbing the lotion to put on his back. "What about him?"

"No feelings?"

"Not on my end."

"But he has them?"

"I think so, yes."

He goes quiet while I cover his body.

"I know I don't have a right to ask what I'm about to ask, but I'm curious." I lift a brow. "If I...if we do the things you're used to. Would that keep you from wanting to do it with anyone else?"

I stare at him, a cocktail of emotions swirling inside me. There are so many things I want to say, and they're all on the tip of my tongue, ready to leap off. But I say something completely different.

"Are you asking me not to sleep with anyone else?"

He runs his hands through his hair. "I know I don't have that right."

"You're right. You don't. Just like I can't ask you to not sleep with your wife. You likely will, right?"

"Matías," he says softly.

"Let's not discuss this," I say. "It's not gonna help anything."

I walk away and go into the pool. There's an older man on the other end, and two ladies on lounge chairs.

A few minutes later, Adrian joins me, and after a few awkward minutes, he speaks up.

"I've always wanted to mess around in a pool."

I look at him before snorting. "Are you propositioning me?"

He looks over at the older man who's doing leg kicks as he hangs onto the side. "Just saying."

We relax in the pool for a while, swimming and floating while we talk, and I'm grateful to be away from our previous subject.

As Adrian floats on his back, I notice the older man and the women on the lounge chairs leave. Earlier, another couple came in, but they're currently behind the closure of their own cabana.

"Adrian," I say, getting his attention. He gets to his feet and looks at me. "Come here."

He swims over, looking around and noticing our audience is gone.

"Yes?" he asks in a flirty tone.

"I want you to touch me."

He bites his lip. "Okay." Turning around, he makes sure nobody is around.

"I'll let you know if someone comes up."

His hand tries to slip into my shorts, but with the water and the type of material, it's not exactly easy.

"Guess you'll have to push them down."

He shoves them below my ass, and reaches below the water to wrap his fingers around my shaft.

"Show me how hard you can get me."

"A challenge?"

"A demand."

"Hmm."

When he begins stroking me, he leans in and rubs his whiskered face against my neck, his lips brushing against my skin when he says, "I'll get you so hard you'll be demanding that I fuck you."

Goosebumps run down my arms as excitement unfurls in my stomach. It's been a while since I've bottomed, but with Adrian, it was mostly our usual.

"We'll see," I say, trying to maintain my composure.

His hand slides up and down my shaft, lips and tongue making their way down my neck as his free hand curves around my ass.

"I think you want me to be inside you," he whispers huskily.

I moan when his finger slides between my cheeks.

"Have you missed me, Matías? And the way I fuck you?"

His finger glides over my hole, my cock hardening in his grip.

He doesn't let me respond before continuing. "I've missed being inside you."

I pant, beginning to thrust into his hand.

"Feeling your tight ass clench around my cock."

"Adrian," I murmur. Distant noises become louder, and my eyes scan the area. "Someone's coming."

He pulls away and I quickly snatch my shorts up. It takes

several seconds of adjusting, but I'm composed by the time the couple come around the corner.

"Maybe we should go back upstairs," I say, still trying to adjust myself so I can get out of the water.

"Good idea," he says with a smirk. "I guess I accomplished the challenge."

I grin as I walk up the stairs. "I guess so. Let's see what else you'll be able to accomplish tonight."

CHAPTER THIRTY-NINE
ADRIAN

Like the good husband that I am, I check in with my wife before I head to a sex club with the guy I've been sleeping with.

I scoff at myself. Disappointed, and yet, not willing to stop.

"So, what should I expect tonight?" I yell from my room as I change for the second time.

"A good time," Matías yells back.

"Black slacks and a white…no, maybe a blue button-up? I don't want to look like I'm there for a business meeting."

He laughs. "What do you want to look like you're there for?"

A thrill runs up my spine as I think *to be fucked*.

"Uhh…you know. Not that."

"I'm sure you'll look fine." His voice and steps get closer. "Let me see."

He emerges through the doorway in all black. The shirt fits him like a glove, showcasing his fit body.

"Well, I don't think you'll look like you're there for a meeting in this," he says, eyeing my nearly naked body.

I stand in front of my bed wearing only my socks and underwear as I stare down at the clothes on the mattress.

"Should I go like this?" I say, turning to face him, arms to the side.

"You can end up like that," he says. "But let's not start off that way."

"Are we gonna…" I leave it there, hoping he'll finish the sentence for me. He doesn't. "You know, do things there?"

"Do you want to?" he questions, picking up a pair of pants from the bed.

"I'm not sure."

He grabs a shirt and hands them both to me. "We can figure it out when we're there. No pressure. Wear these."

I step into the pants and then grab an A-line tank before slipping my arms through the dark purple button-up shirt.

"You look perfect," he says with a smile. "I'm gonna make a call and then we can go."

I nod and finish getting ready. Fifteen minutes later we're on the street, hopping into a cab. Almost thirty minutes later we're pulling up to a building that's far from the lights of The Strip.

"You've been here before?"

He steps out of the cab and I pay the driver.

"Yeah. Twice."

When we get to the door, he shows his ID to the man behind the desk, and mentions me being his guest. I also have to hand over my ID, and then we get a short lecture on rules before we're allowed in.

The main room has a circular bar in the center, and tables lining the walls. The lights emit a golden warm glow in an already dim room.

Music plays over the speakers at a decent level, and people mix and mingle, wearing a variety of different outfits.

The women vary the most—ranging from sexy lingerie to tight-fitting dresses. The men are mostly in dress pants and collared shirts. Some are in see-through black tops, leather pants, and both sexes wear corsets.

As we walk farther in, I notice hallways that branch from each side of the room, and when I gaze upward to inspect the stunning chandelier, I notice there's a second level.

"Where are we going first?" I ask, my body already thrumming with excitement.

Matías grins. "Do you want a drink?"

I shake my head. "I already feel tipsy."

"Then let's get started."

He leads me to the left, where we enter a hall where the rooms have no doors. There are four—two on each side, and every one of them is massive.

Matías chooses one to walk into, and I follow behind, immediately noticing two giant-sized beds and multiple bodies on each. My eyes try to track everything that's happening, but it's hard to focus.

Moans and the sounds of bodies slapping together fill the room. On one section of one of the beds are two women, fully engaged in oral sex. Another section has what appears to be two couples, perhaps swapping, or maybe full on sharing. They all touch and kiss each other, taking turns with one another.

On the other bed are three men interacting with each other and a woman and a man. In front of the beds, with about three feet of distance, is a long leather couch where people sit and watch.

"Wow," I say under my breath.

"A room for voyeurs and exhibitionists."

"Are you either one of those?" I ask.

"I don't mind either one."

"What's in the other rooms?"

He smiles and turns around. We find one room that's outfitted with wooden X's, and some of them have people strapped to them.

"What are those called?"

"St. Andrew's Cross."

"And they're being..."

"Flogged. Or whipped. Or caned."

I feel my body temperature going up. "Let's keep looking."

We visit the other halls, finding that one leads to what appears to be a strip club. But without people crowding stages and throwing money. Men and women dance on a stage as other people watch from their booths.

Eventually, we make our way upstairs, where I find each room has a closed door. Some have small windows in them, so I peek inside and get to watch as a couple have sex on the bed. The man turns his head and finds me there, a small smirk on his face. He turns and says something to the woman, who in turn looks in my direction. They switch positions and really put on a show.

I tug on the collar of my shirt, swallowing as I watch.

"Want to go inside one of these rooms?" Matías asks.

"With a window?"

"Do you want to be watched?"

"Maybe."

"I have to go down and get a key. You're gonna be okay up here?"

"Yeah." I turn to look at him. "Yeah, for sure."

He grins and turns to leave. I continue to watch the couple until the man pulls out of her and comes all over her ass and back.

I move onto the next room with a window and look

inside. This room is set up differently. There's no bed, but there is a table. There's a man bent over it, ankles and wrists restrained as another man walks around him, holding what I now know as a riding crop.

His skin is already slightly red in areas around his ass and thighs. Since I can see him from the side, I spot his erection below the table, and what I'm pretty sure is pre-cum leaking to the floor.

Holy shit.

I feel overheated, so I step back and try to collect myself. As I lean against the wall, I hear steps rounding the corner, and I couldn't be more excited to know Matías is on his way, and we'll soon be behind one of these doors.

However, when the man starts walking toward me, I realize it's just another patron.

He watches me the whole time. His eyes roaming up and down my body as he inches closer.

He's attractive—wearing a form-fitting lace shirt tucked into black pants. I can only see hints of skin, but he's clearly well-built.

"Hey," he says, coming to a stop in front of me.

"Hey."

He peeks over my shoulder and into the room behind me. "Enjoying yourself?"

"Uh, yeah. It's my first time, so."

His brows lift slightly. "Interesting, and are you curious about," he gestures through the window.

I laugh nervously. "I was just looking."

He crosses his arms over his chest and unabashedly checks me out again, but then all of a sudden, Matías is behind him.

"Hello," he says in a cool tone, walking around the man, his eyes on me before he faces him.

"Oh. Are you—"

Matías doesn't let him finish. "He's mine," he states clearly. "He's with me."

"I see," the man says, eyes moving from Matías to me. "Well, I apologize."

Matías gives him a tight grin. "No worries. We'll be in room thirteen if you're interested in seeing what you can't have."

He takes my hand and leads me down the hall to door number thirteen.

My chest vibrates with excitement. At his claim. At his authority. At him telling this man he can watch us.

Matías closes and locks the door once we're inside, barricading me with his arms. "I can't leave you alone for a minute."

I grin. "To be fair, you left me alone for more than a minute."

"And that means you get to flirt with other guys?" he asks, one eyebrow arching upward.

"I wasn't flirting."

He leans forward and takes my bottom lip between his teeth before pulling away. "And why is that?"

My tongue swipes over the area he bit. "Because...because I'm with you."

He kisses me. "Good." Backing away, he continues. "We only do what you're comfortable with, so tell me when you want to stop."

I nod.

"Use your words."

"Okay." Another jolt of excitement runs through me.

Matías turns and walks away, and I finally get a good look at the room. There's a bed and a bench with restraints on the corners. There's a dresser with a bowl of condoms on top and who knows what inside the drawers.

"Come here," he says, standing near the bench. "And take off everything except your underwear."

I walk over to him, staring into his eyes as I undress. My heart races in my chest.

"Now take off my clothes."

Stepping forward, I begin unbuttoning his shirt. He watches me with rapt attention, and I keep flicking my eyes up to meet his gaze.

This is such a simple act, but there's something about the command and the intimacy of undressing him that makes it exciting.

As I undo his belt and unzip his pants, he stares at me with unfiltered lust. When I realize his shoes are still on, I get to my knees and take them off before tugging his pants down to his ankles.

He steps out of the material, and when I move to get to my feet, he puts a hand on my shoulder.

"Stay down there."

On my knees, I peer up at him and wait. I don't even have the need to talk or ask questions. I just want him to tell me what's next.

"Put my cock in your mouth."

I reach into his boxer-briefs and pull out his erection, quickly sliding it between my lips. The window is behind me, so I don't know if that man is still there, if he left, or if there's five other people watching. I don't care. I just want Matías's dick in my mouth.

He gently runs his fingers through my hair as I suck him, rocking his hips slightly. "That's it," he says. "You're so good."

I moan around him, eyes meeting his as I continue to take

him deep into my mouth. He fucks my face for a few minutes before he takes a step back.

"Stand up."

I get to my feet in front of him, our bodies nearly touching. He grabs my face and leans in to kiss me. His tongue swiping across mine as his erection presses into my stomach.

"Turn around," he says after pulling away. "Put each knee on either side."

My stomach rests on the wider part of the contraption, which is at an angle, while my knees rest on the smaller leather benches. Out of the corner of my eye, I see someone at the window, but I don't fully look. The thought that someone is watching is both exciting and terrifying.

Matías runs his hand across my ass, fingers curving over my balls until his hand strokes my cock through my underwear. I suck in a breath and moan.

He stays behind me, his hands running down my thighs before his nails scratch upwards. It's not a deep or painful scratch, but just enough to cause me to shiver.

His hands continue to roam, exploring my body and appreciating every part.

"I want to taste you," he says in a gravelly tone.

"Okay."

Matías pulls the back of the waistband of my boxers down over my ass, keeping my erection concealed. A moan rumbles in his chest at the reveal, his fingers sliding over my hole.

His hands spread my cheeks even wider and then he's licking me up and down.

"Oh, my god, Matías," I moan, squeezing the bench.

Like a starved animal, he consumes me. His tongue travels low, teasing my balls, and it moves all the way up the crack before repeating the path. He takes several minutes to push the tip into my hole, tongue fucking me until I'm a panting mess.

"Matías. Oh, god. Please."

He moans and grunts, making noises like I'm the best thing he's ever tasted. Like he never wants to stop.

And I don't want him to. It feels so good. My body is tingling, sparks going off on every nerve ending.

"More. I need more," I beg.

He pulls away, and then his hand comes down on my right ass cheek.

"Ah!" I cry, then immediately want it to happen again. "Yes."

He does it again.

"Fuck!" I wail. "Matías. I'm so hard. Please."

His hand reaches into my boxers, cupping my balls before stroking my erection. "You're dripping."

"Yes," I say with a whimper.

"I'm not letting them see your cock," he says as he teases me with his fingers. "Get down."

He pulls my boxers back up before I get to my feet, covering me up. I watch him walk to the dresser and open the top drawer, coming back with packets of lube.

Matías sits on the smaller, left bench, farthest from the window. His own erection strains against the material of his boxer-briefs.

He rips open the packet of lube and coats his fingers, pulling me closer with his other hand.

"Stand right here. Just like this."

He positions me in front of him, and when I look over his head, I spot a couple people at the window. I'm so desperate for his touch, I hardly register that we're being watched in this intimate moment. It doesn't feel wrong or weird, because what I'm doing with Matías feels too right.

Matías slips his hand up the right leg of my boxers, his slick fingers finding my hole. I spread my legs and put a hand on his shoulder.

One fingertip breaches my entrance, and I suck in a breath before biting down on my lip. Matías looks up at me, his other hand holding my thigh.

"This is mine."

The words are spoken with finality.

I nod.

"Say it."

"Yours," I say in a throaty whisper. "It's yours."

He pushes deeper, and my head drops back with a moan as my fingertips grip his shoulder.

Matías thrusts in and out with one finger before adding a second.

"Oh, yes," I moan, reaching for my cock.

He bats my hand down. "Not yet."

I let out a whine that morphs into another cry of pleasure as he expertly works his fingers inside me.

As he finger fucks me, he uses his other hand to rub up and down the underside of my erection.

"So hard for me," he croons. "Do you want to come?"

I nod, frantic. "Yes. Yes."

"Shouldn't I come first?" he questions. "Since you came earlier today?"

Once again, I nod. "Yes. You should come."

Matías reaches into his underwear and pulls his erection out, stroking himself. After a few minutes, he removes his fingers from my ass and reaches for another packet of lube.

"Get on my lap," he commands.

I straddle his thighs and watch as he puts some lube on his hand before running it up and down his shaft, then getting some more in his palm.

He pulls my cock from the slit in my shorts, and it twitches, seeking more attention. A drop of precum glistens on the top, but Matías only strokes himself.

He closes his eyes and moans, and it drives me crazy.

"Matías." It's a plea.

His eyes open and he puts his free hand on my lower back and pushes me forward.

"Get closer."

My erection touches the back of his hand as he strokes, and I find myself grinding against him, desperate for any kind of friction.

He lets go of himself and puts his arms out to the sides.

"Rub against me."

I grip the other side of the bench behind him, immediately bringing my dick to his, rubbing against the slick shaft.

My moaning is frantic and wanton. It's not nearly enough, but it still feels good. My hips rock and rotate, and sweat begins to bead at my hairline.

"Okay. Sit back," he says.

I groan, but I listen.

Matías reaches for both of our erections, stroking them together.

"Oh yes, yes," I say, immediately satisfied.

"You like that?" he asks.

"I love it. God, please don't stop."

His hand curves around the top, touching the sensitive head.

"I don't think you're desperate enough."

"I am," I say, thrusting into his hand.

He lets go, then focuses only on himself.

"Matías."

A growl rumbles in his throat. "I love the way you say my name. I never want to hear anyone utter it. Only you."

I moan, trying to grind into him again.

He reaches around me, his hand going down the back of my boxers where his fingertips tease my hole.

I shift to allow him to do more, but it's clear he's just driving me to the brink of insanity.

Matías keeps stroking, watching my face as I whimper and moan. My cock rubs the back of his hand, and he doesn't move it, so I revel in the small amount of friction.

"You want to see me come?"

"Yes. God, yes," I beg.

"Are you gonna clean up the mess?"

"Yes," I growl. "I'll clean it."

My hips move in pace with his hand. I need to come too. I'm beyond desperate.

"Oh, fuck," he grunts.

His cum shoots out of him in ribbons, landing on his stomach and dripping over his fingers.

"Yes," I cry.

He's reduced to grunts and groans, his muscles tense as he releases. Then he sucks in a quivering breath and opens his eyes to look at me.

"Look what you do to me."

My eyes inspect the mess, and I reach down and grab his hand, licking the cum from every part of it.

He hums his appreciation, and as I suck on his fingers, I grind against his erection.

"You're so desperate for it, aren't you?" he asks.

"I am," I moan, licking around his thumb.

"You're leaking all over me."

"I know. I need to come. Please."

"Keep begging."

"Matías, please. Please let me come. I need it."

"Mmm," he moans, reaching for my cock.

He teases it with fingertip touches, smearing the precum around my head.

I sit back and watch, whimpering as I wait for him to grip it tight.

"Please," I say, my voice a small whisper. "Please, please, please."

"God, you're so fucking perfect," he says, finally wrapping his fingers around me. "Come for me."

It only takes four strokes before my orgasm bursts out of me. I let out a deafening roar as he continues his movements, milking me for every drop.

My body turns to Jell-O afterward, and I collapse on top of him, my forehead against his temple, my chest on his. We're both a sweaty mess, but he still wraps his arm around me and rubs my back.

It takes a few minutes before I feel like I can breathe fairly normally. I pull away, and Matías grabs my hips, angling his head up for a kiss.

I press my mouth against his, parting his lips with my tongue.

I feel so overcome with emotion, and I don't know why. I want to say things I have no right to say. I want to cry and beg for his forgiveness for how I treated him before. My head is all over the place.

He seems to sense my frantic thoughts, and he puts his hand on the back of my head, gently brushing through my hair. "It's okay."

CHAPTER FORTY
MATÍAS

"DID YOU HAVE FUN?" I ask Adrian as we make our way into the hotel room.

"I did," he says with a smile. "I sort of expected whips and chains and punishments." He laughs nervously.

"Oh, is that what you're interested in?" I ask with raised brows.

His cheeks blush. "No. I don't know. In some ways, I still feel like I did all those years ago—trying things for the first time. I've not had much experience since college."

I take his hand and squeeze, and then lead him to the couch. "Well, there's a variety of things that can happen in places like that. But I'm not in the lifestyle like most people. I enjoy the level of control I can have. I like power play. Things like that. I'm not requiring people to call me by any titles, or dolling out contracts. We have agreements and boundaries, and that's what calls to me.

"Well, I think you liked when I called you sir," he teases with a smirk.

I sit on the couch and face him. "I'm not opposed, and I am your boss, so you should call me sir."

He chuckles. "Noted."

"You don't have to have sex, or be fully naked to have that power dynamic. I told you what to do, I kept you from coming until I was ready, and just those things can be thrilling. I don't have to whip you. Plus, I didn't want anyone at the window to see what was mine."

His lips twitch. "You say you do this to keep from getting attached, so is that what you're doing with me?" He looks down when he says it, not wanting to meet my gaze.

"With you, everything's different," I admit. "I feel like I'm out of control with you. In fact, I am. You hold all the power. You always did." He looks up at me, confusion marking his brow. "In college, we did whatever we had to in order to keep us a secret. We holed up in my room, we snuck around in yours, we didn't go on dates. You controlled what we did. And now, you're married. You could choose to stop what we have. It's all up to you."

"Matías, that's not—"

"It's fine," I say, cutting him off. "Having control in the bedroom is one thing. It's fun and exciting, but I'd let you do anything to me. I don't want to keep from cuddling or falling asleep together. And that's scary for me, because I know it could all come to an end. Again. But it's you, Adrian. There's something between us, and I could never turn it down."

His brows are drawn in as he chews on the inside of his lip. He's fighting with himself over his feelings or what to say.

"I want to be honest with myself," he says. "I want to be honest with everyone." A long silence follows his statement. "I don't know when." He stares into my eyes. "I don't know when, Matías, but I'm going to try to figure it out. I don't need my father's money anymore. But he still has connections. He found out I'm working for you, and I don't know what that means. I don't know if or what he might try to do.

And I'm not sure how to bring this up with Charlotte or my mom and sister."

I squeeze his knee. "Okay."

With a sigh, I let the conversation end there. I should look at this like a fling. Something casual—no strings attached, but it's not possible. Adrian and I come with strings, and as soon as we're near each other, they start to tie knots, drawing us close. I could cut them, but why would I want to live without a part of me?

"We leave tomorrow. Back to the real world."

"Yeah," he says through an exhale. He turns his head as it rests on the back of the couch, looking at me. "It'll be different, but...I still want to see you."

I grin. "You know where I live. And work."

He smiles. "Indeed, I do."

The journey home goes faster than I wanted. I know I'll see him again. It's inevitable, but it will still be different. He'll have to have excuses now. Lies to tell. I'll be second to his wife and that's a punch to the gut. But I don't have a right to complain.

I pull into my garage and pop the trunk. We walk around to remove our luggage and put it at our feet.

"Well," he says, scratching the back of his neck. "I guess I'll see you later."

"You definitely will," I say with a grin.

He comes in for a hug, but when he goes to pull away, he stops and studies my face. Then he leans in and kisses me.

I cup the side of his face with my hand, deepening the kiss. You'd think we hadn't spent days doing this, because we kiss like it's the first time. Or last.

When we disentangle ourselves, he takes a breath and grabs the handle of the suitcase.

"See you."

I lift a hand and watch him walk out of the garage and head to his house.

CHAPTER FORTY-ONE
ADRIAN

In my bedroom, I lift my suitcase to the bed and start unpacking. The shower is on in the connected en-suite, so I have a few minutes to prepare myself for seeing Charlotte after this weekend. The guilt will likely be written across my face.

I do feel bad, but at the same time, I finally feel like I did something for me. For my happiness.

I'm here in this house, with a ring on my finger, for her. It started because of our parents, but for a while, she's been telling me she needs me. She's heard it from her father for way too long. She doesn't think she's capable of being on her own—of being strong enough to fight through her addiction and be in recovery without me. And while I don't mind being that pillar of strength for her, it feels like I'm being used. Resentment grows inside me.

As I'm taking out the last remaining toiletry items, the bathroom door opens, and she jolts.

"Oh, god." She laughs. "You're home."

"Sorry," I say. "Didn't mean to scare you."

She touches her hair. "No, it's fine. I guess I lost track of time." Charlotte walks over and wraps her arms around me.

I return the hug and kiss the top of her head. "I'm gonna finish up and go make something to eat. Are you hungry?"

"No, I ate not that long ago. I'll just finish getting ready, and I'll meet you down there so you can tell me all about your trip."

"Okay."

I remove the small toiletry bag and put it on the bed before I zip up the suitcase and store it in the closet.

Charlotte goes back into the bathroom, and I head downstairs to start looking for something to eat.

I hesitate at the window, looking through the blinds at Matías's house across the way, wishing things could be different.

By the time I'm sitting down to eat my chicken and cheese quesadilla, Charlotte comes downstairs.

"Hey. Did you talk to your dad?"

I groan, rolling my eyes. "No. Why?"

"He told me he'd been trying to get in touch with you."

"You talked to him?"

"Yeah, he called me."

She sits across from me at the dining room table.

"What did you say?"

"That you were on a work trip."

"That's it?"

She looks confused. "I mean, we talked a little about the area and the house. He was just asking how things were going, Adrian."

I fight the scoff that threatens to come out. "What else did he ask about?"

"Just how you were liking your job." She plays with the

place mat. "Oh, I told him how your boss is our neighbor, and how that's a crazy coincidence."

"What?" I exclaim, putting my food down. "Why are you telling him about my life, Charlotte? I moved so he wouldn't be so heavily involved, and now he has a little spy in you."

"I'm not spying," she shouts, standing up. "He cares about you. He's just checking on you."

"I don't need him to. You should know we don't have a strong relationship."

"Yeah, well you don't seem capable of having strong relationships with anyone," she spits before turning and fleeing upstairs.

I sigh and rub my head, wishing I was still back in Vegas.

At work the next day, I find myself scanning the room for Matías. Right before lunch, my phone rings on my desk.

"Hello?"

"Adrian."

"Mr. Cruz," I say, a smile on my lips.

"Can you meet me in my office, please?"

"Yes, sir."

He clears his throat before hanging up.

Instead of sprinting across the floor like I want to, I take my time and casually make my way to his door, giving it two knocks before turning the knob.

"Yes, sir?" I say before stepping in.

He grins at me from behind his desk. "Please, come in."

I close the door behind me and walk toward him.

He has lunch on his desk. Enough for two.

"Thought we could go over some paperwork," he says with a small grin.

"Oh, of course." I sit in the chair on the opposite side of his desk. "We mustn't get behind on paperwork."

He hands me a Styrofoam container with a crooked smile on his face. "How are you?"

"Good. You?"

I open it up and find a turkey club inside.

"Pretty good. I was going to text you last night, but..."

He lets the sentence end there, because he doesn't need to finish in order for me to understand what he's getting at.

"Oh. Well, I always have my phone on me." I look him in the eye. "So you can text whenever."

"Good to know."

I take a few bites of my sandwich as he stabs a fork through his salad. After a few minutes, I say, "My dad knows I'm working for you now. And that you're my neighbor."

His brows go up slightly. "And what does that mean for you?"

"I don't know. I haven't talked to him. He's been trying to get me to answer the phone, but..." I shrug.

"He can be unhappy about that, but what does he expect from you? To quit your job and move? You just did that."

"No, I'm definitely not catering to him anymore. He's unpredictable, though, so I expect he could just show up at any time to lecture me."

"Have you ever thought about telling him to fuck off?" he asks right before taking a bite.

My snort turns into laughter. "Yes. Many times."

After a minute of silence, he speaks up. "I don't know why parents think they can keep their kids from being who they are. He's bullying you and threatening you simply to keep you from being happy. And all for the sake of his company?" He takes a breath. "Sorry. It's just—"

"No, you're fine. I get it. He's just always been that way. My mom, too, but she's less vocal about it. She's not really concerned with my every move, especially now. Dad has this hatred in him. I don't know why. You'd think gay people did something to him personally, because it's almost as if he's holding a grudge."

Matías shakes his head. "Well, I don't know. Hopefully he leaves you alone."

I roll my eyes as I take another bite, doubtful that'll ever happen. And then a thought hits me, and I just say the words without even thinking about them.

"He'd probably only leave me alone if I came out."

Matías stares at me as I register what I'm saying. Now that the initial thought is out there, more keep coming, and the words fall from my lips.

"He'd be so angry or embarrassed, that he'd likely just disown me and never speak to me again." I pause, putting my food down as I sit back. "That thought bothered me when I was younger and needed him, but I don't need his money anymore. I don't care about running his company. And it's not as if I'd be missing out on an incredible family dynamic."

Matías continues to watch me as I talk, but he doesn't say anything. It's almost as if he's holding his breath, afraid to break this train of thought I'm having.

A phone call interrupts everything.

Matías answers. "Hello? Oh, hi, Mr. Wright. Of course. Yes. I'll be there. Okay, goodbye."

When he hangs up the phone, he looks at me. "I have to go talk to the boss."

"Oh, okay," I say, getting up from the chair.

"I'll text you later."

He stands and walks around the desk, grabbing me by the

tie. Pulling me closer, he plants his mouth on mine. The kiss is quick, but it sends a jolt of electricity through me.

"Okay." I swipe some random papers from his desk. "I'll get these back to you." I walk to the door, opening it while saying, "I'll get right on it, sir."

He fights his grin, shaking his head at me.

<h1 style="text-align:center">CHAPTER FORTY-TWO</h1>
<h1 style="text-align:center">MATÍAS</h1>

Besides running to Adrian's office to get my papers back, I don't see much of him for the rest of the day. I have to stay late to finalize a few things and send emails, so he's gone by the time I emerge from my office.

I end up driving to a Nicola's pizza parlor to pick up dinner, and then make my way home. When I pull up, I spot Adrian in front of his house, looking for something in the backseat of his car.

I know I should just drive into my garage, close it, and head inside, but apparently I do things I shouldn't quite a bit these days. Grabbing the pizza box, I walk into my driveway with the excuse of going to my mailbox.

Adrian turns and watches me, a grin on his lips. "Hello."

I smile. "Hello."

On my way back to the house, I stop midway, and he walks through the grass, stopping about five feet away from me.

"Pizza night, huh?"

"Yep. Didn't feel like cooking." I nod toward his car. "Did you lose something?"

"Huh?" He glances behind him. "Oh. No, uhh—"

His front door opens, and his wife's head pops out. "Did you find it?" She notices me. "Oh. Hi!" she says cheerily.

I lift a hand and give her a tight grin. "Hi."

She steps out, and I hear a low groan come from Adrian's throat. He turns and looks at me, his face expressing his discomfort.

"How are you?" Charlotte says, coming to stand next to Adrian.

"Can't complain," I offer, giving a slight nod as my eyes bounce between the two of them.

I watch her eyes scan over the pizza box in my hand. Then she looks at me. "I'd still love to have you over for dinner sometime. Please tell me you have a wife or girlfriend, so I can have a friend, too." She laughs but Adrian clears his throat, looking uncomfortable.

"Uh, no," I say with a small smile. "I'm gay, so having a wife or girlfriend probably wouldn't work out."

Her eyes widen, and her cheeks turn pink. "Oh, gosh. I'm sorry."

"It's not a problem."

My eyes find Adrian who clearly takes what I said as a direct message to him. It's not what I intended, but.

"Well, either way. You could come or if you have a...significant other, he can come too. What do you think, babe?" she asks, putting her hand on Adrian's arm.

He watches me for a couple seconds. "Uh. If he wants to, yeah, I guess we could put something together. Maybe just a barbeque. I could invite some other neighbors."

Adrian's trying to make sure this isn't just us three, which would make for a very uncomfortable dinner.

"We'll figure it out," she says, waving his idea off. "We can't do Friday. It's date night. But Saturday might work."

Adrian shifts, eyes flickering to me. He looks like he's ready to burst out of his skin.

"Saturday. I'll keep it open. Thanks."

She nods, smiling at me.

"See you tomorrow," I tell Adrian before I walk back into my house.

Definitely shouldn't have come out to talk to him. If I had just gone inside, I wouldn't be invited to dinner, and I wouldn't know that he and his wife have a date night planned.

Three hours later, around ten o'clock, my phone vibrates with a text message. Without looking at it, I know it's from Adrian.

Hey

Hello

I know he's reaching out regarding the whole *date night* comment, but there's really nothing to be said. As much as it may hurt, they're married, and will do married people things, even if he's not fully invested.

Sorry about earlier.

Sorry for what exactly?

You know what.

It's fine. I'm not supposed to be affected.

Doesn't mean you aren't.

It's not even like you think. It's just dinner.

Dinner is a date night activity, and again, don't feel you have to defend yourself. It's not me you owe loyalty to.

Well, that makes me feel like shit, and besides that, it still feels wrong.

We're both aware that what we're doing is wrong. Do you want to stop?

He doesn't reply, and my stomach turns. But twenty minutes later, it finally vibrates.

Come out back.

I quickly put on my house shoes and make my way to the back door. I slide it open and step onto my patio before walking forward, searching the shadows for a familiar figure.

He appears around the collection of emerald-green privacy trees, marching up the couple of steps that lead to my patio.

"Do I want to stop?" he questions, throwing my words back at me.

My hands slip into my pockets as I stare back at him, but he rushes toward me, catching me off guard. I stumble a little when his body crashes into mine, but he holds on to me as his lips land on my own.

I take my hands from my pockets and snake them around his body as his tongue forces its way into my mouth. One hand goes to the back of my head, fingers tugging on the strands. I moan into his mouth as he grinds against me.

I end up pushed against the glass door behind me as his hands travel all over my body.

He pulls away from my mouth to say, "No, I don't want to stop. I never wanted this to stop."

With an exhale, I lean my forehead against his. "I know you're going to have to do married couple things. That doesn't mean it won't hurt, but I understand it."

He sighs before turning to stand on my side, his back now pressed against the same glass door.

"I know what I'm doing is fucked up. I think about it constantly, but I don't want to stop. I don't even want to pause while I get it sorted. I'm gonna try. I have to figure out a few things first, but I'm gonna try."

I nod once. "Okay."

"I should get back."

He doesn't make a move to leave. He just watches me.

"Yeah. You should."

"I don't want to."

"I don't want you to either."

He leans in and kisses me. This time it's softer. When he pulls away, he gives me a small smile before walking away.

I can't help but think that one of these days it'll be for

good. The trauma from the past still haunts me, and I know he's capable of cutting me off for someone else.

With a sigh, I turn and head back inside. I knew starting something with Adrian wasn't a smart idea. Not just because he's married, but because he's still in the closet. Because now there's two reasons why he can never be with me the way I'd want.

But he's my number one weakness, and I'm afraid there's nothing I wouldn't do to have even just a small part of him.

CHAPTER FORTY-THREE

ADRIAN

At almost five o'clock on Friday, I make my way to Matías's office.

"Come in," he says after I give the door a couple quick knocks.

He barely glances up, then notices it's me and looks again, giving me a smile. "Hey."

"Hi. Can I come in?"

"Sure."

I close the door behind me and linger next to it. "So, Saturday."

His head inclines back as he realizes what I'm here to talk about. "Saturday."

"It'll be a barbecue. I invited Diane and Greg from across the street and two houses down, and Martin who's right on the other side of me. And Carl and Leslie."

"I recognize maybe two of those names."

I laugh. "Well, you should get to know your neighbors more."

"I'm friendly when I see them, but I don't go out of my way to strike up conversations."

265

"Well, anyway, it's a little neighborhood barbecue, and it starts at four."

"Why are you so far away?" he asks, changing the subject.

"Oh." I step forward. "Just trying to keep things professional."

He smirks. "Like on our work trip?"

"Yes. I was very professional."

He pushes away from his desk, the chair rolling back enough to reveal his thighs. "It's been too long since I've seen you come."

My body instantly heats up. "A week does feel like forever in this instance," I agree.

"I'm afraid I'm already forgetting what you taste like."

I swallow, getting turned on where I probably shouldn't.

"Which part of me?"

Matías gives me a wicked grin before crooking his fingers, gesturing me over.

I'm next to him in a handful of strides. He sits up and starts undoing the belt on my pants.

"Wh-what are you doing?" I ask, nerves and excitement swirling in my gut.

"Don't worry about that. What should I bring to the barbecue?"

He unbuttons and unzips my pants, tugging them down.

"Uhh." I glance at the door, then back at him. "I don't know. Matías, this is—"

He grabs my hips and positions me in front of his desk, facing the door. Thank god the blinds on his window are closed.

Behind me, he pulls my boxers down.

"Should I bring chips? Drinks?" he asks.

I let out a nervous laugh, because why are we talking about this while I'm being undressed in his office?

His finger traces the line of my crack and I suck in a breath. "Matías."

He groans, leaning forward to kiss the top of my ass cheek, planting a trail of them across the curve.

"We're just having a friendly conversation," he says, squeezing the flesh of my ass.

"Yeah," I say on a breath. "Extremely friendly."

"Very professional."

He pushes down on my back, making me bend over the desk.

"Oh, god."

"I just want a little taste," he says, before spreading me open and swiping his tongue up my crack.

"Holy shit."

He pulls away. "You're gonna have to be quiet, Mr. Kennedy. There are still employees out there."

"Oh." I whimper. "Yes, sir."

A sexy growl rumbles in his throat, then he licks me again. More than that, he fucking consumes me. His tongue pushes into my hole, fucking me with it while making sinful noises of pleasure.

His sounds are muffled, but I have to clamp a hand around my own mouth to keep from being too loud.

Paper crinkles under me, and my other hand tightly grips the edge of the desk. He swipes over my hole like a madman. Like I'm the best thing he's ever had. Perhaps like I'm the only meal to keep him sustained.

His grip on me is tight, and I'm almost ready to beg him to fuck me right here and now when he pulls away, sucking in a deep breath.

"God. I could eat you all goddamn day."

His finger presses over my hole and I suck in a breath. "I'd like that."

"I bet you would," he says, giving my ass a light smack.

I stand up and papers fall to the floor. I bring my underwear and pants back up, tucking my erection under the waistband.

When I turn, he's casually sitting in his chair like he didn't just fucking eat my ass over his desk during work hours.

"So, what should I bring?"

I shake my head as I snort. "Just yourself is fine."

He grins. "Get on your knees."

I kneel in front of him and watch as he undoes his pants and pulls his cock out. It's so hard, the veins pushing against the skin. There's a drop of pre-cum on his tip, and I want nothing more than to lick it up.

"Look what you did to me."

I bite my lip, watching him wrap his fingers around his erection. "Sorry."

He smirks. "Later tonight, I'll replay what just happened, and I'll take care of this."

"Not right now?"

He gives his cock another stroke. "No. Not right now. We're at work, Mr. Kennedy."

I bite back my grin. "Right."

Matías leisurely strokes himself in front of me before tucking it away.

"That'll be all, Mr. Kennedy."

My eyes flicker up at him. "I want to watch. I want to be able to see you when you come tonight."

His brow arches slightly. "Hmm. We'll see."

I stand and get myself situated. "Thank you for the uhh… conversation. I'll be thinking about it for the rest of the evening."

"I hope so," he says with a grin.

I make my way to the door and give him another glance before I walk out.

CHAPTER FORTY-FOUR
ADRIAN

"This is exciting. We haven't had a date night in so long," Charlotte says from in front of the mirror where she puts on her earrings.

"Yeah, I know."

She walks up to me, pulling on my tie. "You might get lucky tonight, mister."

I force a smile on my face while my stomach churns.

It's not like it'll be the first time I've had sex with her. I can do it. She's never gotten my best. If she had girlfriends, I'd definitely be talked about. She'd mention my lack of enthusiasm, probably. How I don't initiate it ever. Perhaps, and most embarrassingly, the times when I couldn't keep it up or finish.

But it's not like it's her. It's hard to do those things with someone you're not attracted to. And not just *I don't think you're cute enough*, because she's pretty, but I'm not attracted to the female body. It doesn't do anything for me, and the act is in fact, uncomfortable.

"Not to put a wet blanket over tonight," she starts, walking toward the closet.

"Charlotte, please," I groan, already knowing where this is going.

"Your dad wants to talk to you. Just call him and get it over with."

"Not tonight."

"That's fine. Also, my parents are planning on visiting in a week or two, depending on Dad's schedule."

I inhale deeply through my nose, running my hand over my forehead while trying to keep from having an outburst.

"We should leave soon. Reservations are in thirty, and it's at least twenty minutes away."

Charlotte slips her feet into some heels as she sits on the edge of the bed, then grabs her purse from the dresser and gives me a smile.

"I'm ready."

Since our garage is still full of boxes and furniture that we need to get rid of, the car is parked in the driveway. As we're getting to the doors, Matías walks out wearing some running shoes, shorts, and a tank top.

We make eye contact before he gives us a tight smile and wave.

Charlotte waves back, but I don't. He puts in his earbuds and then takes off down the block.

I spend most of our date thinking about him. I think about what he did to me earlier today in his office. I think about how I shouldn't be thinking about that while I'm on a date with my wife. I wonder if he's mad. I wonder if he'll try to go on a date just to get even. I think about way too many things at once, and realize I've been a terrible date.

"You look amazing, by the way," I tell Charlotte.

Her face lights up a bit. "Thank you." Silence stretches. "I've been feeling like things have been off between us," she admits. "I think we need more date nights. The move has been stressful for us both."

I don't know how to tell her it's not just the move. Did she not feel the distance before? Was I better at masking my feelings prior to coming here? I don't want to promise to be better knowing I can't keep that promise. I don't want to agree to more dates, but I also can't just say, 'Well, I'm gay, that's why things are off. Let's get a divorce.'

I sigh. "Yeah, I've been really overwhelmed," I tell her, since it's not a lie.

"Talk to me," she says, reaching for my hand. "We used to be such good friends."

I give her a small smile. "I liked when we were friends."

She blanches and I realize I may have made a mistake. "Well, I'd like to think we still are."

"Of course," I say. "But our relationship didn't really start out in a normal way."

"Well, no. But that doesn't mean it isn't real."

I bite my tongue. "You're not upset that we were forced into this?"

"Of course I was. You remember how angry I used to be, but it's clear our parents had our best interests in mind. I've become so much better since being with you. I'm like a whole new person with a new outlook. You've helped me so much, Adrian. You still do. I don't want to let you down, which is why I try so hard to stay sober."

"Charlotte," I start, not knowing how to word what I want to say. "I want you to stay sober for yourself. You shouldn't do that for me, you know?" She nods, looking down at the tablecloth. "You're so strong. You've come so far, and I know you can keep it up."

She glances at me, a smile on her lips. "Thank you."

"And I don't think our parents had *our* interests in mind at all. Maybe yours, definitely theirs, but not mine."

She looks like she's about to say something, but the waiter arrives, bringing us some dessert.

Our previous conversation is never brought up again, but it sticks in my brain, eating away at me.

I won't be able to do this much longer. I know that. But how do I give her this news and make sure she doesn't spiral? She'll be hurt enough as is, but I don't need her slipping into bad habits, and that pressure is heavy.

Before we leave the restaurant, she slides into my side of the booth and takes a couple of photos of us since she said it's the first time she's been dressed up in a while.

In the car ride home, she rests her hand on my leg, her fingers making circles and tracing lines. I feel tense but she doesn't seem to notice.

As we pull into our driveway, I notice a couple lights on in Matías's house, and wonder what he's doing.

In the room, she kicks off her shoes and walks toward me, wrapping her arms around my waist and resting her head on my chest.

I know where this is going. It's even an understandable next move for a married couple. Our first date night in a while should lead to sex, since it's been a while since we've done that, too.

And while I used to be able to just grin and bear it, I now have Matías in the back of my mind. He's right next door, knowing I was on a date tonight, possibly worried about me having sex right now.

It's strange and wrong, but it feels like I'm cheating on him too.

"I'm gonna use the bathroom real quick," I tell her, extracting myself from her grip and rushing off.

I close and lock the door and then turn on the faucet. I stare at myself wondering what the hell I'm supposed to do. My stomach is in knots. I try to come up with an excuse. Maybe I'm sick. Maybe I got food poisoning and it's already working its way through my system. Maybe I have someone call me and pretend there's an emergency, but what the hell would that be? My job doesn't have late night emergencies that would require me to leave.

I even think to text my dad and tell him to call me, just because it would keep me from what's sure to come as soon as I step out of the bathroom. But I really don't want to talk to him, especially not in front of Charlotte when I know what the conversation will be about.

When I finally exit the bathroom, Charlotte's already changed and wearing a pair of silk shorts and a matching tank top.

"I'll be right out. Just want to freshen up," she says as she passes me. Her grin tells me everything.

I strip out of my clothes and put on a T-shirt and pair of sweatpants before I climb under the covers.

My phone buzzes when I plug it in, but not from being charged. It's a message from Matías.

Hey

I glance at the bathroom and still hear the faucet running. I type out a quick response.

Hey

Still want to watch?

It takes a second before I realize what he's referring to. I told him earlier today that I wanted to watch him come. But my god this isn't the right time.

Of course

I've been thinking about you all night.

I've been thinking about you too.

The water in the bathroom shuts off. There's some movement, but she'll be out here any second now.

I want to taste you again. I want to make you as desperate as you were at the club in Vegas.

My heart is in my throat, beating rapidly as my body heats up. Matías is turning me on through texts while I worry about my wife coming out of the bathroom to try to sleep with me.

. . .

I feel like I'm always desperate for you.

Good.

Three dots appear, letting me know he's typing something else out. I anxiously await the message, and then the bathroom door opens.

I wonder if my face shows the amount of guilt and fear that I feel. Can she hear how fast my heart is beating?

"Good. You're still up," she says with a grin as she climbs into bed. "Who are you talking to?"

I make the phone go dark. "Nobody."

The phone buzzes in my hand, and sweat prickles under my arms. For all she knows, that could be an email. I don't look at it.

Her hand lands on my stomach under the covers, moving down toward my waist.

"You know, maybe you're right. I should just talk to my dad and get it over with," I say.

Her hand doesn't stop moving. She pushes my shirt up to touch my skin, her fingers dancing under the waistband of my sweats.

"Yeah, that's good," she says, scooting closer.

"He's probably still awake," I say.

She stops moving. "You want to call him right now?"

"I mean, I should, right? Like, that's what you said."

Charlotte pulls away completely. "You said earlier that it wouldn't be today, but now you want to?"

"I don't ever want to talk to him, Charlotte, but you keep telling me I need to, so—"

"Not at ten o'clock when we're in bed and I'm clearly trying to have an intimate moment with you. Are you that oblivious or just completely disinterested? Do you even know how long it's been since we've had sex? Because I can tell you."

"Are you really keeping track?" I say, my guilt turning into defensiveness and anger. "That's real great, Charlotte. I didn't know that just because *you* want to have sex, I also have to want to have sex. Not everyone is in the mood all the time. I know I'm a man, but I can't just deliver when you're ready."

"Oh, my god," she exclaims. "That's not what I meant at all."

"Well, that's how it sounds. I'm supposed to be here for you when you need me and want me, but my needs and wants don't matter."

Her mouth drops open. "What are you talking about?"

I get out of the bed, taking my phone off the nightstand.

"Just forget it."

"Where are you going?"

"Downstairs."

"Good. Thanks for the *wonderful* date night. It's been a blast," she says sarcastically.

I stop at the closet for an extra blanket. "Yep. Definitely."

"You know, people cheat on their spouses when they're not happy," she says.

I freeze, turning to look at her. She stares back at me, unflinching.

It's a threat. She's trying to scare me into thinking that's what she'd do, but all she's done is uttered a statement that rings true to me.

I know people cheat for different reasons or for no reason. It's never justified, but in this case, it feels like she's exactly right.

I'm not happy. Haven't been happy in a long time. And look at what I'm doing. I'm finding that happiness somewhere else. But it's not because I'm bored, or another girl is giving me attention I don't think I get at home. It's not because I need my ego stroked and my wife doesn't do it for me. It's not because I have to go out and see if *I still got it.*

Matías is the one person I've ever felt true happiness around. Who I've been my true authentic self with. No fear. No stress. No discomfort.

I'm with him now because it feels like it's the one thing keeping me from doing a deep dive into depression. He's keeping me afloat in a situation where I've always felt like I'm drowning.

I don't reply to her. I simply walk out of the room.

CHAPTER FORTY-FIVE

ADRIAN

WE DON'T KEEP alcohol in the house, but I could go for a drink right about now. I pace through the living room, then make my way into the kitchen to grab a bottle of water.

For nearly thirty minutes, I wear paths into the floor, unable to sit still.

When my phone vibrates, I pick it up off the couch where I tossed it and look at the screen. There are two messages from Matías. One from forty minutes ago, and another just now.

> I'm about to go into my office, which is downstairs and at the back of the house. Are you able to sneak out?

> I'm assuming not. I'll see you tomorrow then.

I quickly type back a response.

. . .

Sorry. I'm still up.

Oh okay.

Your office?

There's a window. You said you wanted to watch.

I glance toward the stairs. It's too risky. She might still be awake, and even if she isn't, she could come downstairs at some point.

However, something about Charlotte is that she's stubborn as hell. She won't be quick to apologize, and she'll thrive while giving me the silent treatment.

I feel bad about the fight, knowing I started it. I didn't mean to, I just meant to put off having sex. My real feelings came out, but she's unaware of what I'm talking about, and I know that's only my fault. But it doesn't make me any less upset that what I want in life has never been thought about.

I should apologize.

And I will.

But not right now.

Give me ten.

I quietly make my way upstairs and stand outside our bedroom door. It's only partially cracked, but the lights are off, and I hear the soft sounds of her breathing. She's asleep.

Back downstairs, I slip on a pair of tennis shoes, pocket my phone, and carefully make my way out the back door.

Like a thief in the night, I creep through the shadows, watching for any neighbors who might be out late. Luckily, the space between our houses isn't too vast, and once I'm behind his place, I go straight toward the window where the light is still on. He has it cracked marginally, allowing for a slight breeze. Or to make sure I can hear him.

He's not inside, so I pull out my phone and send him a message.

I'm here.

I'll be down soon.

Do I just stand out here and look like a perverted peeping Tom?

Yes. You watch me while I think about eating your ass earlier. Watch me jack off to thoughts of you. Watch my cum paint my skin while I imagine what it would be like to feel you inside me again.

My cock twitches inside my sweats. God, this is so not normal. I'd have never thought to do this, but it turns me on so much.

What if I just went inside?

No. Not tonight. We'd need more time than
you probably have.

Okay.

A minute later, Matías walks into the room wearing only a pair of thin pajama pants. He doesn't even glance toward the window. He simply sits on the loveseat that's on the far wall, giving me a frontal view.

He scoots down a little, legs spread wide, and he closes his eyes as his hand slips into his pants.

I swallow, attempting to get even closer.

His movements are slow at first, teasing. I can't see anything except the movement beneath the gray material, and yet it's the hottest fucking thing I've ever watched.

Matías swallows, his Adam's apple bobbing up and down. His teeth sink into his bottom lip as his hand moves a little faster.

God, please let me see it.

He releases a moan that barely reaches my ears. I lean in, desperate to hear everything.

A small wet spot appears on the light gray pants, and I lick my lips. God, I want to be in there. On my knees. Mouth open.

I put my hand down my sweats and wrap my fingers around my erection.

Matías lifts his hips, pushing the pants to his knees and revealing his perfect cock. He reaches into the small table drawer next to him and removes a bottle of lube.

Before he pours the liquid into his palm, he shoves his pants all the way down, kicking them off to the side. He's completely naked in front of me and my mouth salivates. I want to be on top of him, under him, in him. I don't care. I just want him. He's intoxicating.

The lube coats his fingers, and then he lifts one leg, planting his foot on the cushion, and begins to finger himself.

"Oh, fuck," I mutter to myself.

I can hear the wet sound of the lube as he works his middle finger into his ass, thrusting in and out. His body is like a work of art, carved to perfection, and on full display to me.

After a couple minutes, he takes more lube and begins stroking his erection while simultaneously finger fucking himself.

My entire body nearly bursts into flames. I'm so hot. I find myself matching his pace as I jerk my own dick. My free hand touches the window as I stare inside. If anybody saw me, they'd call the cops for sure, but luckily nobody lives behind him, and the trees block his neighbors on the side.

His moans and grunts sporadically drown out the slick sounds of the lube as he works himself closer to orgasm.

My hand grips my cock tighter, moving quickly up and down my shaft. My own heavy breaths and grunts probably filter into his office, but not once does he acknowledge that I'm here. And somehow that's even hotter.

"Oh, fuck," he moans, muscles flexing. "Oh. Ahh!"

His noises are sinful, taking me to the edge.

"Oh, god," we both murmur at the same time.

Matías cries out as his orgasm spills out of him. White lines and drops of cum land on his stomach and chest.

I push my pants down in the front with my left hand,

stroking vigorously with my right, and then I come on the side of his house and in his grass.

"Oh, fuck. Fuck," I say through gritted teeth.

My body twitches with every drop I spill, and when I open my eyes, I find Matías coming toward the window.

He's still naked and covered in cum, the evidence running down his abs in rivulets. His still hard cock points directly at me as he gets closer, and in a barely there whisper, he says, "Goodnight," and closes the window.

CHAPTER FORTY-SIX

MATÍAS

I MAKE a point to be purposefully late to the barbecue, only because I don't want to be the first guest to mingle with the married couple.

I come with a pack of soda and two bags of different types of chips. Martin, one of the neighbors I do know, shows up on the porch right after I ring the bell.

"Hey," he says with a friendly smile.

"Martin. Hi. How've you been?"

"Not too bad. You?"

"Pretty good," I answer with a smile.

Footsteps approach and the door begins to open.

"Yeah. You look good," Martin says, giving me a thorough once-over.

I turn my head and find Adrian there, and based on his expression, he overheard.

He quickly paints a smile on his face as he greets us.

"Hey, guys."

"Hey," I reply.

"Thanks for the invite," Martin says, holding up a plastic grocery bag. "I brought a few things."

"Come in. You can put everything in the kitchen."

Martin walks in first and instantly begins talking to someone else already in the house.

I meet Adrian's eyes as I step inside. "Hello. Sleep well?"

He smirks, cheeks blushing, but doesn't answer. Instead, he asks his own question. "Was Martin hitting on you?"

I smile back at him. "So, the kitchen?"

He makes a noise in his throat and closes the door. "Yeah."

Martin's talking to another man that I know I've seen several times, but whose name doesn't come to me. But besides them, there's nobody else in the house.

Adrian takes the bag of chips from me and puts them on the island in the middle of the kitchen, and I put the drinks next to some other ones that are displayed near the sink.

"I gotta get back to the grill," he says. "Greg might be burning my food. Y'all can come out back."

Through the sliding glass door, I see Charlotte talking to Diane, a woman I've talked to quite a bit. Pretty sure she's married to the guy Martin was talking to.

"Hey," Charlotte greets us with a wide smile. "Thanks for coming."

"Of course. Thanks for the invite," I say with a small nod.

They have a rectangular table on their porch, with a large umbrella open and sitting in the middle, blocking out the sun.

There's also a couple of chairs near a fire pit that's several feet past the main seating area, and while I'd much prefer to be as far away from the group as possible, I guess it would be weird for me to choose to sit out there.

"So, you guys all know each other, right?" Charlotte asks, gesturing between all of us, including a couple already sitting at the table.

Martin speaks up first. "I know this guy right here," he says, an arm going around my shoulder briefly. "And I know Greg and Diane, but I don't think I've met you two," he says to the couple at the table. "I'm Martin. I'm down at 479." He extends his hand.

"Carl," the man says. He gestures to the woman at his side. "My wife, Leslie."

Leslie shakes Martin's hand, a warm smile on her face. "Nice to meet you."

I lift a hand at the Black couple, who look to be about mid-forties. Carl has a salt and pepper beard and a bald head, while Leslie has chocolate brown curls, and a smattering of freckles on her cheeks.

"I'm Matías," I say.

They nod and smile, and I turn to Diane. "How are you?"

She grins. "I'm good. I missed you this morning."

I laugh. "I slept in for once. Sorry to miss our morning chat."

Diane smiles, the fine lines deepening around her mouth. "It's good to sleep in once in a while."

I met Diane almost five years ago, when I first moved into this neighborhood. She just turned forty-nine, because the last time I saw her, she mentioned it being the last year she can say she's in her forties.

On Saturdays, I'm usually out front doing yardwork or cleaning my car inside and out. She always stops by during her walks with her little Yorkshire terrier to talk to me, and we also run into each other on my evening jogs when she's once again out for a walk with her other dog, a long-haired chihuahua. She says they can't be walked together because they don't know how to act.

Adrian puts on some low music, and everyone starts talking about where they grew up, how long they've lived here, what they do for work, and general *get to know you* questions.

"The food will be done soon, guys," Adrian announces from the grill that sits a few feet from the table.

"It smells good," Diane says.

"Let's hope it tastes good," Adrian says with a laugh.

"I'm pretty talented on the grill," Carl announces. "Next time we can do it at my house."

"I'm always down for a good meal," Martin says, eyes sliding in my direction to give me another up and down.

I turn my gaze to find Adrian looking at Martin.

"So, how long have you two been married?" Diane asks Charlotte.

"Oh. Not too long. About two years."

"That's damn near still newlyweds," Diane's husband says. "We've been married for fifteen years. Makes me feel ancient."

Diane playfully smacks him. "Greg, it's been sixteen years."

"Oh." Greg laughs.

"Any plans for kids?" Diane questions.

Charlotte shifts, looking uncomfortable.

"Not sure," she says. "Haven't thought much about it."

"Well, you still have time. Or you can choose to never have them, like we did. Either way, as long as you're happy."

Charlotte flattens her lips into a tight smile. "Right. As long as we're happy."

"I don't think I ever want kids," Martin chimes in from my left. He takes a sip of his drink. "What about you?" he asks me.

"Maybe," I answer. "One day. Not for another five years or so," I say with a laugh. "Maybe longer."

Adrian turns to look at me; there's an expression on his face that I can't read.

"Are you married yet?" Leslie asks.

"No," I reply with a smile. "I guess I need to start there, but even then, the process of having babies would be different for me." Leslie's brows knit in confusion. "I'm gay," I tell her.

"Oh. I have a friend who's been a surrogate twice. The first pregnancy was for a gay couple, and they all still get together from time to time. She's been able to watch the baby grow up. That's definitely an option."

I nod. "Yeah. We'll see."

"Food's done," Adrian announces.

Everyone gets up and goes in and out of the house to load their plates with chips, hot dogs, and burgers, and to refill their cups.

We sit outside at the table, and Charlotte chooses to sit next to Diane and across from Leslie, and when I sit at the other end, Martin plops into the seat at my left. Adrian takes the one to my right.

For the next forty minutes or so, we all eat and talk—topics bouncing from one thing to the next, and plenty of cross conversations as well. It's clear there's some tension between Adrian and Charlotte. They hardly speak to each other, but they're putting on friendly faces for everyone else.

"Looks like we're the only single ones here," Martin says, nudging me with his elbow.

I incline my head. "Oh, yeah."

Adrian's talking to Greg, but I know he hears Martin, because his body goes stiff.

"I don't know about you," Martin continues, his voice quiet. "But I'd love to have dinner with you. Just us, you know."

I turn and look at him, trying to figure out how to respond.

"Oh, hey," Adrian announces loudly. "I have some corn hole boards. And I should also have this giant beer pong yard game. The buckets are large and you just set them in the grass. We don't have beer, but it could still be fun."

Charlotte looks annoyed but quickly hides it when a few people show interest.

"I'll go grab them. Can you help?" he asks me. "Might need to move a few boxes in the garage."

I stand and follow him inside. We end up in his garage where he digs into a box and pulls out a large drawstring bag.

"Okay, Martin's clearly hitting on you, and had I known he was harboring a crush, he wouldn't have been invited."

I laugh. "So this is your plan? College games in your backyard just to keep me from accepting his dinner invitation?"

"First of all, people of all ages love games. You and I were pretty good at beer pong back in the day. You could be my teammate again."

"Mm," I murmur, crossing my arms.

"What? Do you really want to date that guy?"

"No."

"Good. Grab a board, will you?" he says, gesturing to the wooden boards in the corner.

"When can you get away?" I ask him.

"What do you mean?"

I step forward, my hand on his hip as I lean in and lick his neck. "I mean, when." Kiss. "Can." Kiss. "You." Kiss. "Get away?" A final kiss on his chin.

"Oh."

"For a decent amount of time without any concern."

"Um. I don't know. I'll figure something out."

I step away. "Soon."

He nods, and I go and grab the corn hole boards.

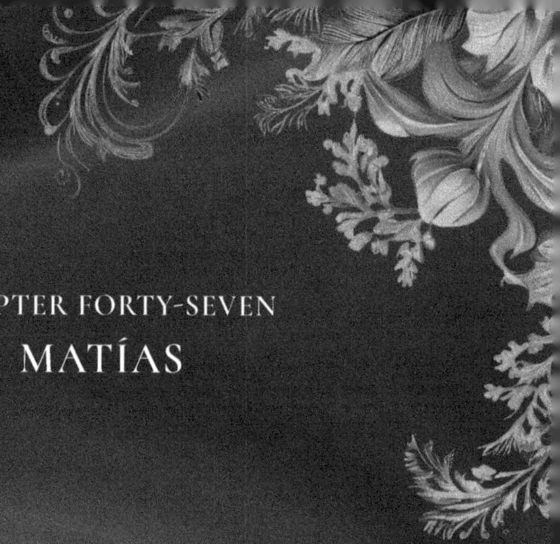

CHAPTER FORTY-SEVEN

MATÍAS

"Okay, we have to defend the buckets. Once it bounces, smack that shit away. Don't let them win."

Leslie and Carl laugh from the other side of their buckets.

"We're gonna win," Leslie says in a sing-song voice.

"Hey, Matías has good aim. He can win this for us."

"Oh, my god. Just throw the ball," Charlotte says.

"It's not even our turn," Adrian replies, neither of them actually looking at each other.

Charlotte waves him off then leans in to say something to Diane. They giggle.

"Anyway," Adrian says. "Okay, go ahead."

Leslie gets ready, bouncing the ball on the patio before it hits the edge of one bucket and falls to the side.

"Ha!" Adrian exclaims.

"Oh, shush," Leslie says with a laugh. "Come on, babe. You got this."

Carl tosses his ball over, but he also misses.

"All right, man. You can do it," Adrian says, touching his arm before snatching his hand back.

I aim and get it in one of the last two remaining cups.

"Yeah!" Adrian and I yell.

"Okay, okay. Just don't take your eye off the bucket," I tell him. "You got it."

"Booo!" Carl says from the other side.

The game quickly became competitive, and there's been a lot of friendly trash talk, but we have to win this.

"Keep our streak alive," I tell him.

"No pressure then," he says with a laugh, looking at me briefly.

I grin.

Adrian holds the ball, ready to throw it, and I hold my breath and watch as it leaves his hand, hits the edge, rolls along the side then falls inside.

"Fuck yeah!" Adrian yells, arms in the air. We do a double high five before he turns back to our opponents. "You can't beat us. Nobody can."

"Yeah, yeah," Carl says, waving his hand in the air. "We'll have a rematch soon."

Diane and Greg end up leaving first, then Leslie and Charlotte go inside, leaving me, Adrian, Carl, and Martin out here.

Martin's talking Carl's ear off about some car, so Adrian and I sit in the chairs that surround the fire pit.

"I guess tonight wasn't too bad," I say.

"Nah," he replies, shaking his head. "Less people than those college parties."

"Thank god."

He smiles. "This was fun. All things considered."

"Hmm." I lift my chin. "Yeah, something seems up."

He shrugs, but doesn't go into detail. Not sure I want details, so I leave it alone.

"I'll probably head out soon. I don't wanna be the last person here."

"Makes sense."

"How did you enjoy the show last night?" I ask, standing up.

He peers up at me. "Quite a lot. More than I thought I would."

"Did you make a mess in my backyard?"

Adrian bites his lip, a smile forming. "Maybe."

"Such a dirty boy."

His lips part as he sucks in a breath, then he lets out a throaty moan.

"I thought I heard something similar to that last night."

He stands up, putting his hands in his pockets. I glance around and notice the girls are still inside, and the guys are sitting at the table, their backs to us.

"It was the hottest fucking thing I've ever seen. Let alone been a part of."

I smirk. "I have another idea we'll have to try. Text me later?"

He nods.

Walking toward the guys, I say, "Well, I'm outta here. I'll see you two around, yeah?"

"Oh, yeah," Carl says. "We'll need a rematch of this damn game. I refuse to lose more than once."

I laugh. "Sounds good. Tell the ladies I said bye."

I walk across the yard and make my way into my house, grateful to have gotten through it with no issues, but desperate for alone time with him that's not at work.

Hopefully he can get away soon.

The thing about affairs is that nobody involved is ever truly happy. The person getting cheated on feels the absence of their partner. The person sleeping with that partner feels like they're not getting enough time. And the person doing the cheating has to feel the guilt and stress of trying to get away with it.

It's an ugly situation for everyone, and yet, it doesn't stop people from doing it. Selfishness overpowers everything, and I'm not afraid to admit that I'm selfish enough to keep this up —because he is *mine*. He always has been. She's just been borrowing him.

CHAPTER FORTY-EIGHT
ADRIAN

CHARLOTTE and I haven't revisited our fight. After the barbecue, we didn't speak to each other. She went upstairs while I cleaned up, and when I woke up the next morning, she was gone. She came home briefly in the afternoon just to leave again. It was nearly one in the morning when she walked back inside.

She's still asleep when I get up for work this morning, and I know we'll need to sit down and talk soon. Maybe now's the best time, if there is such a thing. I don't want to wait until we're in a happier situation just to drop this bomb.

Throughout the work day, I'm distracted. I go over all possible outcomes and scenarios for when I tell Charlotte the truth. I debate on whether I should tell her everything, but decide it's probably best if I don't. Knowing I've been sleeping with our neighbor who is also my boss isn't going to help. She'll already need to maneuver through the minefield of my coming out, telling her I want a divorce, and possibly having to move back to Chicago. Dropping another bomb would be too much. Plus, I don't want Matías caught up in this. She'll tell her dad, who will in turn tell mine, and it'll become too much to deal with.

At three o'clock, I have a meeting with my team, so I put everything aside and focus on my job. At four, we leave the conference room to go back to our desks, and I spot Matías for the first time today. Based on his expression, it seems like he's had a stressful day. He rubs his forehead like he's trying to massage a headache away. His eyes meet mine as he's about to turn off to go to his office, and he gives me a small grin.

I smile back but let him get to what he was doing.

In my office, I have a phone call with a client, send out a half dozen emails, and then send one more to each member on my team regarding our meeting today.

It's after five when there's a knock on my door.

"Come in."

It creaks open, and Matías fills the doorway. "Hey."

I stop typing and lean back in my chair. "Hey."

There are still people in the cubicles behind him, their voices filtering into my office. "It's been quite the day," he says.

I nod. "Yeah. Pretty busy."

He sighs. "I could use a drink. Do you want to get one with me?"

"Yeah. Definitely. I just need to finish this. Give me fifteen minutes or so."

"I'll meet you in the parking lot."

"Okay."

With a brief smile, he nods and spins around to leave.

I don't think to tell Charlotte I'll be late. For one, we're still not talking, and based on her disappearing act yesterday, she doesn't seem to think we need to inform each other about our whereabouts. Plus, my job sometimes has me home late anyway. It wouldn't be abnormal.

Twenty minutes later, I meet him at his car.

"So, where are we going?" I ask.

"At first, I was thinking about this place called Ginny's, but it's about thirty minutes from where we live, and if we're gonna drink, then we'll only be able to drink one before we have to sober up to drive home."

I smirk. "Nice to know you're still abiding by those rules."

"Laws," he amends with a grin. "Yes. I'm still against drunk driving, as I'd wish everyone would be, but anyway." He sighs. "This is where you being my neighbor is a problem. I was going to invite you to my house. For a drink or two," he says with a glint in his eye.

"For a drink."

"Right, but, well, you live next door, and I suppose your car being home and you not being there would be an issue."

"Hmm." After a couple minutes, I shrug. "Let's go. It'll be fine."

He raises his brows. "Yeah?"

"Yeah," I say with a nod. "I'll see you in a little bit."

"Okay."

He climbs into his car and takes off, and I follow behind just a couple minutes later.

The only good thing about being in the closet, is that there's no way she'd suspect anything weird if I say I'm going to my boss's house. Or even if I just said I'd be at the neighbor's.

When I pull into the driveway, I lock the car and walk through my front door. I hang the keys on the hook nearby before jogging upstairs.

Charlotte isn't home. Considering I had the car all day, that's interesting.

However, it works out for me now. I head back downstairs and walk outside and across the yard.

I ring Matías's doorbell and he opens it just a few seconds later.

"All good?" he asks as he takes a step back.

"She's not home."

He inclines his head slightly, but doesn't say anything else.

We both remove our shoes and suit jackets, while Matías removes the button-up shirt as well.

"I have a little bar over here," he says, walking into his living room.

I follow behind, noting the warm tones in his furniture and decor. Brown curtains that are just a shade darker than the couch. Brown and beige pillows are placed along the cushions and beige, wooden tables hold candles and small decor items. There's a row of three pictures behind his couch that look like landscape photos taken in the fall.

"Nice place," I tell him as he opens a cabinet at a wooden bar against the wall.

"Thank you."

I dig my toes into the soft, white rug under my feet. "So, whatcha got over here?"

I make my way to his side, and he pulls two glasses from the bottom shelf, handing one to me. In a little shelf on the door, he points to a few bottles of liquor—gin, whiskey, and vodka.

"I also have wine."

I shake my head. "Whiskey is fine."

He pours mine first, handing it to me. "I know you're not gonna drink it straight. Give me a sec and I'll grab something."

I laugh. "I suppose I'm mostly a beer guy, but I don't

drink a whole lot these days, so plain whiskey is a little scary."

We go into his kitchen where he pulls a can of Coke out of the fridge. "This good?"

"Yeah." I take the can and pop the top, pouring some into my glass.

He holds his glass up and I clink mine against it. We take a sip before I put it down on the counter and step toward him.

"I know you invited me over for a drink or two." I put my hands on his hips. "But I think I remember you saying you had an idea for later."

Matías sets his drink down. "Yes, but that's a different place. Hopefully you can get away on a weekend night."

"Okay, well, I'm intrigued. Now, are you gonna kiss me?"

He smirks before leaning in and touching his lips to mine. One of his hands is on my lower back while the other is at my neck. His tongue slides into my mouth, and my hand moves to his ass.

Our kissing escalates to lots of touching and grinding. He turns and pushes me against the counter, kissing along my jaw.

"I really did plan to let you have a drink or two," he murmurs between kisses.

"Mmhmm," I say, my fingers drawing down his back. "We still can."

"I was going to talk to you, too," he says before biting into my neck.

I gasp and let out a shuddering breath. "Yeah, we can. Later."

"Okay then. Let's go upstairs."

CHAPTER FORTY-NINE
MATÍAS

ADRIAN GOES TO THE WINDOW, looking out between the slats of the blinds.

"Your room faces my house."

"It does."

"That's my bathroom window."

"Is it?" I question, coming up behind him.

"Yeah. The bathroom connected to my room."

My hands travel down his torso until I get to his belt. I undo it along with the pants, shoving my hand inside.

"Next time you shower, you could let me know. I'll watch you from here."

"You'll only see my upper body," he says, leaning into me.

"Then you can Facetime me and put your phone where I can see you."

"You're a perv."

"I am."

"Mm." He nuzzles his head into my neck. "I love it."

"Maybe *you're* a perv."

He chuckles. "Maybe."

I kiss the side of his head before I disentangle myself and step to the side. "I'll be right back."

"Okay."

I disappear into my bathroom and get cleaned up, prepared to have the tables turned today. I remove everything but my underwear before I walk back into the bedroom where Adrian's draping his clothing over the upholstered, barrel shaped accent chair near the window.

Walking straight up to him, I hand him a bottle of lube and say, "I want you to fuck me."

He takes it, looking into my eyes. His tongue swipes over his bottom lip as he gives me one nod. "Yes. Fuck yes."

Adrian yanks me into him, his mouth devouring mine in a viscous kiss.

"God, I've been waiting to feel you again. To feel how you clench around me," he says through heavy breaths.

"Fuck," I groan.

"You have no idea how often I thought about this. How frequently my memories of us would pop into my head."

"Well, you don't have to think about it anymore. You can do it. Fuck me, Adrian. Remind me that I'm yours."

He makes a noise low in his throat. "You are."

"Remind me. Claim me." I let my tongue dance across his bottom lip. Lowering my voice, I say, "Hard. Fast. Deep. Show me how much you missed being inside me."

Once again he smashes his lips against mine, shoving my boxer-briefs down at the same time. He pulls away, turning me toward the chair and pushing me until I'm forced to kneel on the cushion.

I spread my legs as far as they can go, my hands gripping the back of the seat as he buries his face between my cheeks.

"Oh, god," I cry out, his tongue gliding over my hole.

He laps at me like I'm a puddle of water and he's dying of thirst. His hands squeeze my ass as he hungrily devours me.

I pant and moan, begging for more, and he finally relents.

Easing away, he caresses my ass, and then I hear the cap of the lube pop open. A few seconds later, slick fingers begin pressing against my entrance.

I angle my head over my shoulder. "Yes, give it to me."

His free hand traces a line down my spine. "Look at you. How did I go so long without having this? Without being able to see you like this anytime I wanted?"

I push back a little, his fingers sliding in deeper. He rotates them inside me.

"God," I growl. "Fuck me, Adrian. I can't take it anymore."

His fingers curl up. "I want you to be ready for me," he says.

"I am."

"You think you are," he says, tone deep and low. "But I'm going to fuck you with eight years of passion, desire, and need. I'm gonna fuck you with everything that I am."

"Oh, yeah," I moan.

"Do you have a condom?"

"In my nightstand."

He takes several more minutes to stretch me and get my body prepared for him, and then he walks away to get the condom.

Every second feels like a minute, and I'm afraid I might combust if he doesn't fuck me soon. The tear of the wrapper sends chills down my spine. The cap of the lube opening has my toes curling. Feeling his fingers at my entrance has me sucking in a breath.

When his cock finally prods at my hole, I tighten my grip on the chair, arch my back even more, and try to remember to keep breathing.

When he starts pushing in, he groans. He slips past the ring of muscle and I exhale just as he sucks in a shuddering breath.

"So tight," he says. "So fucking tight."

Adrian begins slow, keeping himself tame as I adjust to the size of him, but his fingers dig into my skin as he holds me firm around the waist.

He pulls almost completely out before thrusting in with a little more force.

"Yes!" I cry.

It spurs him on. He draws back again, repeating the long and slow strokes until he can't hold back any longer.

His hips move faster, his cock going deep inside me, stretching me open. I haven't been with anyone like this in I don't know how long. While the sensation isn't brand new, it's not what I've been used to, and I almost forgot how good it can be.

Maybe it's just because it's him.

"Matías," he grunts. "Oh, my god."

"You feel so good," I tell him.

"Yeah?" One hand slides up my back, gripping my shoulder.

I release a moan as he moves. "Yeah," I say on a breath. "God, yes."

"I never want to stop," he says. "I want to be inside you forever."

"Yes, yes," I chant, wanting nothing more than for this to never end.

He slows his movements, holding my ass cheeks apart as he pulls out. I clench around him, drawing him back in slightly.

Adrian moans. "Do it again."

I listen, giving him what he wants.

"Fuck." The word is drawn out, husky and dripping with lust. "I've always loved the way you take me."

"And I've missed the way you fuck me."

Another groan of appreciation leaves his throat. He pushes at my right leg, so I pull it in, and his foot comes to rest on the cushion next to it. The front of his body leans over the back of mine, one arm snaking around my middle as he rocks into me.

"Tell me I'm the best you've ever had. Tell me nobody else made you feel the way I do."

He's not seeking the truth. He wants to hear what he wants to hear.

"You're the best," I say between grunts as he thrusts. "Only you." I moan. "Only you make me feel this way."

But it's one hundred percent the truth, and he probably doesn't even believe it, because he's never understood just how much he means to me. How much he's always meant and will always mean.

"God, Matías," he groans. "I...I...This is...Fuck!"

He never finishes the thought. He fucks harder and deeper.

"You're mine," he says, but not with conviction. "You're mine. Mine. God, tell me you're mine."

I'm nearly over the back of the chair, his force pushing my body closer and closer to the window. I put my hand on the window seal to keep my head from slamming against the blinds.

"Yes," I cry. "Yours. I'm yours, Adrian. I've always been yours."

He makes a deep, throaty noise, his body shifting slightly. His hands caress my ass. "Mine." They curve around my hips and travel down the fronts of my thighs. "Mine." One hand touches my cock, fingers wrapping around it. "Mine."

"Fuck. Yes. God. Please," I beg.

He strokes me, smearing my pre-cum around my head. "God, you're so hard."

"For you," I moan. "You make me so hard."

Adrian releases me, but only to grab my waist and fuck me relentlessly. I replace his hand with my own, my body bent over the chair as he gives me everything he has.

His words are nonsensical. They don't form cohesive sentences, but it wouldn't matter if he was reciting poetry. I'm unable to focus on anything but my impending orgasm. It's getting closer and closer.

I beg for more and more. I want it deeper. I want it harder. I want to feel him after he leaves. I want the memory of him to stay with me while he's over there with her. I want to be able to convince myself that it's me that he wants.

"Matías," he moans, his breaths short and staccato. "Matías. Oh, god."

"Yes, yes," I cry, my fist flying up and down my shaft. "Come inside me. Give it to me, Adrian."

"Oh shit," he cries.

At the first twitch of his cock, my orgasm explodes out of me. "Fuck! Oh, god. I'm coming."

His dick throbs and releases inside me as I bring myself to completion, completely unaware or concerned about where it's going.

I drop my head onto my forearm that's bent across the back of the chair, sweat dripping down the sides of my face as my cock drips onto the cushion below me.

Adrian's body collapses on top of mine, breathing into my back before planting a few kisses there.

I lift my head slightly and catch sight of a car pulling into the driveway of their house. He pulls out slowly, unaware.

He lets out a breath, his fingers trailing over the curve of my ass.

I stand, my legs feeling boneless as I do.

I spot his wife exit the car, and when the door closes, it gets his attention too.

"Oh, shit," he murmurs, stepping to the side.

"I don't think she can see inside," I say, but I move away as well.

He looks at me, searching my expression to see if seeing her has ruined this moment. At least that's what I'm thinking. Has this amazing experience just been tainted by the arrival of his wife?

Adrian steps forward, hand cradling my face before his lips press a soft kiss to mine. He eases away, but continues to stare at me. There's something in his expression. Words left unsaid, resting on his tongue. He gives me a small smile instead before turning to head to the bathroom.

CHAPTER FIFTY

ADRIAN

We realized after we cleaned up that Matías came on my pants, so we took some time to clean it up as best we could before getting dressed and heading downstairs.

I look at our abandoned glasses. "I guess we'll need to try the whole drink thing another time," I say.

His lips twitch. "I'm not mad about how it ended up."

"Me neither." I step closer and brace him between my arms as he leans against the kitchen counter. "I wish I didn't have to leave."

He starts to shake his head, his lips flattened into a line. "You don't have to say it."

"I know, but I really want to be here with you."

He nods once. "I'll see you tomorrow?"

"I guess I have to go to work."

He smiles. "You most certainly do. Unless you want to be fired."

I kiss his cheek, then the corner of his mouth. "What if I suck up to my boss?"

"You can try."

I chuckle, my hand grabbing his. I intertwine our fingers,

looking at the connection before I meet his gaze again. Bringing his knuckles to my lips, I plant a kiss on them.

He pulls my hand to his mouth and does the same.

"I still want to talk to you."

My brows knit slightly. "Should I be worried?"

"No, but it's a conversation we should have."

"Do you want to tell me now?"

He shakes his head. "I'm sure you need to get home."

I nod once. "I do. I need to…I think it's time to talk to her."

He doesn't look happy or relieved. He doesn't show almost any emotion. Then I realize he probably doesn't believe anything will come of it. He doesn't have any hope.

Matías barely dips his chin in acknowledgement. "We'll talk tomorrow."

I lean in to give him another kiss, and then I make my way to the living room where I put on my suit jacket and shoes.

Reaching for his hand, I give it a squeeze before kissing him one last time. "See you."

"Don't forget to call me when you shower," he says with a wink.

I laugh before I open the door and walk out into the night air. I fight the euphoric, post-coital smile on my face as I cross his driveway and into my yard.

Steeling myself, I take a breath and twist the knob, only to find it locked.

I sigh and knock, waiting to hear her steps come closer. When several seconds go by, I knock even louder. Several more seconds pass, and I'm about to walk around to the back, but then I hear footsteps heading toward me.

The door opens, and instead of being met by the face of my wife, I'm met by the stern face of my father.

"Adrian," he says, jaw clenching. "Nice of you to join us."

Though I'm thirty, and at the door to a house I bought, I'm suddenly feeling like a child caught sneaking back into the house by his parents. My father's always had that ability. The one that makes you feel like a kid even after you've become an adult. He's a formidable man, and he knows it and takes pride in knowing people fear him.

I stare at him as he blocks the doorway. "Am I allowed in my own home?" I question, taking a step forward. "Why are you here?"

He finally steps back. "I'm here because apparently you are incapable of answering your phone when I call. I'm here because we need to talk."

"Where's Charlotte?" I question once I'm in the living room.

"In her room," he says with a slight shrug, like he isn't sure.

"I think driving out here was a little unnecessary."

"Oh, I didn't drive. I flew."

I roll my eyes as I make my way to the kitchen. The flight is an hour and half. Even more unnecessary when the drive is only four hours, but of course my father would rather fly.

He follows me to the kitchen, his dress shoes clicking across the floor. He's dressed in a suit, like he hopped on a plane right after a business meeting. I'm actually not sure I've ever seen my father dressed casually.

"Does she know," he says in a quiet but firm voice.

"Know what?" I question, opening the fridge.

"Based on my conversation with her, I can tell things between you two aren't going too well. She seems very upset. Does she know?"

I slam it closed and look at him. "Know. What?" I ask through gritted teeth.

"That you're fucking your boss," he says with barely disguised disgust.

His words launch at me, and I blanch, surprised even though the statement is true. Luckily, I can hear the water running upstairs and know Charlotte has just gotten in the shower. I still keep my voice down.

"What are you talking about?"

My heart gallops in my chest and I'm afraid that not only can he hear it, but if he looks close enough, he'll see it threatening to burst through my skin. He can't actually know. He's only guessing. Assuming. And it pisses me off that he's right.

He crosses his arms over his chest. "You move out here with some line about needing a new start. Wanting to get out from under me and find your own path, only to run straight to that boy and get under him."

I bite down on my teeth, grinding them as I try to figure out what to say first.

"I didn't know he worked there until I got here."

"Sure." He uncrosses his arms and places one hand on the edge of the counter. "But you do find yourself *under* him."

I shoot him a look and shake my head. "This conversation is ridiculous."

"It is," he agrees. "I hate that I can't trust my son to move his wife to a new town and NOT start fucking some boy. I thought you outgrew this. I thought you made the decision to work for me—to one day run the company. I thought you put these ridiculous thoughts out of your head and gained some sense. But no. You sneak off next door to fuck the same boy you—"

"He's not a fucking boy!" I shout, louder than I meant to.

Dad jolts back slightly, eyebrows up before his face settles into a sneer. "I knew it."

I shake my head, remembering he's aware Matías is my

neighbor thanks to a conversation with Charlotte. "I don't want to run your company. I'm staying here."

"Your wife is still fragile. She looked ready to break the minute she saw me. Not only are you cheating on her, but you're cheating on her with a...*man*." He looks me up and down like I'm trash. "You're going to send her into a tailspin. She'll be back to her old ways in no time. You can't move her away from her family and everything she knows and then abandon her this way. Are you only concerned about yourself?"

I cross my arms. "I didn't force her to come. She chose to follow me here."

"She's your wife. Of course she came with you."

"And funny you're talking about only being concerned with myself. Since when have you ever been concerned with anyone but yourself? You threatening to disown me was for who? You said I wouldn't have a family, a job, a future if I didn't do exactly what *you* wanted me to do. You said I needed to marry her so she could have a strong and stable figure in her life. You wanted me to be the father of a child that wasn't mine. You and David forced us together in some marriage-of-convenience situation, except it was only for your convenience. So she wouldn't embarrass him or bring negative press to your business dealings. I've been *anything* but selfish. Everything I've done in life has been to appease you! And now her. Everybody needs something from me, but what about what I need? Huh?"

If anything, he looks slightly surprised by my outburst, but not necessarily moved. Which isn't surprising.

"What you *need* is to be a man and step up to the plate. What you're doing isn't any different from any other man out there."

"That's what you have with Mom? You're with her

because once upon a time your father and her father forced you together? Or were you allowed to meet and fall in love with her on your own accord?"

I know it's the latter. I've heard the story about them meeting in college. Love at first sight according to Mom.

He doesn't reply to my question.

"What's your plan here, Adrian? You're gonna have this little thing on the side forever? Stay married and continue fucking the neighbor? Wait until your wife finds out? Because trust me, son, they always do. And then what?"

I rub my eyes and then sigh. "Maybe I'll do what I've been wanting to do since I was in college."

His expression hardens even more, eyes narrowing. "Which would be?"

"Whatever I want."

His nostrils flare. "We don't get to do whatever we want in life. We do what is needed."

"I feel sorry for you then. You're clearly living a life you never wanted." I cross one foot over the other as I lean into the corner of the countertops.

"I've worked very hard for the life I have, for the life I gave to you and your sister. And now you want me to hand it over to someone who doesn't share my blood?"

"If you spent a little more time being a better father rather than being a businessman, then maybe I wouldn't have minded working with you. But tell me, do you really think I'd want to work for or with someone who hates the person that I am? Who says vile things to me? I should want to work for someone who threatens me because they can? Who uses their power and authority to scare me into doing things?"

He's quiet for a few seconds. "If you think you'll always work for someone who is going to cater to your feelings, then you're wrong. Every boss you have will be an asshole. Every supervisor has to use their authority to keep people in line."

I give him a small grin. "See, that's the problem. You're not my boss. Or my supervisor. You're my father. I only ever wanted you to be my dad—someone I could go to for advice and support. Someone I could be honest with. Vulnerable even. But you don't allow that. I've never felt comfortable going to you for anything, and that's not my problem. It's yours."

The shower cuts off upstairs, and both of us glance up when we hear the floor creak with her footsteps.

"So, you're telling me this...thing. This—" He waves his hand in the air. "You're telling me you have no interest in your wife."

He says the last part in a quieter tone, and somehow it feels like he's trying to protect my secret.

I stare at him, knowing this is just part of the journey I have to take. "You've always known the truth. Haven't you? You hoped you were wrong. You hoped I'd change. Or keep up with the lie. But you've always known."

He takes a deep breath and sighs, pressing his forefinger and thumb into his eyebrows, like I've just given him a migraine.

"You can't tell her." He meets my gaze and repeats it. "You can't tell her. She won't be able to handle it."

"She'll be fine. She has you on her side, apparently. And her own father. She can go home, and you two can watch over her. That's your priority, right?"

He opens his mouth, but a door opens upstairs.

"How long are you in town for?" I ask.

"Not long. I have work to do."

I nod my head. "Did you rent a car?"

Charlotte emerges from around the corner, wearing pajamas. "I got an Uber and picked him up from the airport."

"I'm happy you both arranged this meeting without letting me know," I say with a tight smile. "I'll take you to a hotel," I tell him, pushing away from the counter and heading to the front door.

"Adrian," Charlotte says with surprise. "He can stay here." She looks at my dad. "You can stay here. We have a—"

"We have an air mattress that's still in a box in the garage," I say, cutting her off. "And a spare room that doesn't even have curtains up yet. He's not staying there."

My dad gives her a thin-lipped smile. "I'll stay in a hotel."

"Will you be coming by tomorrow? I can make lunch or maybe we can go out."

My father smiles again, this time a little more genuine. "I'll let you know. I may have to fly out in the evening, but I could probably do lunch."

She nods once. "Okay. Yeah, let me know." Her eyes slide to my face, but she doesn't say anything, only turns away.

I grab the keys and walk out the door.

CHAPTER FIFTY-ONE
ADRIAN

"She's a good woman," Dad says when we're in the car.

"She is. Don't you think she deserves better?"

"Better than you?"

I nod, backing into the street. "Better than someone who is incapable of loving her the way she should be loved."

"I'm sure you love her," he says, looking out his window.

"Not in a way you should love your spouse. I'll never be what she wants, just like she can never be what I want."

"And what you want is that *man*?"

He manages to make the word *man* sound like a slur.

"Dad," I say with a sigh.

"I'm truly asking. You said you wanted to be able to talk to me and be honest. Well, it's been a long time coming. So let's talk. You want to leave your wife and be with a kid you knew in college? Is that the only..." He hesitates, stumbling over his words. "The only...uhh...experience you've had?"

"If we're gonna talk about this, it's going to be about me and not about him or anyone else. What I want is to be who I am and have the freedom to make decisions for me, whatever those might be. I don't want to be afraid of your reactions anymore, because you know what? This is already a scary thing for me. But having your words in the back of my head, your threats and your disgust...that lives with me and I'm tired of it. I'm an adult, and you have to get to the point where you understand that your children become their own people with their own lives and it has nothing to do with you."

I stop talking when we get to a light, expecting him to say something, but he doesn't. We go through two more lights before he says anything.

"I think we're due for a long talk. Maybe many. But I'm gonna say this for now," he states as I pull into a hotel parking lot. "If you're telling me you're gay and that you're going to break apart your family, then I want you to be sure about what you're doing. You were with this man in school—something I chalked up to experimentation and messing around. And if he has been the only person you've had this... experience with, then I'd say you need to get some more experience under your belt. You say you're attracted to men, and he's a man, but he's not the *only* man. You can't throw away everything to be with the only man you've ever been with. He holds memories. First times, I imagine. It's special for most people, but firsts don't equate to forevers. It hardly ever works out that way. I'd just think about it, if I were you."

I'm taken aback by his response. My brain is working overtime to filter through his words to find the cruelty I'm used to, and then he opens the door.

I look over at him, but he's not looking at me. He gets out, closes the door, and gives it a couple pats before walking to the front of the hotel.

Instead of going straight home, I drive around for a little while.

Technically, I just came out to my father. I didn't say the

words, but I didn't have to. Like I told him, he always knew. The truth has always been between us.

He may not like it, and may not understand, but it's not for him to do either of those things.

His words about Charlotte not being able to handle this confession swirl around in my head, and I suppose the fear of sending her into a spiral has always lived within me. But does that mean I live a lie forever? She deserves better. We both do.

When I get home, she's asleep, so I pull my blankets and pillow out of the closet and lie on the couch. Sleep doesn't come easy, but I eventually close my eyes so I can end the day.

In the morning, I only go into the room to grab my clothes. She doesn't stir as I open and close the closet. I shower in the bathroom in the hall, get dressed, and then make my way to the car.

I greet a few people on my way to my office, but as soon as I'm at my desk, I'm bombarded with calls and emails. Work is demanding, but it keeps me from daydreaming about other things.

Matías is absent from the office for most of the morning. A meeting I have runs a little late, cutting into my normal lunch time, but when I make my way back to my office, I stop in my tracks when I see my father.

He's near the elevators, his phone in hand.

"What are you doing here?" I ask when I approach.

He looks up, his brown eyes meeting mine with a hint of surprise in them. "Will you be able to make it to lunch with Charlotte and I?"

My brows furrow. Is he serious? "I didn't think I was invited."

He pockets his phone. "Well, you are."

"And what's supposed to be discussed at this lunch?" I question, looking around.

"Nothing. Anything." He gives a nod and tight-lipped smile to someone who stops to wait for the elevator. "I'm leaving afterward."

I take a couple steps away, trying to get to a spot in the hall that's away from all the foot traffic. He follows.

"Are you planning on telling David?" I ask in a quiet voice.

"I think if you're going to go through with this, then you need to tell Charlotte before her father finds out. Don't you think?"

Once again, it feels like he's taking my side, which doesn't seem right. I don't trust it.

"Are you okay with...this?"

He sets his jaw. "No. But what can I do at this point?"

I want to ask him what his problem is. Is it with gay people in general? Is it simply because I'm gay? Is it because of his business and legacy that he keeps going on about? But now's not the place to get into that.

"Well, you tried your best," I say with a smile that holds zero amusement.

His eyes find something over my shoulder that steals his attention, but I continue to watch him. His hair is more gray than brown these days, but it's the only thing that really shows his age. While he has some lines and wrinkles, they're not too deep. He still takes really good care of himself—the picture of health. He'll be around a while, and running his company for at least another ten years. He has time to find someone else to take over. He's got capable employees. I spent many years there, and I'm probably not even the most qualified person.

His expression changes slightly, so I turn to find what he's looking at. I step back. It's Matías.

He spots us, his steps slowing as his eyes bounce between my father and me.

"Mr. Cruz," my father says, stealing my breath as I look at him.

I look back at Matías who simply gives a courtesy nod.

"I was wondering if it was possible that you allow my son a longer lunch today so he can eat with me and his wife?"

His tone is polite if not robotic. But the last two words have a bite.

Matías glances at me then nods to my father. "Of course. Enjoy your lunch."

He walks away, and I stare at my father with what has to be a dumbfounded look on my face.

"What?" he questions.

I sigh and shake my head. "Nothing. I'll be right back."

Back in my office, I grab my cell and send a message to Matías.

> Hey. Sorry about that. I wasn't expecting him to be here today. I didn't even know he was in town until last night. It's a whole long story that I'll explain later. But I'll be back as soon as I can.

I pocket the phone, go back out to find my dad, and ride the elevator down with him. He offers to drive; he apparently rented a car sometime this morning.

He types an address into the GPS and begins the drive to the restaurant in silence. After a few minutes, I say something I probably shouldn't. But I don't care.

"Matías is someone you'd really like and respect. If you

met him in any other capacity, I think you'd appreciate him as a person. He has a good head on his shoulders. He's smart and cares a lot about his work."

Dad's quiet for a little bit. "Yes, that's unfortunate then. Though I don't know if I'd agree, because someone who cares about work and has a good head on their shoulders probably wouldn't have an affair with their married co-worker."

I sigh and look out the window.

We don't speak again until we're at the restaurant, sitting with Charlotte at a round table.

She looks a little surprised to see me, but we don't greet each other. I just sit down and wait for the waiter to arrive.

After we place our drink orders, my father looks at Charlotte. "How do you like the area? Do you miss Chicago yet?"

She smiles a little, eyes flickering in my direction before answering. "I do miss Chicago. It's a bit smaller here. Not what I'm used to, but you know, it's fine."

My father nods. "You could come visit." A quick look at me. "You both could. It's not too far away."

"Yeah, I was thinking about going back for my father's birthday. I know he likes to have these big extravagant parties."

"And he's turning sixty, so it'll be extra big," my dad says with a small laugh. "Have you talked to your mother?"

I look over the menu as they have their conversation, wondering why the hell I was invited in the first place.

"Yeah. I guess she's been busy redecorating their new place."

"Oh yeah. Her and Suzie may have found a new hobby," my father says, talking about my mom. "She's already talked about wanting to re-do our guest room."

"What's her plan?" Charlotte asks.

"Oh, I don't know. She has her own plans. I nod and agree, and she's happy."

Charlotte laughs. "You guys are so great together." A pause. "I guess some people are just meant to be. Soulmates. Do you believe in that?"

I fight to keep from looking over my menu. I let out a soft sigh and pretend to read some more.

My dad clears his throat. "I believe in soulmates," he says, surprising me. "But I believe there are different types. Most people think a soulmate is the one and only person you're meant to be with forever. I think you can have a platonic soulmate. I think you can have a romantic one. I think you can even have more than one."

I finally lower my menu, watching my father with confusion on my face. I've never heard him talk about relationships at all.

"More than one? Doesn't that defeat the purpose of a soulmate?" Charlotte asks.

"No. Not to me, anyway. Sometimes people come into your life and change it in a way that alters your path, your outlook, or fixes a part of you. That doesn't mean you have to be with them forever. They served their purpose."

I swallow, hanging on his every word.

"But Suzie...she's your soulmate, right? Your forever."

My father looks at her, but I see his eyes shift slightly in my direction, like he's just now aware that I'm here.

"She's my forever, yes. But she wasn't my first soulmate. She wasn't my first love, either. A series of events led me to her."

This is news to me. Mom has always talked about their relationship with this fairytale haze over it. They met in college—a meet-cute in the quad due to having mutual friends. They had their first date two days later, and were in love and together from then on. They never spoke of other relationships.

The table goes quiet, and then the waiter appears. Conversation shifts into non-important things. My dad tries to pull me in with questions about work, but I answer only what he asks. I'm too focused on what he said earlier. Were his statements for Charlotte or for me? It sort of felt like both.

I was here for her to help her in her journey, but not necessarily meant for forever. Or is he saying that Matías was part of a series of events in my own journey.

After quickly eating, I look at my watch. "I need to get back to work. I have another meeting soon."

"Oh. I can take you back," Dad says.

"It's fine. We don't even have the check yet." I pull out my wallet.

Dad raises his hand. "I got it."

"Thanks. I'm gonna grab an Uber. I'll see you later," I say, looking at Charlotte. I turn my attention to my dad. "Hope you have a good trip back. I'll see you...sometime, I guess."

He nods and I just put my hand on his shoulder before I leave.

Outside, after I order a car, I check my text thread with Matías and find he hasn't replied to my last message.

Once I'm on my floor, I go to his office and knock.

"He's not here," Lucy says from behind me. "Just left a little bit ago."

"Oh. Okay," I say. "I'll just send him an email."

Behind my desk, I pull out my phone again.

Hey. I want to talk to you. Are you coming back to the office today?

. . .

I wait ten minutes before I start focusing on work. I go the rest of the work day without a reply and without seeing him again.

In my car, before I head home, I try again.

Matías. What's going on?

A few minutes later, my phone vibrates. I'm already driving, but I chance a glance at it anyway.

I'm guessing your father didn't tell you.

My heart plummets. What did my dad do?

CHAPTER FIFTY-TWO

MATÍAS

Ten minutes later, there's a knock on my door. When I open it up, I'm met with the concerned face of Adrian.

"What did he do? What happened?"

"Do you want to come in?"

He strides through, going into the living room where he stands, waiting for me.

"What's going on?"

I sigh, take a sip of the drink in my hand, and then go sit on the couch. "Your father came to visit me this morning. In my office. He told me he knew what we were doing. He said he could go to my boss and get me fired for inappropriate conduct. He said I was taking advantage of you."

"What the—" He runs his hands through his hair, staring at me in disbelief.

"He then said that if I cared about you, I'd leave you alone until you came to a decision about what you wanted your future to look like."

"This has nothing to do with him!" he shouts. "And you're taking advantage of me? How?"

"Adrian," I tell him calmly. "Come sit."

I put my glass on the table and shift to face him as he drops to the cushion next to me.

"Please don't tell me he's scared you with his threats."

"He's right. It is inappropriate. I could get in trouble if anyone were to find out. We would have to disclose our relationship to HR, and even then, I don't know how everyone would feel."

"But he—"

I cut him off by lifting my hand. "Besides that, I understand the other part of what he was saying."

"You *understand* him?"

"Hold on," I say in a gentle tone. "He definitely seems angry. I don't think we ever expected he'd be happy about this, but based on what he said, it seems like you two had a discussion."

"Well, yeah. Even today at lunch, he was saying these confusing things. I don't know if he's on my side or not. He knows, Matías. I never confessed to having an affair with you, but he knows. He's also aware that I don't want to stay with Charlotte. He tells me he won't tell anyone. He says I need to be sure."

I nod. "His concern is that you're throwing everything away for me—the same guy from college. The *only* guy you've ever been with. He doesn't think you have enough experience to know for sure."

"That's ridiculous."

When I don't say anything right away, he stares at me.

"It's ridiculous, Matías. You know that, right?"

"I've had years of experience, Adrian. I've had terrible experiences, great experiences, and mediocre ones. I've met different types of men. I've learned a lot about myself through each one of them. There's been many lessons throughout time, and you've not had any."

"Don't," he starts.

"I love that I'm your first. That I've been your only. Believe me when I say I want it to be that way forever. But—"

He stands. "No. I'm not listening to this. Are you serious right now? Now you're telling me that I need to go date and sleep around with more men? It's the only way I'll know I'm gay?"

"No, I'm not saying that. I know you're gay. You know that, and you don't have to have sex with anyone to know that. But...I don't want to be presumptuous here."

"What?"

"I want you, Adrian. I want more than what we have now. More than what we had then. Every time we've been together it's been under a blanket of secrecy. Shrouded in lies and fear. I want to know what it's like to be with you in a way I've only dreamed about. You do have a lot to figure out. If you decide to end your marriage, of course I want you to come to me. But I don't want you to continue to feel like you've always felt—deprived. You'll go from a marriage to a woman you never wanted to marry to a relationship with the only man you've ever been with. You don't even know what's out there."

"I don't give a shit about that," he shouts. "You say I don't have to have sex with a man to know I'm gay, but then you tell me I need to have multiple experiences to be sure that it's you I want to be with? Is that what you're saying, Matías? Honestly. That you could even give me the option to be with anyone else makes me wonder if we're even on the same page, because I would never tell you to go be with someone else. I can't even think about you being with someone else, and I'm pissed that you had so many experiences. I'm not grateful that you know yourself better because of them. I'm mad that they even had a tiny piece of you. That they know what you feel like. What you taste like. Because I want you to myself."

My heart thumps against my ribcage. "I'm sorry. I didn't mean—"

"I'm gonna go," he says, walking toward the door. "I can't believe he went to you with threats. I can't believe you both think I don't know what it is I want." He turns to look at me. "I've had eight years to think about it, Matías. You don't think I know myself? I craved you for eight years. I've missed you, longed for you, and thought about nothing else but how I hurt you. How it was the worst thing I've ever done. Even now.

"Leaving you the way I did still remains my biggest regret. Seeing how hurt you were is seared into my brain. Because you...you were everything to me. And when I lost you, I lost a part of myself."

I open my mouth, but the words don't come out. I have too much to say and no idea where to begin. I stare at him, absorbing what he said, and I only get his name out before he's marching out the door.

The Past

Adrian

CHAPTER FIFTY-THREE
ADRIAN

I SEE him watching me when I'm with my friends. I see him when I'm pretending I'm into some girl because my friends say we'd be good together.

It hurts, but I need him to hate me. I need him to not want a future with me, because my father won't allow it. I don't want him to lose out on any internships or job opportunities because my father's being spiteful.

Matías is perfect. He's kind and smart. He's honest and funny. His heart is warm and full of love, and he'll be okay. He'll find someone who can give him what I wish I could. But he can't think there's a chance for us. Otherwise he might wait forever. He's that loyal.

I bump into him one day and pretend I didn't know it was him. I acted like I was too much in a rush to even see his face, but I'm always aware of his presence. I feel him the moment he comes into my radius.

Seeing the hurt on his face when he saw me with my arm around a girl whose name I don't even remember made my heart split down the middle. There are many nights that I cry under my blankets, wondering what the hell I'm doing.

Without him, I laugh less. I miss who I was when I had him, and I hurt myself by hurting him. I'm now depriving us both of what brought us happiness. But I have to believe it's for the best. I have to believe he'll move on and be happy. If it can only be one of us, it has to be him.

I'll never find another Matías. Nobody will make me feel the way he did. He became my best friend. The romantic part was icing on the cake.

I will always love him, but staying with him will hurt him in the end, because I have nothing to offer. Just more secrecy. More lies.

He doesn't know it now, but maybe one day he'll understand that by doing this, he's getting the chance to live open and free in a way he could never have with me.

Present Day

Adrian

ADRIAN

My emotions drive me, sending me across the lawn and into my house where I know it's time to finally have this conversation. I can't take it anymore.

"Charlotte. Charlotte!" I call, getting louder each time. "Charlotte!"

"What's going on?" she says, coming down the stairs with a furrow in her brow.

"We need to talk."

"Adrian, not right now," she starts, turning around to head back up.

"No, right this second," I yell. "We've been avoiding each other and it's not helping the situation." I take a breath and try to calm down. "Please. I need to tell you something."

She stops, looks at me with some apprehension, but comes down the steps.

I choose to sit at the dining room table and wait for her to take her seat on the opposite side.

"What is it?" she asks, her voice a little shaky.

I take a breath and stare into her eyes.

"I want you to know that I care about you so much. You're

exceptionally strong and smart, and capable of anything you put your mind to. I'm proud of you and your growth. You've gone through things I couldn't imagine, and—"

"Adrian, please," she says, her voice cracking. "What are you saying?"

"Charlotte, we were forced together by our parents. They used me to keep you in line, to watch over you, to be the father of a child everyone knew wasn't mine. Your father cared more about his business dealings than your well-being. He was embarrassed and didn't want you to taint his name and what he had going on with my father. And my father," I say, voice cutting out. "He was also embarrassed of me. He hated who I was. Who I am. And this was the perfect way of getting what he wanted from me."

"I don't understand," she says, shaking her head slightly.

"I'm gay, Charlotte." I let the words sit there, and she stares at me with wide eyes, her lips parted. "He's known since I was in college. He told me I couldn't be gay and still be a part of his family. He told me he'd cut me off. I'd have no money, no job, no future. He threatened the guy he knew I was with back then. Said he'd make sure he couldn't get the job he wanted. He forced us apart and continued to control me by ensuring I needed him. He paid for everything. My car, apartment, phone bill. When I first started working for him, he took chunks of my check for the things he already paid for. It took a long time to save enough to be able to be on my own."

Her fingers come to her lips, hand shaking as tears brim in her eyes. "What?" Her voice is barely above a whisper.

"I'm sorry, Charlotte. I couldn't tell you. I never told anyone."

"You couldn't tell me?" she questions. "You married me!"

"Because I had to, just like you had to marry me. You

didn't love me. You didn't want me. We were told what was expected of us, and considering we were both dependent on our parents, we didn't have a choice. We had a good friendship. We got along, we laughed, and we tried. You have to know I tried, Charlotte. I tried to let our relationship develop into something I knew wasn't possible. But there's no denying it wasn't perfect."

She stares at me for a long time, her lips still parted in surprise.

"I love you, though."

The words are like little daggers aimed at my heart. "And I love you." The pause is long, stretching between us as we study each other.

"But," we both say at the same time.

I tilt my head, my lips pulling down in the corners. "Not the way someone should love their spouse."

A sole tear falls from her eye, rolling down her cheek. She leaves it there for a few seconds before swiping it away.

"I don't know what this means. I don't know what to say or what to expect. I moved here with you. I...I don't have anyone else. You've ruined everything."

She gets up and rushes upstairs. I follow her, taking them two at a time, then find her in our room where she's changing out of her pajama pants.

"Charlotte. I'm sorry, but I couldn't keep living a lie. It was killing me to let my father have control over my life. I want to be able to live my life the way I want, not how he's orchestrated, and you deserve the same."

She buttons her jeans and shoves her feet into a pair of sneakers. "Oh, please. Don't pretend like you thought about me at all in this scenario."

"What did you want me to do? Continue to lie to myself? To you? Stay in this marriage even though I'm not—"

I stop myself, realizing how the end of that sentence will sound. I'm not trying to be harsh, but honesty hurts sometimes.

"Not what?" she questions, her eyes still wet. "Not attracted to me? Not in love with me?"

"I think you're beautiful, but—"

"Don't," she says with a bite, holding her hand out.

"Our last fight was over how many times we've had sex. That's how our marriage would be forever. I can't make you feel the way you want. People have the need to feel desired, and I can't give that to you."

She scoffs, rushing past me to go back downstairs. After finding her purse, she takes the keys and bounds through the front door.

"Charlotte. We need to talk about this," I say, following her out.

"You've said enough, Adrian. I don't think I can handle you continuing to tell me you don't love me or find me attractive."

I sigh, finding myself frustrated, but trying to understand that she's angry and hurt.

"I didn't say either of those things and you know it. You're stunning, but I'm not wired to appreciate it the way I should. It's not just you, Charlotte."

She yanks open the car door and throws her purse inside. "You've just completely upturned my life. I can't even look at you right now."

Before I can say anything else, she's inside the car and slamming the door closed. I watch her reverse and take off down the street, hoping like hell that she stays safe.

I drop down onto the front steps and run my hands through my hair. A minute later, I hear the sound of steps on the grass.

Looking up, I find Matías watching me with an expression of sympathy.

I sigh, my shoulders dropping as emotion hits hard. My own tears well in my eyes, and Matías rushes over, sitting next to me on the steps. He wraps his arms around me and I melt into him, lost in the sound of his heartbeat.

"She said I ruined her life."

He squeezes me tighter, kissing the top of my head. "She's upset. She'll realize later that what you did was set her free. You've both been trapped."

"I didn't even tell her about us." I pull away. "Should I? She was already so hurt."

He shakes his head slightly. "I don't know."

"I'm sorry for yelling and storming off earlier. I'm really on a roll tonight."

"You're fine," he says, taking my hand in his and rubbing the top of it with the fingers from his other hand. "I'm sorry, too. The impromptu meeting with your father had me in a mood, and his words burrowed into my head, and I wondered if I should let you explore yourself. If that was the right thing to do."

I shake my head. "I don't want to talk about it right now. I don't even know what to do next. I can tell my dad that I told her. She'll soon tell her own parents, and then my mom will know, and I'll have to talk to my sister." I sigh. "And then, I don't know. She may move back to Chicago."

"Yeah, you've got a lot going on."

My phone rings from inside, so I jump up to get it.

"You can come in. I'll be right back," I say, rushing to the kitchen where I left it.

I don't recognize the number, and I'm suddenly worried it's a hospital or the cops.

"Hello?"

"Mr. Kennedy?"

"Yeah?" I ask, looking across the house at Matías as he steps in.

"Do you have a few minutes?"

"Yeah, what's going on? What happened?"

Matías walks a little closer, his face a mirror of what I imagine mine looks like.

"My name's Raphael. I'm from Liberty Mortgage, and we'd—"

"Oh, fuck off," I say before ending the call. Matías cocks his head. "Fucking scam calls."

Matías visibly relaxes and we both begin to laugh.

"Jesus Christ. I thought it was gonna be bad."

"You're gonna have to block that number."

"I've blocked three already. They're so fucking annoying."

I pull at my tie, then unbutton my shirt before taking them both off and tossing them onto the back of one of the dining room chairs. I finally toe off my work shoes, leaving them in the kitchen.

"Well, I guess I'm gonna go," Matías says, taking a couple steps backward. "If you need to take off tomorrow, that's fine. Let me know and I'll cover for you."

I walk him toward the front door. "Thanks. Yeah, I'm not sure what will be best in this situation. To stay here and argue about it all day, or leave and let her cool off until she's ready to talk."

"Just let me know."

I nod, stopping a couple steps from the door. "Thank you."

"I'm sorry it didn't go over well."

"I guess I didn't really expect that it would."

"Like I said, you're giving her a chance at a life she

deserves. To find someone who can love her the way she wants."

I rest my hand on the doorknob. "I thought I was doing that for you, too. But you know how much I hurt you. How mad you were at me and for how long. I've just done the same thing to her."

His brows knit together. "You thought you were giving me an opportunity at something better?"

"You deserved better than what I could've given you back then...which was nothing."

"I had everything I needed with you. I told you I was willing to wait."

I grab his hand and squeeze it. "It's amazing."

"What is?" he asks with a smile.

"How all this time can pass, and yet, I still look at you and feel exactly as I did when I was twenty-one."

His expression changes slightly, smile falling, eyes widening. "The same way?"

I step forward, grabbing the side of his face with one hand and pressing my mouth to his. I give him a couple quick kisses. "Maybe not exactly the same. Maybe more."

Matías wraps his arm around me, pulling me into him as he deepens the kiss. After a minute, he pulls away.

"Maybe we should discuss this more later."

I nod. "Yes, we should."

"Okay. Well, I'm gonna go."

He opens the door and steps onto the porch.

"You make me feel like everything's gonna be okay," I tell him as he walks down the steps.

He turns around and looks up at me. "It will be." Matías winks, his teeth pulling his bottom lip into his mouth briefly.

"God," I say, grinning like a fool, three tiny words on the

tip of my tongue as I stare down at his handsome face. "You drive me crazy."

He chuckles, but turns and heads back to his house. I watch him the entire way, only going inside once I can't see him anymore.

I flop onto the couch with a sigh, feeling split down the middle. I'm elated to have Matías, but I'm nowhere near in the clear when it comes to Charlotte, or even when it comes to coming out to everyone I know.

There's a tiny, pin-prick of light at the end of the tunnel, but the journey seems long.

The doorknob turns and the door opens, making me whip around to face it.

Charlotte stands there, her expression a mix of shock and sadness.

"Are you fucking him?"

CHAPTER FIFTY-FIVE

ADRIAN

"Charlotte," I say, standing up, heart in my throat.

She didn't see anything. We didn't do anything once the door was open.

Except I stared at him like a love-struck teenager as he walked home. But I never saw her or the car.

"Are you fucking our neighbor?" she yells, pointing toward his house. "Your boss?! Are you?"

"Charlotte, please."

"No, Adrian. I leave for fifteen minutes, and come back to find him leaving our house, and you standing there with a smile on your face like you don't care that our marriage is over."

I get up and walk around the couch, but she moves away like I have an infectious disease.

Her eyes study me, and then something hits her. She gasps lightly, and I watch as her eyes widen. Several long seconds pass by as she watches me, holding onto a thought in her head.

"You said your dad found out in college." Another long pause as she puts things together. "And you told me you knew him. Our neighbor. You said you went to school together."

My heart drops into my stomach.

"You didn't tell me right away, though. You didn't tell me he was your boss. You didn't tell me you knew him in college." After a few seconds, she says, "It's true, isn't it? It's him." My fear and guilt keep me from finding the words. I just stare at her, my heart rate spiking. "Goddammit, Adrian, fucking tell me! I already know!"

"Yes, he's the guy from college."

"And?" she questions, eyes wild with anger.

"Charlotte, let me explain."

She laughs a humorless laugh. A short choking sound. "Of course. Now you want to explain. How fucking dare you. How dare you!" Her voice bounces off the walls.

"I'm sorry, Charlotte."

"Sure you are," she says, more angry than sad right now.

"I know nothing I say will make this better. Nothing I tell you will make you understand, but—"

She whirls around. "But what? What, Adrian? You don't regret it? You don't wish you could take it back?"

I look at her, knowing she won't want to hear the truth, though she thinks she does. It's going to make an already painful situation hurt even more.

"I feel bad that I hurt you."

"What a fucking cowardly answer," she sneers. "You fuck someone else but don't have the balls to tell your wife that you did it because you wanted to. That not once did you think about me. That my feelings weren't even in your head, because all you could think about was yourself. You fucked him knowing it was wrong. You fucked him knowing it would hurt me. You fucked him. You fucked him. You fucked him!" she yells, tears now streaming down her face.

"Charlotte, I've loved him since I was twenty-one!" I shout.

She blanches, eyes wide.

"I know that hurts to hear, but it's true. He's the only person I've ever been myself with. We were forced apart by my father using threats and manipulation. Just as *we* were forced into this relationship," I say, gesturing between us. "My whole life I've been forced to pretend and lie. I've never lived for myself, Charlotte. I made decisions my father wanted me to make. I married you and knew I could never love you the same way. I wanted to be there for you, and I was. I supported you and cared for you, and I don't regret those things. I don't, Char. You needed me."

A sob breaks free, and she covers her mouth.

"Seeing him again brought everything back, and yes, I made decisions I knew were wrong. I knew they'd hurt you. I know I'm fucked up for that, but it felt like I was finally making decisions for myself and not for anyone else. I was doing something I wanted to do. I was reclaiming what was taken from me. It was a hundred percent selfish, and I admit that."

She shakes her head, softly crying. "I can't believe this."

Tears well in my eyes watching her break down. I want to hug her and hold her, but I'm sure she doesn't want me to touch her. I take a few steps closer to where she leans against the wall.

"You deserve better than me, Char. And you'll find someone who will worship the ground you walk on, and I'll be so happy for you."

"Stop," she says through another sob. "Please just leave me alone."

Slowly, I back away, and turn to head upstairs. I go into

the bedroom and sit on the bed, drop my head in my hands, and let the tears fall.

Even though I needed to tell her the truth, and though I knew I needed to end our marriage, it doesn't make this process feel any better. It still hurts, and I'm still heartbroken over it.

CHAPTER FIFTY-SIX

ADRIAN

I wake up at five in the morning after a restless night, and find that Charlotte is gone. I send a message to Matías letting him know I will need the day off after all, but I don't go into details. Not yet.

I send another message to Charlotte, asking her to please let me know she's okay, but it goes unanswered.

After a shower, I put on a pot of coffee and then sit at the dining room table and decide who I need to call first.

Amelia. I call her number.

"What's wrong?" she answers.

"What a way to answer the phone."

"Well, it's six-thirty in the morning and you never call this early. Are you okay?"

"Yeah. Yeah, I'm fine," I say with a sigh.

"Then why the fuck are you calling me at six-thirty?"

"Do you have some time to talk? You going to work soon?"

"I have an hour before I absolutely need to crawl out of bed. What's going on?"

"Well, I wanted to tell you something before it runs

through the grapevine, picking up some bullshit along the way."

"I'm definitely awake now."

With a long sigh, I say, "Me and Charlotte are gonna be getting divorced." I let it sit there, but she doesn't say anything, so I keep going. "Because...well, because I'm gay."

I bite down on my thumbnail, holding my breath and waiting for her response.

"You're...okay. You're getting a divorce."

"Yes," I say with a nod.

"Because you're gay."

"Yes."

Another several seconds go by. "Well, you know, this makes sense."

"What do you mean?"

"Getting married to Charlotte? That whole thing never made sense to me. You didn't know her. You hadn't told me anything about you two dating. We knew *of* her because she was David's daughter, but you never expressed interest. Then all of a sudden you two run off to get married? I remember questioning you about it and you were just like, 'Yeah, it felt right.' It wasn't like you, though."

I rub my forehead and get ready to tell her the part she's never known. "Charlotte was pregnant. The father was an addict who was in jail. They needed her to settle down and have a *decent* partner. They were in the middle of acquiring a new business, and she was getting arrested, and disappearing for days."

"Wait, so...okay, hold on. Dad made you marry her so there wouldn't be negative press about David's daughter? What kind of sense? And obviously you don't have a kid, so she miscarried?"

"Well, yeah. It was for them, but I know Dad was more

than happy to volunteer me considering he knew about me, and thought this was the perfect set up to get me with a woman. Hoping like hell it would stick. And yes, she miscarried. She went through a rough patch after that, and then went to rehab. She's been clean since."

"Damn," she says. "This is crazy, Adrian. I can't believe you didn't tell me!"

"I'm sorry. I didn't tell anyone."

"I'm so fucking pissed. How could Dad do that? How could Mom let him? Because you're gay? Jesus fuck, everyone is gay."

"What?" I ask with a laugh.

"Okay, maybe not everyone. But there's gay people all over the place. He's still acting like this in 2024?"

"I just wanted to let you know, because Charlotte knows now, and I'm sure her parents will find out soon, and it'll eventually trickle through."

"How'd she take it?"

"Not good. There's another detail I may have left out."

"Oh god," she groans.

"I don't want you to think less of me."

"Jesus," she murmurs on the other side.

"There's a guy here."

"Lord have mercy. Adrian, I'm trying to be on your team."

"It's a long story, but it wasn't just some stupid fling or one-night stand. I know him. He's who I was with in college. The one Dad found out about."

"Oh. Well, damn."

"Anyway, that's a story for another time. Charlotte is upset and took off. We haven't talked about what will happen next, but I imagine she'll move back home."

"And you? What are you gonna do?"

"I'm going to finally live."

She's quiet for a little bit. "Good. That's good, Adrian. You're in quite a mess right now, but it's not fair what you had to go through. I wish you would've told me, because you know I always have your back, but that's your journey. I love you. Let me know if you need anything, okay?"

Tears fill my eyes. "Thanks, Ame. I love you so much."

"We'll talk later."

"Okay."

After I end the call, I swipe at my eyes and send a message to my dad.

> Charlotte knows everything, and I told Amelia. I don't appreciate you threatening Matías either.

His response comes a lot faster than I expected.

> Can you come to Chicago soon?

> For what?

> There are a few things we need to go over.

I don't reply, because I don't know what the hell he's talking about. I tell him that the news about my sexuality and affair is out there, and he responds like we need to have a business meeting.

I call Charlotte, but it goes straight to voicemail. I decide to send another message to my dad.

> Charlotte is gone and isn't answering my calls. If you or David hear from her, let me know so I know she's safe.

He doesn't reply.
But Matías does.

> That's fine. Take care of what you have going on. I'm here if you need me.

CHAPTER FIFTY-SEVEN
MATÍAS

On Wednesday morning, Adrian's in my office before I can even start working.

"Hey," he says, coming inside and closing the door. "Can we talk for a minute?"

"Yeah, sure."

He sits across from me, legs bouncing. My heart squeezes, wondering what he's about to say. Is this all about to come crashing to an end? Is he staying with her? Will I, once again, be left behind to watch him fake it with someone else?

"I need to put in a request for time off."

My stomach twists. "Okay," I say slowly. "How much time off?"

He rubs his finger over his eyebrow. "Uh, I don't know. I know I haven't been here too long, but I'll need a few days at least."

I turn on my computer and click a few things before I get the leave request form open. I hit print.

"Are you okay?" I ask him.

He finally looks me in the eye. "I have hope that I will be soon."

My lips turn up into a small smile. "That's good."

"Charlotte left. She's in Chicago. She took the car, so I need to get there so I can drive it back. But while I'm there, I have to have a conversation with my family."

I nod. "Okay."

"She knows. Everyone knows. Not only about me, but about us."

My brows lift. "Oh."

"She saw you leave my house Monday night, and it started a discussion that turned into a fight." He waves his hand in the air. "But yeah, so there's that."

"How do you feel?" I ask.

"It's such a confusing feeling," he says, leaning back in the chair a little. "I feel terrible. I feel guilty and sad, but I also feel relief. I feel hopeful."

He smiles at me, and the heaviness leaves my shoulders. I return the grin before getting up to get the paper from the printer.

I walk to his chair and hold the paper out. "Fill this out and bring it back to me. I'll file it."

He takes it, standing up. "Thank you."

"You're welcome."

Our faces are inches away, but I wait for him.

He leans forward, lips brushing mine.

I kiss him back, softly at first, then I swipe my tongue inside his mouth and swallow his subsequent moan.

"Tell me you're coming back to me," I whisper against his mouth before placing another kiss. "Please tell me you're coming back."

His hand slides over my hip, gripping me tight as he eases away so he can look into my eyes.

"Matías. I'm coming back. I promise you. I'm not letting you go again."

He kisses me, and through his lips and tongue, I search for the truth of his words.

CHAPTER FIFTY-EIGHT
ADRIAN

I GET to Chicago around two o'clock on Wednesday afternoon. I rent a car from the airport and drive sixteen miles to get to my parents' house in Winnetka.

In the driveway of their four-million-dollar home, I sit in the car and try to breathe. After today, I tell myself I'll never have to deal with them again. I'll never have to have this conversation again either.

Once I walk up the stairs, I ring the bell and wait. My father is the one who opens the door.

After a couple seconds, he says, "Come in. Let's talk before your mother gets here."

"I'd really rather talk to everyone at once. Are David and Charlotte coming?"

"Not that I know of."

I sigh and follow him through the expansive foyer and into his study. He makes his way to the mini bar and pours himself a drink before finding his way to the couch.

"Sit, Adrian."

"I think I'll stand," I tell him, simply because I don't want him to think he can still boss me around.

He gives me a look but doesn't fight me on it.

"I see you've made your choice."

"I have."

He takes a sip of his drink, staring out the window to his right, then starts talking.

"I know you think I've been harsh on you." I have to bite my tongue to keep from arguing already. "My father was strict. Overbearing. Whatever you want to call it. It's how I grew up. He seemed to only pass on his negative traits to me. I knew not to go against the grain in his house, because he wasn't afraid to get physical."

Dad stands up and walks to the window now, avoiding looking at me. "We sometimes regurgitate the things we hear or see. I'm not going to blame my father for the things I said to you, because I believe there's a part of me that actually felt that way. However, they were also things my own father told me."

I swallow, wondering what he's talking about. He's never said much about his dad. We hardly knew the man. He lives in Connecticut, but there was a time when me and Amelia were children that he'd come around with Grandma. When she died, the visits slowed dramatically, and we never spoke on the phone.

Dad comes back to the couch, eyes on me. I decide to sit in the chair to his left.

"I loved someone else before I met your mother. She doesn't know, nor does she need to, but that's the truth. For the first two years of college, I believed I had met my wife. I was hopelessly in love. Blinded by it, in fact. Whatever she wanted, I gave to her. If she wanted to do something, I'd do it, even if it was outside my comfort zone. She had me pushing the envelope at every turn. It was fun. I was alive and thriving. I had never known a life like that, because my home life was very restricted." He sighs. "Anyway, my grades started dropping and my father wasn't happy about it. I was doing things I'd never done before—drugs, drinking, skipping class. It was all in good fun, I thought. The typical college experience.

"My dad wanted me to be a lawyer. Did I ever tell you that?"

I shake my head, curious about the change in direction. "He had his own practice, didn't he?"

"He did," he says with a nod. "He didn't think I was doing enough to be successful. I needed to stop focusing on girls and only worry about my school work. Suffice it to say, I did not go into law. Much to his chagrin. But I only came to that conclusion after breaking up with Charleen. The truth of the matter is, she probably wasn't what was best for me. I was young and finally living life outside of my parents' house. I was doing things that didn't align with who I knew I was, but I didn't realize that right away. Sometimes we don't listen to our parents, simply because they're our parents. We want to rebel and fight, and believe that they don't know what they're talking about, but later, you'll come to find out that they had a lot of truth to offer."

"Are you saying—"

He holds his hand up to stop me. "I believed you were doing the same at first. You were allowing the freedom of being out of my house to drive you to do things you'd never thought about—things that weren't who you were at your core. I also had this need for you to work for me simply as a *fuck you* to my father. I wanted him to see that he couldn't get me to work for him, but I would have my own son work for me. I wanted him to see that I succeeded where he failed, because he always thought of me as a failure. I definitely allowed my own problems to interfere with my relationship with you. I see that now. I suppose blindness isn't always related to romantic relationships. You can be blinded by fear, revenge, rage, and spite. I was selfish. I wanted to bend you at my will for my own reasons, and I used language and threats in an attempt to get what I wanted from you. I didn't see that I was my own father until recently.

"Now, don't get me wrong, I still think you'd be a great CEO, and I want you to take over the company when I'm done, but if that's not your dream, then what can I do?" he questions with a shrug. "I didn't do what my father wanted either, so I suppose this is karma."

Everything he's just said swims around in my head, trying to find a landing place in my brain, but there's one thing he hasn't mentioned.

"And forcing me to marry Charlotte? What was your reasoning for that?"

He sighs. "You were alone and seemed unhappy. The main reason for getting you two together was mostly for her. David needed her to get on the right track, and she needed help, so I thought I was doing some good by bringing you two together. I thought you were perhaps into both men and women."

"Did David ever think that maybe he was responsible for his own daughter? That he and his wife should've been the ones supporting and helping her?"

He shakes his head. "No. They were never involved with her. I don't think it ever crossed his mind to pay her any extra attention."

"Yeah, well, maybe if he had done so, she wouldn't have taken that particular journey."

"Maybe."

"I'm not bisexual, Dad," I tell him. "I know I told you it was nothing. I told you I could be with women, but I only said that because I was afraid. I wanted to convince you I was something I was not. I didn't want you to ruin Matías's life in order to keep me in line, so I said what was needed. And honestly, regardless of what your own father did or said to you, it doesn't excuse your clear case of homophobia."

"I was more concerned that you were going to throw your life away over someone who wouldn't be in it forever."

"Why would I be throwing my life away by being gay?"

"I didn't think that you were!" he shouts, putting his glass down. "I thought you were just messing around. I didn't want the effects of this new and different thing to distract you from the life I wanted for you."

"I can't be gay and run a company? My gayness would keep me from making smart business decisions? Who I have in my bed means I suddenly don't know anything about work?"

"Look, I don't understand it, okay? I just don't."

"You don't have to."

"You can't have kids. The Kennedy name ends with you. Who will the company go to then?"

"Oh, my god," I exclaim. "Gay people can have kids if they want to. Do I really need to educate you on adoption or surrogacy? And I won't force my kid to do anything he or she doesn't want to. At some point, this ugly cycle has to end. Your father wanted something for you, and you went against it only to try to force me into your own dreams. What happened? I rebelled. I moved to a different state to get away from you. I will not push my kid away by forcing them into a life they don't want."

He exhales, pacing around before coming to a stop and looking at me. "I'm just trying to say that I'm beginning to understand. I see what I didn't see before. How I was exactly who I tried so hard to get away from. I went about things the wrong way. You clearly…like this person a lot. To do what you did. To end your marriage over him."

I run a hand over my forehead. "I didn't end it over him. Yes, I cheated, but I was cheated out of a lot of life experiences because of you, and my marriage ended because I'm finally ready to live my truth. I'm finally out from under you. I don't need your money or job offers. I'm not afraid of you anymore." He blanches. "I more than like him, Dad, and you can deal with that or not. I no longer care. Tell David what you want. Tell Mom the same. I'm going to get my car from Charlotte, and tell her that I hope to be her friend. I will always be there for her, but not as a husband."

I turn to leave and find my mother stepping into the doorway, a look of shock and sadness on her face. Her eyes flicker to Dad before landing back on my face.

She gives me the tiniest smile, but it's tinged in despair. "Hi, honey," she says softly. "I heard, well, most everything."

I inhale deeply and force myself to stare into her eyes. "I came here to tell you both."

She looks at my father again. "Yes, well, I guess I was late."

"It's my fault. I started talking to him about some stuff," my dad says. "It spiraled."

"Hmm." She walks forward and holds my wrists. "I can't take back how I made you feel growing up. Nor can I change the way others made you feel." She slides her hand into mine and squeezes gently. "I can't erase the words of the past, but together, maybe we can write a new path forward, because if it's the rest of my life without you or a life that involves you and any man you choose to spend it with, I want the latter."

Tears burn my eyes as I look down at her. She's never

been a warm or nurturing person, and she's still not. Her words held almost no emotion, but they were clear and concise. She chooses me.

I nod, leaning in to kiss her cheek. "We'll talk later."

"Okay."

I flee the house before emotions take hold.

CHAPTER FIFTY-NINE

ADRIAN

I DRIVE to David's house, assuming that's where Charlotte's gone. Instead of going inside, I call her from the driveway where I park right next to my car. Surprisingly, she answers.

"Hello?"

"Charlotte," I say with a sigh of relief. "I'm outside. Can we talk?"

"You're here?" she questions, her voice going up an octave.

"Yes."

"I'll be out in a minute."

She ends the call and I end up leaning against my rental car for nearly five minutes before she appears.

Wearing a pair of wide leg pants and a tank top, she walks toward me and rests her hip on the front end of my car.

"I'd apologize for taking the car, but I'm not that sorry."

My lips pull up on one side, forming a sad smile. "That's fine."

She runs her fingers through her hair, making it fall over onto one side. "I guess you're here to take it back."

"Yes, and to talk to you. I just left my parents' house."

"You told them?" she asks.

I nod. "Did you tell your parents?"

She hesitates briefly before nodding, chewing on her lip. "They know."

Pushing away from the car, I move a little closer to her. "Charlotte, I really want to apologize."

She brings both of her hands up, palms facing me. "Please don't. It's not going to help anything."

I remember the words Matías told me before. *Forgiveness is for the guilty party. Not the wronged.*

I nod and silence stretches between us for a minute.

"I'm not forgiving you," she starts. "But I can't imagine what it would be like to be in a relationship with a woman, because that does nothing for me. So I can only imagine what it was like for you."

"Perhaps if we had just stayed friends, and didn't try to have an actual relationship, we would've been fine."

"Well, I know we got married because my dad needed me to look like I had my life together with a decent guy instead of birthing a drug-addicted baby."

"Char, don't. You stopped as soon as you knew. You were doing your best."

She shrugs. "Karma, I suppose. I was terrible. I made stupid decisions and disappointed my family at every turn." Charlotte blows out a breath and looks off to the side. "Anyway, I knew it wasn't a typical relationship, but I did really like you. We got along and laughed, and when it moved toward intimacy, I thought it was natural for us both. I didn't know...I just assumed you felt about me the way I felt about you."

"I should've told you. I should've trusted you to keep it between us, but then you'd just be in a relationship with someone you'd never feel wanted by. Someone you'd never sleep with. And I truly thought I could make it work."

She gives me a sad grin. "We could've had an open marriage."

I smile back at her. "Now you tell me."

We chuckle a little before we fall into silence.

"I wish you would've told me before you started this affair. I wish I had the chance to understand how you were feeling."

"I'm sorry." I pin my lips together. "I didn't have the intention of coming out. I had finally got away from my father, but felt like I couldn't leave you. It seemed like you needed me, and I didn't want to do anything to—" I stop myself, not really willing to say what her father and mine have always said.

"To what? Send me down a dark path again? Well, an affair isn't much better." I study her and she rolls her eyes. "I'm still sober."

"With him...I didn't expect it to happen. Not at first. I had hurt him and he wasn't interested in talking to me. Especially when he found out I was married."

"That changed," she says with a scoff.

"It did," I say softly, not sure she wants me to go into any other details.

"He was your first love?" she asks after a while.

"My only love," I answer honestly.

She looks into my eyes, and I see the wetness in hers. With a single nod, she bites into her bottom lip. "Well." She reaches into her pocket and pulls out the keys, handing them to me. "Here you go."

I take them and hand her the rental's keys.

"I rented it for a week. If you need more time, I'll extend it."

She takes the keys and nods. "Okay."

"Do you know what you're going to do? Are you moving back here?"

"Dad offered to let me stay here. Probably because he thinks I'll end up on the streets otherwise." She sighs. "I need to find a job so I don't have to be here."

"I'll help you," I tell her. "I have money saved."

"You just bought a house. You have a mortgage now. How can you also pay for me to live somewhere?"

"I'll sell it," I tell her. "Find something smaller."

She shakes her head. "Chicago's expensive."

"Let me help you. It's the least I could do."

"That's true," she says before giving me another little grin. "I'll let you know what I plan on doing, and when I'll be back for my stuff."

"I know I don't deserve it, and I'll understand if you tell me to fuck off, but one day, maybe way down the line, I'd love to still have our friendship."

Tears fall down her cheeks and she makes a noise that's between a scoff and a disbelieving laugh. "Fuck off." Then she lunges forward and wraps her arms around me, head buried in my chest as she cries.

I hold her tight, my chin resting on her head as my own tears fall.

"I hate you," she murmurs.

"I know."

We stay like that for at least five minutes before she pulls away, wiping tears from her cheeks.

After several seconds of looking at each other, she backs away. "See ya."

"See ya."

CHAPTER SIXTY

MATÍAS

IT's seven-twenty when my phone rings. When I see Adrian's name on the screen, I breathe a sigh of relief as my heart begins to race.

"Hey," I answer.

"Hey. Are you busy?"

I mute the TV and lean back into my couch. "No. What are you up to?"

He sighs. "I'm in a hotel. Just got done eating. Now I'm lying on the bed before I shower and call it a night."

"How was today?"

Another long exhale. "It was fine. My dad had a whole conversation planned, but at the end of it, he said he was beginning to understand my situation, because it was mirroring his own situation with his father. He couldn't see that he was exactly who he was trying to run away from. But he also said that back in college, he didn't want me to ruin my life over someone who wouldn't be in it forever. He didn't believe I was gay, and thought I was just giving it the good ol' college try." He laughs humorlessly. "Said I must like you a lot now, though."

My lips stretch into a small smile. "And do you? Like me a lot now."

"Mm. Maybe," he replies, and I can hear the smile through his words.

"Interesting. What about your mom? Charlotte?"

"Mom overheard everything. I was telling Dad that he could accept me or not, but that I was no longer afraid of him. That I no longer cared. He brought up the fact that I couldn't have kids, and his legacy would die with me. I guess he thought I couldn't run a company if I was gay. You know, because it does affect job capabilities," he says with a scoff. "Anyway, she simply said she heard and that when it came down to it, if it was a life without me or a life with me and whichever man I chose to be with, then she chose me."

"That's nice," I reply.

"Yeah. Charlotte was still upset, which I get, but I think we'll be okay. I don't know how long it'll take, but I have hope we'll maintain some semblance of a friendship. She's gonna let me know when she's going back home for her stuff. She's trying to figure out what she wants to do. Where she wants to live. I told her I'd help her, but I don't know."

"You're a good guy, Adrian."

He scoffs. "Not sure about that."

"No, you are. What happened between us doesn't mean you don't have a good heart. We're all imperfect, but we're the sum of every decision we make, not just the bad ones. The good in you outweighs any of the bad."

He's quiet for a little while. "Thanks."

"So, you're about to get in the shower?" I ask.

"Yeah."

"You should FaceTime me and set your phone on the bathroom counter. Let me watch you." After a beat of silence, I say, "It's only fair. I gave you a show."

"Hmm."

Noise in the background lets me know he's moving around. A few seconds later, my phone beeps, and when I look at the screen, I see he's started a video call.

I press the button and the room comes into view. He's already propped the phone up in the bathroom, because I watch him walk toward the shower where he opens the glass door and turns on the water.

He walks off screen, but reappears a few seconds later. I watch as he begins to undress, taking off his plain white T-shirt and dropping it to the floor. He gives me his back when he takes off his pants, bending over slightly to get them off around his ankles.

A hum of appreciation rumbles in my throat.

Once he's naked, he turns to the side slightly, letting me see his half-hard cock before he moves to get into the shower.

It's about three feet from where the phone rests, and though he leaves the glass door open, my view gets skewed when he moves forward, covered by the glass.

He's teasing me, but I don't hate it.

After he's soaped up his body, he appears back in the doorway, making a show of cleaning his cock. His hand runs up and down the length a few times, soap suds hiding the beautiful shaft.

His body becomes a blur behind the glass when he steps up to wash his hair, but soon enough, he's back in view. He gives me every angel as he bends and twists to clean every part of his body. I get the perfect view of his ass from the side and from the back. My eyes track the muscles in his thighs and arms as water cascades over them. He finally gives me a frontal view, his hands running through his hair.

I shift, putting a hand in my pants to grab my cock, and

then he leans against the wall of the shower, his hand going to his shaft.

He tugs on it, eyes closed as he gets himself fully erect. My own hand moves up and down, and I quickly tug my pants down past my ass and free my cock from the confines of my boxer-briefs.

Adrian moans and it sends a jolt of lust up my spine. I sit up straighter, watching closely as he strokes himself. A couple minutes later, he stops, turning off the water.

He walks out of the shower, dripping wet and rock hard. I'm transfixed as he gets closer to the screen, his cock staring straight at me.

Off screen he reaches for something, but then his hand is back on his shaft, and I realize he got some lotion.

I thank the heavens for low counters and tall men because he's able to stroke himself directly in front of me without anything blocking him.

His tip is engorged and dark pink, and I wish I could put it in my mouth.

"Oh, god," he moans, setting me on fire. "Fuck."

I can't see his face, but his voice and the visual in front of me is perfect. I spit in my palm and stroke a little faster.

Another sinful moan leaves his lips. It's almost whimpery. It's that desperate sound he makes when he's so close to coming.

My tongue swipes at my lip as I await his release.

"Oh, fuck. Oh, god. Matías," he says, voice like gravel. "I'm coming."

The muscles in his stomach flex and then white ribbons of cum shoot out, landing on the countertop.

"Ah," he grunts. "Fuck." He sucks in a breath and releases a shuddery exhale.

His body continues to jerk and spasm as I watch every

drop of his release leave his body and be wasted on the granite fucking counter.

"Let me see your ass," I say in a commanding voice, but it's a plea. I'd beg if he asked me to.

He steps away, the sink coming on briefly before he's back. He lifts the phone, his slightly flushed face appearing on the screen.

"I thought you were supposed to be quiet."

"There are no rules," I say. "Now show me your ass. I want to come imagining I'm filling you up."

His teeth bite into his lip. "That might be enjoyable."

"You like that?" I ask, languidly stroking myself as I wait. "The idea of me coming in your ass? Watching it drip out of you? Eating it out of you?"

"Fuck," he groans. "You're so filthy."

"I'd do despicable things to you. With you. For you," I say. "I'd do anything."

There's some noise on the other end, and then the phone gets placed down, facing the bed.

Adrian climbs over the covers, looking over his shoulder to see if he's in view.

"Perfect," I say. "Fucking perfect."

On all fours, his ass is displayed to me. He reaches around and runs his finger over his hole, before pulling his cheek to the side, really spreading himself open.

"Ah fuck," I groan.

He arches his back even more, his front half low to the bed as his ass stays perched in the air.

My eyes watch his hole as he clenches it, then drop to his balls and cock hanging between his legs.

Everything about him is a work of art.

"God, Adrian," I moan. "You drive me crazy."

It doesn't take long before my orgasm is rearing up.

"I'm about to come. Oh, fuck. I'm gonna come," I cry.

He looks over his shoulder, and at the first spurt of cum, he turns around. I don't see anything after that, because my eyes are squeezed closed as I come all over myself.

When I finally open my eyes, I find Adrian lying on his back, the phone above him as he watches.

I angle the phone at my cock and hand, giving it a few more strokes, squeezing the remaining cum from the tip.

"Mm," he hums. "You made a mess."

"Yeah. Gonna need to change clothes." I exhale, sinking into the couch.

"I can't wait to see you again."

I bring my face into the screen, an exhausted smile on my lips. "I still have plans for us."

"Well, I'm free."

My smile widens. "That's good to hear."

"I guess I should let you clean up."

"Yeah," I say, looking down at the mess. "Let me know when you'll be back."

"I will. I'll call you tomorrow."

"Okay."

We stare at each other for a few seconds before he smiles. "Bye."

"Bye," I reply with a grin.

CHAPTER SIXTY-ONE

ADRIAN

"So, Mom says you have a boyfriend," Amelia says, her voice booming over the speakers in my car as I drive home.

I laugh. "I suppose so. What else did she say?"

"Not much. She overheard your convo with Dad. Said she had no clue about any of it. Dad never let on about anything."

"Yeah, but it's not like I could even open up to her. Dad wasn't the only one who made little homophobic jokes."

"Some people will always be homophobic assholes, but sometimes people can change and grow. Especially when it comes to their kid."

"Are you saying Mom is capable of growth and change?"

"She didn't say anything too crazy. She asked if I knew. She said she, quote, doesn't know what it means, end quote." Amelia laughs. "I don't even know what she means."

"Well, I guess we'll see how things develop, but it'll be hard to forgive Dad for everything. Plus, Mom was also on board with this forced wedding."

"Well, she said Dad told her you and Charlotte had been secretly hooking up anyway. So, she presumed there were some sort of feelings there already."

I scoff, shaking my head. "So Dad just lied to everyone."

"Basically. Mom seemed a little pissed about it."

"Regardless, I'm not taking any steps. So if they want to make a change or show some effort, then it's on them to reach out."

"Yeah. I understand. But when do I meet the boyfriend," she says in a sing-song voice.

"Let's give it a minute," I say with a laugh. "We still have some stuff to talk about."

"Fine. It's almost August now, so I'll give you until November. I'll have time off around then for Thanksgiving, and I expect to be invited over."

"Okay." I chuckle. "Thanks for feeding me the gossip. Let me know if they have anything else to say about me."

"Will do."

"Love you."

"Love you more."

Once she's off the line, I bring up Matías's name and press *call*. It rings a couple times before he answers.

"Hello?"

"Hi," I say, a stupid smile on my face. "I'm on my way home."

"Oh, that's good." I can hear the joy in his voice. "What time?"

I glance at the GPS. "Maybe around four-thirty."

"Okay, well, I have an idea if you're up for it."

"I'm up for anything."

"You come home, eat, shower, change, and do whatever you need to do to prepare yourself for a night with me."

My smile is wide when I reply. "Okay. And then I go to your house?"

"No. I'll send you an address. I'll meet you there."

"Do I need to wear anything specific?"

"Nothing specific, no. I'll bring what you need."

"Hmm," I murmur, biting on my lip. "I'm intrigued."

"Good."

"I can't wait to see you."

"I can't wait either," he says, voice softening a little. "Drive safely. Text me when you make it home."

"I will."

There's a brief pause. "Bye."

"Bye."

I increase my speed just a little, desperate to get home.

To get to him.

I pull into my driveway at four-fifteen, so I know Matías is still at work. I send him a message that I've arrived safely, then I eat a sandwich and clean up the house a little before I hop into the shower.

While I clean myself, I think about him watching me in the shower in the hotel. My time with Matías, both now and back in college, has brought me so many new experiences. Things I've never thought of doing or trying have filled me with so much excitement. I know now that if there's anything he ever wants to do, I'm highly unlikely to say no. I haven't had a lot of time to try out new things, so I'm definitely willing to take advantage now. So if that means watching him through his window, or having him watch me through the phone, or whatever he has planned for tonight, I will meet it with exhilaration.

My cock hardens as I think about him. I give it a few strokes, but then force myself to stop. I'll be seeing him soon. I don't need to come now. I want him to have all of it.

After I rinse, I step out and decide to send him a photo.

It's mostly my torso, hinting at the short-trimmed curls around my cock.

Currently preparing for tonight. What about you?

Jesus Christ.

I smirk and put the phone down, reaching for a towel. I dry off my body, and then my hair before I grab the bottle of lotion.

My phone vibrates on the counter. Matías has sent another message.

I'm also preparing.

A photo comes in afterward, and it's a shot of his bed, but on top of the covers is a variety of objects that have my lips parting.

A flogger and riding crop get my attention first, then I notice some leather straps and a thin chain. Beside those is a small silver object with a diamond on one end.

I stare at the phone for a while, unsure how to respond. I just keep looking at everything in the picture and imagine how everything will be used.

I'm excited and a little nervous.

Don't be nervous. You know I'll take care
of you.

My heart flutters, and I quickly finish getting ready. I decide
to wear a pair of black chinos and a dark gray button-up.

I'm ready.

93073 West Anders Avenue, Wyndgrove MI

I'll meet you at the gate.

Okay. See you soon.

CHAPTER SIXTY-TWO
MATÍAS

I'VE ALREADY GONE INSIDE to put my things in the room I've rented. This time, instead of using the main house, I rented a room in the carriage house. There are only two rooms inside, each with their own entrance.

When I spot Adrian driving around the corner, I call him.

"Hey," he says.

"There's a parking lot a half-block down."

"Okay. I'll see you soon."

A few minutes later, I watch him strolling toward me, one hand in his pocket, as the other arm swings at his side.

God, he makes walking sexy.

When he gets closer, he gives me a shy smile before looking at the mansion. "This is quite the place."

"Mmhmm," I murmur before stepping forward and putting a hand on his lower back, bringing him closer before I plant my lips on his.

He makes a small noise before melting into the kiss, his hands coming to a rest on my sides.

"It's good to see you," I say when I pull away.

He grins. "I told you I'd come back."

I don't mention my fear that he wouldn't, I just nod and smile.

I press the button on the gate again, and inside, we stop at the gate guard shack so Adrian can give his ID over to them to register as my guest.

Once that's done, we walk past the main house and toward the left.

"We're over here," I tell him. "I've never been in this room."

He nods, a small smile on his lips. I wanted him to know that I'm not taking him to a room I've been in with other people.

I stop at the door, turning to face him. "Rules." His brows lift, a smirk on his lips as he crosses his arms. "I want you to do everything I say. I want you at my mercy, but that doesn't mean I won't stop if you want to stop. You just have to let me know."

"Unless you plan on electrocuting me, I don't think I'll be needing to stop. I'm a big boy."

My eyes run down his body and back up. "Indeed you are." I lean in, my lips against his. "So, you'll be a good boy for me, then?"

His body loosens, a slight shiver running through it. "Yes."

"Good. Come."

I turn and twist the knob, walking inside. After Adrian steps in, I lock the door behind him and find my way to the high back chair in the corner. I sit there, my right leg resting over my left knee as he takes it all in.

He stops by the bed where I unpacked all my toys, glancing back at me. My lips curve into a grin.

Adrian moves around the room with all the curiosity of a child. On one side of the bed, he inspects a black leather tantric chair, and then goes to the familiar spanking bench on the other side. He gives me another little smirk when he runs his fingers across the leather.

Moving on, he studies the deep red walls, touching the molding and intricate designs before inspecting the dressers and opening a few drawers.

A black chandelier hangs above a red plush couch in the center, and black wall sconces hold the faux candles that give off a warm glow. Red floral arrangements are displayed in black vases, and I have to admit, it's definitely better than the other rooms I've been inside here.

After a quick disappearing act into the connecting bathroom, he returns and walks straight toward me.

Dropping down in front of me, his hands rest on my knees, skating gently up my thighs. "Where do you want me?"

My body roars to life, and I have to fight myself for control. Part of me wants to throw him on the bed and have my way with him, but the other part wants to take this slow. I want to enjoy every second. I want to take him to the edge where he begs me to push him into euphoria.

I take one of his hands and bring it to my mouth, kissing his knuckles. "Stand up. Get undressed."

When he gets up, I do the same, but I make my way to the bed where I grab the leather harness and leash.

I turn and watch Adrian take off his clothes. Putting them neatly on the chair I just left.

He grabs the waist of his boxer-briefs, looking at me with raised eyebrows.

I shake my head. "You can keep those on. For now."

Walking forward, I secure the harness on him. "I've been

dying to see you in this." Once it's in place, I hook the leash to the center ring that's in the middle of his chest. "Perfect." I give it a tug, pulling him into me so I can give him a chaste kiss.

Turning around, I walk him to the edge of the bed. "Take off my jacket, will you?"

He nods, eyes assessing me as he begins to unbutton my suit jacket. He takes it off my shoulders and holds onto it.

"You can put it down."

Adrian tosses it to the bed behind me.

I elect to keep the rest of my clothes on for now, wanting to focus on him. With another little yank on the chain, I lead him to the tantric chair.

"Straddle this and lean your torso right here," I say, helping him into place.

In this position, his ass is up at an angle, and his body gets to rest on the soft material.

I walk two of my fingers down his spine before placing my palm on the curve of his ass. I raise it and come down with a quick smack.

He gasps, his body shifting slightly.

At the bed, I grab the riding crop and then drag the end up the back of his leg until I get to his ass. I give it a couple quick hits before letting it dance up his back.

"You look so incredible right now," I tell him, bending down to bring my face close to his. "I love knowing I have you all to myself."

He releases a soft moan, eyes focused on me. "I'm yours."

I stare at him for a few seconds before saying, "That's what I like to hear." I crouch down next to him, the riding crop in my hand and poised over his ass. "Tell me again. Who do you belong to?"

His teeth sink into his bottom lip. I let the leather tip of the crop come down on his ass.

He gasps before grinding into the chair. "You." Another moan. "I'm yours, Matías."

I grip his chin between my forefinger and thumb, leaning in to kiss his lips. "Yes, you are."

I put the riding crop down and let my fingers dance underneath the waistband of his underwear. His breath hitches as my fingers slide into his crease. Adrian arches his back even more.

"Desperate little thing, aren't you?"

He nods, a moan on his lips.

"Do you like when I play with you?"

"Yes." He groans when I gently press into his hole.

"I'll be right back."

I go and grab the lube from the end table, bringing it back with me. His perfect peach shaped ass teases me, stretching the white cotton material. I caress it again, squeezing the flesh in my hand.

Before I lube my fingers up and start fingering him, I have to taste him. I need my tongue to explore the area first. I need my fill.

Behind him, I tug down the material just enough to expose his hole to me, then I lean over the bottom half of the chair and bury my face between his cheeks.

"Oh, god," he moans.

I lick upward before twirling my tongue around his entrance. I keep him spread open with my hands as I taste every part of him. I lick across his taint, teasing his balls with the tip of my tongue before journeying back to his hole. I prod at it gently before downright attempting to fuck him with my tongue. I push in as far as I can, moving my hands to his hips where I pull him back. When I die, I want to be suffocated while tongue-fucking his ass.

"Oh, god. Matías. Fuck." He moans between gasps. "So good. Oh, my god."

He begins moving, grinding his cock into the chair as I devour him.

I pull away to look at his glistening hole, then I bring my hand down on his right cheek, the sound reverberating in the room.

"Fuck," he hisses. "Yes."

"Keep grinding into the chair," I tell him, reaching for the lube.

After coating my fingers, I spread some around his entrance before sliding inside.

"Oh, yes," he moans, voice shuddering.

"I want to come inside you."

"Yes," he agrees quickly.

"I want to be inside you. Bare. Nothing between us."

His hips continue to rock, giving him friction on his cock while fucking himself on my fingers. "Okay," he pants.

I smirk, because I think I have him so blissed out, he'd agree to anything.

I stop moving my fingers, and place a hand on his back, stilling him.

"Adrian. I was tested just a couple weeks ago. I'm negative. I'm assuming you were only with your wife and that you're also free of any—"

"Yes," he says quickly, trying to move again. "Yes, I want you inside me."

"Stand up," I tell him, removing my fingers from his ass.

He lets out a small whimpery groan, but he stands.

"Finish undressing me."

Without hesitation, and with a scrape of his teeth across his bottom lip, he unbuttons the deep maroon vest I have on, gracelessly shoving it off my shoulders before nearly ripping every button off my black button-up shirt. I get out of my shoes while he unfastens my pants, shoving them down my legs.

"In a rush?" I ask with a quirk of my lips.

He nods. "Yes." Then he pulls down my boxer-briefs, freeing my erection.

His tongue darts across his lips, eyes flickering up at me for permission. For an order.

I take hold of the leash and tug him into me. "Remove your underwear."

He shimmies out of them, staying close to me. With a hand on his jaw, I lean in and kiss him, sliding my tongue between his lips to dance with his. Then I pull away, the chain in my hand as I direct him to the bed.

With a soft click, I unhook the leash and drop it on the floor. I bring the lube to the bed and lay down.

"I want you to ride me. I want to stroke that beautiful dick until you cover me with your release."

Adrian moans, reaching for the bottle of lube. After squeezing some onto his fingers, he reaches around to massage it into his hole. I pour the liquid into my hand before coating my cock.

He crawls over me, his muscular thighs trapping me between them. With a hand on my stomach, he uses his other to take hold of my shaft and slowly guide me inside him.

His heat envelopes me, inch by inch. The slow pace is the most delicious form of torture.

"Fuck, Matías," he cries, head back as he releases a sinful moan. "You're so big."

"And you take it so well," I say, rubbing his thighs.

With my still-slick hand, I reach out and begin stroking his cock.

"Oh, god," he breathes, fully seated now.

"Rotate your hips."

He listens, and his body moves like he's performing the sexiest lap dance.

"Fuck yeah," I groan. "You're so tight, baby."

His breath leaves him with a small sound. He lifts up slightly, then drops back down. He continues this until the strokes are longer, his ass nearly coming completely off of me before he slides back down my shaft.

"You're so fucking perfect."

"It feels so good," he says, his eyes focused on me as his movements begin to quicken. "I never want to stop."

Adrian drops lower, using his arms to brace himself as his hips rock back and forth. I grab his waist, closing my eyes as I enjoy the sensation. His weight comes down on me as he nips at my throat.

"I love riding you," he says in a gravelly tone, his mouth moving to my ear. "I love having you inside me."

"Mm," I moan, taking his earlobe between my teeth. "What else do you love?"

"Everything. Oh, god."

He pulls back, hips moving faster, while still keeping me deep inside him.

I wrap my fingers around his shaft again, stroking him as he closes his eyes. He's chasing the orgasm, and I can't wait until he reaches it.

"That's it, baby," I say. "Give it to me."

He's gasping between whimpers and grunts, and then his eyes fly open and meet my gaze.

"I'm about to—"

I keep stroking. "I want it. Give me what I want, Adrian."

"Oh. Oh, fuck!" he cries.

He stills just as the first spurt of cum shoots out. He moves again, releasing more white streams onto my stomach.

"Oh, yeah," I groan. "That's it. Make a fucking mess."

"Matías," he gasps. "Fuck. God. Yes."

"Mmm." I milk everything out of him. I tug and squeeze until not even a drop comes out of him.

He exhales, body sagging and chest heaving. His cum is still warm and thick against my skin.

"Holy shit," he says through a breath, slowly getting up.

Once he's off, he drops to his side then rolls to his back. He's a fucking beautiful, satiated mess on white satin sheets. Sweat glistens on his head and neck. His limbs are loose and his cock is still hard. If I could take a photo of him like this I would. I'd look at it every single day and wonder how the hell I got lucky enough to have him, lose him, and get him back again.

I take my cum-covered hand and stroke myself before adding some more lube.

"Turn over."

He rolls before getting up on his knees.

"Fuck, your ass is incredible."

He sways it back and forth before I hold him still with one hand and guide myself inside with the other.

I take my time at first, wanting to watch the way he opens around me. I spread his cheeks and slowly dip in and out, loving that I can be inside him without a barrier.

When I can't take it anymore, I thrust in deep, making him cry out as his arms give out on him.

I take hold of the leather harness and pull him back up, and then I continue to use it as leverage. I pull on it as I thrust, keeping him upright.

"I love being inside you. I love the way you take me. Oh god, Adrian," I cry out, slamming my hips against his ass. "You're so fucking good. So good, baby."

"Yes, yes," he chants. "Fuck me."

"I can't wait to fill you up. I want to watch my cum leak out of you. Marked. Owned."

"Fuck," he growls. "Yes. All yours."

"Mine," I say with a grunt. "Mine. Mine." I punctuate each one with a deep thrust. "I'm about to come. Oh, shit."

I release the harness and hold his hips, fucking him with long, deep strokes. A few seconds later, my orgasm hits, and I slam into him pouring my release inside him as I roar into the room.

My cock twitches inside him, filling him with every drop. I pull out slightly, just to push in again, feeling how slick he is with my release.

"Oh, my god," he groans.

When I pull out completely, I do it with leisure, watching his ass release me. I spread him open and watch as my cum drips out.

"Fuck." I drag the word out, using my finger to dip inside him. "Look at you."

He whimpers and then more cum pours out.

I smear the liquid over his hole, my fingers massaging it in like lotion, then I lean forward and swipe my tongue up his crease.

The gasp he sucks in is loud and long, his body trembling.

I let him go and he collapses on his stomach. I drop down next to him, lying on my side. When his eyes flicker open, he gives me a sleepy smile.

"I don't think I can move," he says.

I grin, my fingers dancing over his arm and shoulder. "I like seeing you like this."

He snorts. "What do I look like?"

I run my hand through his hair, feeling the sweat at the roots. "Happy." My eyes trail down his body. "Absolutely wrecked." He laughs. I drag my knuckle down his jaw. "Mine."

His eyes close briefly, but he has a little smile on his lips. He shimmies over and kisses my lips before dropping back down. "Definitely all those things."

My mind flies back in time, remembering a very specific moment between us. It wasn't the first time he took my breath away, because he did that often. He did that when he spoke to me in class for the first time. When he forced us into a friendship I was sure he didn't need. When he invited me to his place for parties. When he asked if I was dating some guy. When he told me he was gay. When he admitted to being attracted to me.

But one of the most prominent memories was after we had sex. When he was on his knees next to the bed, admitting just how deep his feelings went.

I try to mimic his words from back then.

"This might not be the best time to say this," I start.

His eyes open and he turns to his side, a little worry in them. "What is it?"

"I love you, Adrian. Not sure I ever stopped. I think my love for you was always there, tucked away and hidden under hurt and anger. But the moment you came back into my life, everything I used to try to mask those feelings started falling away."

His wide eyes stare back at me. "Matías," he says in a whisper, so much emotion expressed in just my name.

I close my eyes, a smile on my face. "You wonder why I never want anyone else to call me by my real name. It's because the way you say it. The way my name falls from your lips is like a prayer to a god. It's always uttered with so much reverence, need, or adoration." His teeth dig into his lip, and I reach out to cradle his cheek. "Anyway, I needed to tell you how I felt. You don't need to say anything, but I want you to know where I stand. You have a lot to sift through and figure out right now, but I'm always going to be here."

His brows dip slightly, a hint of frustration in his features, and fear wraps its hands around my lungs.

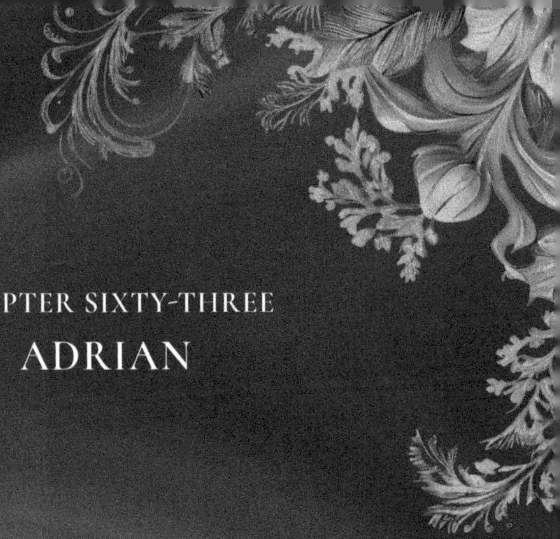

CHAPTER SIXTY-THREE

ADRIAN

"Are you kidding?" I ask.

He eyes me with trepidation, giving me a slight shake of his head like he's confused.

"You think I still have things to *sift* through?" I put my hand on the side of his face, my fingers at the back of his head. "I've told my family about you. I told Charlotte about you. I'm getting a divorce." I huff out a breath. "Being out to them has lifted a weight from my shoulders, and one that needed to be removed a long time ago, but..." I pause, my thumb brushing against the side of his face. "But being with you." I let loose a sigh. "Matías, being with you feels like freedom. Like home. Like a warm blanket on a cold night." I shake my head, unsure there are even enough words to express how I feel. "Being with you makes me feel like I'm invincible. Like nothing could ever happen that we wouldn't find our way back from. We're inevitable."

He leans in close, pressing his lips to mine in a firm kiss that lasts several seconds.

Our foreheads connect and he brushes his nose against mine.

"I love you, too," I whisper against his lips. "Did you ever think I didn't? You are the love of my life."

His lips land on mine again, this time followed by his tongue plunging into my mouth as he releases a moan.

He pulls away briefly. "So, no need to test the waters?" he questions.

I inhale. "Don't bring it up again."

He chuckles lightly. "Okay." Easing back, he looks in my eyes. "And you're mostly out."

"I'm out to anyone I was ever worried about being out to. I don't need to call up any friends or anything," I say with a chuckle.

He chews on his bottom lip. "Work," he says simply. "We'd have to tell HR."

I nod. "That's fine."

"But also, I've been having conversations with the VP. It's what I wanted to talk to you about. I just became the director six months ago, so I have a while in this role before I can move up, but he's been talking to me about an opening at another company that might allow for a faster promotion. It's still in software development."

"Is it still local?" I ask quickly, afraid he's about to pull the rug out from under me.

"It is. Fairly," he says with a shrug. "About thirty minutes away."

I release a breath. "Okay. That's good."

"It won't happen for a little while."

"So we still have time to sneak around in your office?" I question with a grin.

He laughs. "Definitely."

"Good."

"We still have a few things to discuss, but for now, let's

enjoy the rest of the night. We don't check out until tomorrow afternoon."

"Ooh. Plenty of time to try other things," I say, wiggling my brows.

He grins. "Let's test out this jacuzzi tub first."

"Sounds good."

Matías stares at me for a few seconds. "I love you."

I touch his cheek. "I love *you*.

EPILOGUE

Adrian
Eight months later

"Where should we put the cake?" Amelia asks, holding the white box in her hands.

"Over here," I say, clearing off a space on the kitchen counter.

"All right, honey. I have the food setup on the table. They're all covered and in the warmers," Matías's Mom, Lucia, says as she walks back into the kitchen.

"Thank you."

I glance at the time to see we have maybe twenty minutes before he drives up. He's not big on parties or people, so his surprise party consists of me, Amelia, his mom, and his step-dad.

This is the first time we've hosted anything since the house has been completely put together. Three months ago, we moved into a new place that sits halfway between South River and Ashberry—where he now works.

Today actually marks the end of his first week there, and while I miss seeing him every day at work, at least we can now come home to each other.

It didn't take us long before we realized living next to each other was pointless. I spent every night at his house, so we started looking for a place that would have our commutes to work fairly even, and then we listed our homes.

Charlotte and I are on better terms. She decided to stay in Chicago, and after living with her parents for six months while working at a bank, she found an apartment.

She's asked how Matías and I are, which is definitely progress. She hasn't spoken to or seen him, and I wouldn't ask her to do that.

My mom has met him. She was kind if not a little stand-offish, but that's always been her nature. She's trying though. She calls to see how we're doing or will tell me to pass her regards to him. Her reaction has been better than I imagined.

Dad didn't talk to me for a little while. However, after finding out Amelia came to have Thanksgiving dinner with Matías and I instead of going over there, he decided to call me.

It was a brief conversation, where he asked if I was plan-ning on hosting Thanksgiving dinner every year. When I replied with a just as prickly *maybe* he asked if I'd be visiting them for Christmas. I told him we'd probably be busy, but mostly because I'm just not ready to forgive him so soon. He hadn't been making any effort, and was still trying to use his power as a father to get me to do what he wanted.

He asked to be told about our next Thanksgiving plans, and I told him he could come visit us if he wanted. His response was a small huff, but it wasn't a no. Since then, he's checked in with me here and there, mostly about work and a little about whatever new hobby Mom picks up, but it's something. At Christmas I got a call and was told "Merry Christmas to you guys" so there's that.

Amelia, however, loves him. Sometimes it feels like she likes him more than me. She'll call him on the phone to ask about something, or talk about some show they both watch. I can't remember the name, because it's something I have no interest in, but they both love it.

Lucia's rearranging some balloons while I get the camera Matías bought me for Christmas. He remembered what I said in college about liking taking photos, and said that even if I'm going to stick with my job, I should have a hobby that I enjoy. So, I've been taking pictures again, and I can't wait to capture the look on his face today when he walks in.

The garage door goes up.

"Okay, he's here!" Amelia screeches, grabbing her little party horn.

His step-dad, Charles, stands a little behind me as I aim the camera at the door, while Amelia and Lucia stand on either side of it. The garage begins to close, and the door opens.

"Happy birthday!" The four of us shout the greeting, mostly in unison, and then Amelia blows her horn right after.

I snap several photos, capturing the surprise at both the loudness, and then the recognition of who's here.

His face splits into a smile and then he looks at me, his eyes softening and head tilting just slightly. The shutter clicks a few more times, catching the appreciation in his gaze.

I lower the camera and smile at him.

He hugs his mom and Amelia, then shakes Charles's hand before pulling me into a hug.

"Happy birthday, baby."

He kisses me on the mouth. "Thank you." A brief pause. "So, I'm assuming you're not really sick."

I laugh. "I needed an excuse to not go into work today."

He grins and squeezes my hand before turning to his mom to talk to her. After a few minutes, he excuses himself to get changed, and then we all sit down at the dinner table to eat.

Once we're done, Amelia grabs the cake, and we light the candles and sing happy birthday to him as he sits in embarrassment at the attention.

His parents leave first, since they have over a two drive to get home, but Amelia sticks around for a little while, and the three of us sit in front of the TV and talk for a couple of hours.

"Well, I'm gonna get to the hotel. I'll swing by around lunch time, but then I fly out early the next day."

We stand to give her a hug. "Thanks for coming out."

"Anything for my brother," she says. "And you too, Adrian."

I put my hand on her head and mess up her hair. "You're still a brat."

Matías chuckles. "I'm glad I got to see you."

"Me too. Happy birthday again."

"Thanks."

Once she leaves, the two of us plop back down on the couch.

Grabbing my hand, Matías looks at me. "Thank you for today. For doing all of this."

I smile and lean in to kiss him. "You don't have to thank me."

"No?" he says with raised brows. "I was about to offer to show you how thankful I am for you...in the bedroom," he says, jerking his thumb toward the stairs. "But if you don't need to be thanked—"

"No, no. I definitely need to be thanked. It was so much hard work."

He smirks, leaning forward to capture my mouth with his. "I love you, Adrian. You're the best thing to ever happen to me."

My hand goes to the side of his face as I kiss him again. "I love you. I'll never be able to express just how much, but I'm glad we have the rest of our lives for me to try."

He hums low in his throat. "I like the sound of that."

ACKNOWLEDGMENTS

Thank you so much for reading! Going into this one, I knew it was going to split the audience. Hopefully, if you got this far, you knew what you were getting into with the cheating. I wanted to be clear about the content in marketing, because I know people have strong feelings about the cheating trope. I'm glad you gave it a try!

I don't condone cheating in real life, and don't believe there to be any "good" reason for doing so, but this is a story of fiction, and meant to bring two soulmates together regardless of circumstance.

I want to thank Tyla Rae for being my alpha reader and giving me so much confidence and many laughs with her commentary.

Huge thanks to my beta readers for being willing to read it and give me their thoughts and opinions.

Victoria from Cruel Ink & Design for being my editor and always finding time to squeeze me in.

Shout out to my street and ARC team for everything they do and share. I'm so appreciative of you all!

The biggest thanks goes to my husband, because he's always here to listen to me rant and vent. We also throw ideas around with each other, and I'm so happy to have him here with all his knowledge and support when I'm struggling. Love you, boo! You're my everything.

I want to thank you again for reading my book. I know

there's millions out there, so I'm grateful that you picked mine. I'm already planning the next one. Please follow me on social media so you don't miss out on what's next!

Until next time.

ABOUT THE AUTHOR

Isabel Lucero is a bestselling author, finding joy in giving readers books for every mood.

Though born in a small town in New Mexico, Isabel currently lives in Delaware with her family. When not completely lost in the world of her next WIP, she can be found reading, or in the nearest Target buying things she doesn't need.

Isabel loves connecting with her readers and fans of books in general. You can find her across all social media platforms.

www.isabellucero.com

ALSO BY ISABEL LUCERO

Think Again

Dysfunctional

The Prince of Darkness

Splintered

Lights, Camera, Passion

Kingston Brothers Series

On the Rocks

Truth or Dare

Against the Rules

Risking it All

South River University Series

Stealing Ronan

Tasting Innocence

Breaking Free

Tempting Him